ENDLESS FIRE
Aethon Arises
by
R E Kearney

Also by R E Kearney
Future Furies

This book is a work of fiction. Names, characters, places and incidents are the product of the author's imagination or are used fictitiously. Any resemblance to actual events or persons, living or dead, is coincidental.

This book is the intellectual property of the author and as such cannot be reproduced in whole or in part in any medium without the express written permission of the author.

ISBN-13: 978-1977728258
ISBN-10: 1977728251

*To Barb, my loving wife, best friend
and the Editor in Chief.
Without her encouragement and assistance I could not
and would not have written this story.*

ENDLESS FIRE
Aethon Arises
by
R E Kearney

Acknowledgments

Many thanks and my sincere appreciation to Tim Flanagan and his associates at Novel Design Studio www.noveldesignstudio.com for their cover design, social media production and all of their other assistance coordinating the publication of this book.

Table of Contents

"Everyone is different. We all suffer from the disease of being human. There are a thousand cures but no antidotes."
James Altucher

EL PRESIDENTE

Puerto Rico! Independencia! Independence! Liberacion! Puerto Rico! Puerto Rico! Puerto Rico! Cheering crowds shouting, musicians playing and horns squawking rattle Robert's windows yanking him from his dreams and tossing him onto the floor. Rubbing his aching head, he wanders to his room's window. Below his Condado district hotel room, Independence Day celebrants fill San Juan's Avenida Ashford for as far as Robert can see.

Heading the parade is the independent nation of Puerto Rico's first President, its former Governor Justo Negocio. Tall and muscular with graying black hair, he is striding ahead of a wall of laser-light banners, Puerto Rican flags with dark-blue, freedom fields and placards carried by a river of his shouting and dancing supporters. Negocio is their champion leading them forward now just as he led them to independence one year ago.

Before these joyous Puerto Ricans fly drones broadcasting their celebration worldwide. Above and behind Negocio, flies a squadron of aerodrones also hauling banners. Robots roll along intermingled in the crowd. Some celebrants parade riding hoverboards or hoverscooters or electric unicycles, but the majority march on foot.

Robert notices that all of the banners and placards are acclaiming Puerto Rico's first year of independence from the United States except for two. Scrawled upon one of the differing banners is *Close Fort Buchannan*. Its sister banner demands, *US Army Go Home*. As the protestors surge closer, he notices a limping, partially uniformed man is carrying one of the anti-Army signs with his prosthetic hand. Next to him a woman carries the other anti-Army sign with her prosthetic hand and arm.

"What are you watching? Why don't you come back to bed?" Asks a young, dusty-skinned, black haired woman lounging naked in the bed.

"I'm watching your President Negocio. I have a meeting with him later today about establishing some special security system for him."

"Good. I'm glad. He needs more protection. Somebody lased at him last week. He's stirred up a lot of trouble. In America, not everybody is happy about his declaring Puerto Rico an independent nation. They're calling him a revolutionary and traitor. I think that's why they sent some more soldiers and other people to that old Army fort."

"Fort Buchannan?"

"Yeah, that's it." The woman pats the side of the bed, "But, let's not talk about that. Why don't you bring your boney body back to bed?"

"Well, ok then." Smiling happily, Robert returns to the bed. "I don't meet with him until this afternoon"

"Wait. What is this? I didn't notice this last night in the dark." The woman probes, as she gently traces her finger tips across a scar on the right side of Robert's chest. "It looks and feels like the letters M-K."

"Yeah. You're correct. The letters M-K. The initials of Mugavus Komfort. She 3D bioprinted the biocompatible nanomaterials for the tissue to repair my bullet wound. She thought she should sign her work. Very funny, eh? She thought she was funny. Anyway, it's a souvenir of my visit to Ethiopia where a very crazy American who desperately wanted to kill me, missed my heart and only wounded me."

"Why did he want to kill a sweet fellow like you?" She continues circling the MK with her finger.

"Well, as I remember, he just did not appreciate me trying to stop him from destroying the Washington D.C. Mall, and inadvertently, collapsing his uncle's government."

She stops tracing his wound and locks her eyes on his. "Wait a second. Now, everybody knows about the slaughter at the capital, but I don't remember any stories involving you. What I heard was that a massive military computer failure caused the weapons to malfunction and that's why it's been hushed up. Los muertos no cuentan cuentos, you know."

Robert chuckles while rubbing his shoulder. "Well computers were involved, but it was a man who went crazy and..."

"Robert Goodfellow, are you in there?" A slightly Spanish accented man's voice calls from the hall followed by someone knocking. "Mister Goodfellow, I need to speak with you, immediately."

After struggling into his trousers, Robert hurriedly opens the door.

"Good morning, I'm Justo Negocio." He announces as he strides into the room passing Robert, "How are you this morning?"

"Well I..."

Spying the woman in the bed, Negocio nods toward her and then smiles at Robert, "Oh, I see that you are doing quite well this morning. Muy bueno de verdad. Really good."

"Good morning Rita," he steps toward the woman with his hand extended and a broad smile on his face. "How are you this morning? Did you keep our friend safe and out of trouble last night?"

"Yes, he was never in danger. I made sure that he was out of Club Kronos early and safely in bed."

Grabbing Negocio's hand, Robert snatches his attention away from Rita and back to him, "Sorry sir, I wasn't expecting you. I didn't think we were scheduled to meet until this afternoon."

Two quick shakes and Negocio drops Robert's hand, "That was your schedule, not mine. Plans change Mister Goodfellow. Plans change. I need for you to start now. Throw on your clothes and let's go."

"But, I..."

"But, what? Do you want this gig or not?"

"Well yes, I..."

"Bueno. Meet you down in the lobby in ten minutes, then. Say your goodbyes, quick and let's go." Waving his hand at Rita, he backs toward the door, "Pleasure seeing you. Good work Rita."

After Negocio is gone Robert angrily reproaches Rita. "So, you're a prostitute he hired for me?"

"No! I most certainly am not!" Rita retorts indignantly. "I am a patriotic citizen of the independent nation of Puerto Rico. I was instructed to protect you, and that's exactly what I did."

"Now wait…" Rita's statement startles Robert. "…why do I need protection?"

"You don't realize how precarious it is here right now, Robert. If you think all of those aerodrones and robots surrounding President Negocio during the parade were just to haul banners then you're naïve. They aren't for show. They are laser armed and deadly."

"To protect Negocio. That I understand." Robert taps his chest. "But, I'm no threat."

Puerto Rico is still struggling to free itself. Separate itself from the mainland. So it's a bit of a mess with legal and political disputes and infighting. Some American businesses that had property here are actually sending in goons and criminals. They've been attacking visitors and residents. Extortion, you know. Threatening to embarrass us and scare away our tourists, if we don't give them what they want. So, I did what I needed to do to get you away from the two men I suspect were following you last night."

"Two men? Following me?"

"Yes, two men." Rita motions uses her hands to indicate the size of the men. "Very large, too. Heavy. Strange reddish skin and they seemed to be sweating a lot. The clothes they were wearing and their uncomfortable appearance made them impossible to miss. They watched us the entire time we were at Club Kronos. I'm surprised that you never noticed."

Then with a coy smile, Rita adds, "But by then, I do believe I had won your undivided attention. You certainly didn't seem to mind my protection plan last night."

Robert returns her smile and winks. "No. No, I didn't. I must admit. And you? Was it all work for you?"

"I wouldn't have invited you back to bed this morning, if it had been. It was a pleasure doing the business of pleasure with you." Rita stretches and sighs with satisfaction. "Estás bueno! I may have to protect you again, real soon mister Goodfellow."

"Really? Me? Is that you speaking or just Negocio's money talking?" Robert points toward himself. "I must tell you that I'm normally not pursued by beautiful women…well…or any women…actually. I'm a bit of a computer geek, you know."

Smiling and shaking her head in exasperation, Rita points toward the bathroom. "You are such a manganzon. Just get dressed geek. They're waiting for you."

With his right fist raised victoriously, Robert struts toward the shower. "As Star Trek movie star LeVar Burton once said, I fly my geek flag proudly. Absolutely."

ALERT AND NERVOUS

Robert arrives in the lobby to find Negocio chatting with two women. He has them enthralled. Near the hotel entrance stand two broad-shouldered, muscular men eyeing everyone approaching or entering. As Robert nears Negocio, one of the men suddenly appears in front of him blocking his path. He is surprised. The big man moves with the light-footed speed and agility of a cat.

"He's with me Hector," Negocio raises his hand to calm his bodyguard. "Go with Rubio and summon our glider."

"You're a little late Mister Goodfellow. We don't have time to waste. Come with me." Pivoting, he begins striding toward the exit.

Without hesitating or skipping a step, Negocio exits the hotel and steps directly into his arriving autonomous, electriglide human transport. Following him, Robert is not nearly as coordinated. Stumbling upon the transport's entrance's curved threshold, he tumbles into the transport's cabin. Only Hector's strong-armed assistance saves him. Groaning and rubbing his scraped shin, he climbs onto the seat across from Puerto Rico's leader. He starts to buckle his safety restraints, but when he notices none of the others are wearing them, he drops his.

"I must say that I expected a little better from you, Robert. I need speed to succeed. I require surprise to keep my opposition off balance. So far they still think I'm just a joke. So, I have to stay a step ahead. Move before they do. Puerto Rico must become completely self-reliant to overcome their meddling. We have to be ready...no...we are ready to stand on our own as a nation. Puerto Ricans just have to realize it and act like it."

"Well...yes...ok. But, where do I fit into this?"

"My friend, Dame Gutefrau of SPEA, recommended you. I understand that you are known to have a particularly valuable set of skills in cyber and physical security which you will provide when paid the proper price. You're a digital mercenary. Is that not true?"

"Well, it's a living, yes..."

"And you're also Canadian. Aren't you? Canadian military in fact? Not American? Not restricted directly by US Science Suppression laws? You're working in an independent, foreign nation now, you know."

"Uh yes, I'm an officer in the Canadian Air Force Reserve...but..."

"Good. We have a deal then." Looking away, Negocio runs his hand across the inside of the transport's door, massaging the padding. "What do you think of my new ride, Robert? Just received it yesterday."

Robert surveys the interior. "It's different. I feel like we're sitting in the yoke of an enormous, pearl-colored, boiled egg. Having an egg shaped exterior with contoured solar panels as its upper half is a new design to me. I don't recognize it."

"It's Chinese, Robert. Beijing Transport Innovations delivered it yesterday. It's an all-electric, gliding, autonomous automobile. I call it my auto-auto. Reinforced, 3D printed graphene makes it light, strong and almost invulnerable." Negocio pounds his fist against the transparent graphene window. "Stop some of the strongest lasers."

"It's just what we need here. Robert. We can't produce oil or gasoline, but we have bountiful sunlight, wind and waves, which can produce electricity. So, why should we send our money to some environment-wrecking, oil company? Makes no sense. Does it? No. So, I've mandated that Puerto Rico will use only what it produces. Self-sufficiency is the truest form of independence and freedom. That's my philosophy of Economics." Negocio proudly proclaims.

Like a student attempting to impress a professor, Robert instinctively agrees. "Well, you're not the first to see the wisdom in that. Small self-supporting states are proving stronger and more secure than large dependent states. Estonia for example is..."

"Whap!" Proudly, Negocio slaps the seat. "Now that Puerto Rico is finally no longer forced by America's hydrocarbon laws to use internal combustion engines, I've banned the import of all non-renewable-energy fueled engines. No more internal combustion engines. No ICE in Puerto Rico. America's oil companies are fighting it, but they cannot stop us now that we are independent and free of them. Congress can pass all the laws that they want mandating Americans to use their gasoline, but here the petroleum power period has passed. Fossil fuels are for fossil fools living in the past. Finally! Puerto Rico is joining the fossil fuel free world!"

Animated and excited, Negocio bounces in his seat. "And since it is Chinese manufactured, US security can't hack it and grab control of it. Last month, somebody in the US hacked our Ponce police and shut down all of their equipment. A very dangerous and nasty hack attack that they perpetrated just to show us they could. Just before the hackers released the Ponce police, they taunted us with the message, *We still own you.* So, this auto-auto is another successful step in our escape from American control."

There is no denying that Negocio is a man with plans. Robert decides that he is just the type of person Puerto Rico needs to steer it into the future. Intelligent. Innovative. Imaginative. A leader dedicated to advancing his people.

"By the way Robert, three dozen of these auto-autos will arrive tomorrow. They're government property, so I'm assigning one to you for your use while you're here. Yours will be just like mine, here, except without the ballistic proofing of mine." Negocio smiles and hands Robert an auto-auto control fob.

Robert studies the fob. "Thank you, this will be a new experience for me. Never had my own personal transport, before. Always use community-share conveyances or ride with someone."

Ahead, at the edge of the street, workers are replacing a miles-per-hour speed sign with a sign stating kilometers-per-hour. Negocio points toward them. "It's taken longer than I expected, but we've also converted to the metric system. Time for Puerto Rico to abandon another obsolete US practice and join the rest of the world."

"Well, we use both systems in Canada. But personally, I'm a fan of the metrics. It's more science based." Robert smirks, "I think we keep miles and feet and pounds around, just so visiting Americans don't whine and get lost."

Placing his finger against his lips and cupping his other hand behind his ear, Negocio whispers, "Shh. Just listen to that. Beautiful battery power. No exhaust fumes. No noisy engine. And thanks to aerodynamic lift engineering, its spherical tires barely touch the pavement. Breathe deep our exhaustless air. Soak in the silence."

Robert smiles enjoying Negocio's enthusiasm. Obviously, he is his nascent nation's biggest fan and promoter.

Negocio leans close to the auto-auto's window. "What's that? I believe I hear the song of our national bird, the Puerto Rican Spindalis. That is definitely the sound of Puerto Rican progress. Shh."

Security guard Hector hesitantly clears his throat and quietly attempts to correct Negocio. "Actually the Spindalis lives in the bush not in old San Juan sir. I doubt that you…"

"Yes Hector, I know that. I was exaggerating for effect…oh…just be quiet." Frustrated, Negocio freezes his attention on the street scene.

With a grimace and an audible groan, Negocio watches an internal combustion engine vehicle approach and pass them heading the opposite direction. He sniffs the air, snorting as if the vehicle had filled the city with fumes. Exaggerating his discomfort at the vehicle's engine noise, he covers his ears.

With his hands still protecting his hearing, Negocio instructs the auto-auto. "Play Lamento Borincano by Marc Anthony."

As the music begins, he uncovers his ears and describes the music to Robert. "This is one of my favorite old songs. It was originally written by composer Rafael Hernández Marín in 1929. In his song, he describes the harsh conditions impoverished Puerto Rican farmers had to face on a daily basis. So long ago, but still a lot of similarities to today. My favorite part is the last line when he sings Yo te adoro, Puerto Rico, y eso nadie lo va a quitar, which roughly translates to, I adore you, Puerto Rico, and no one can take that away."

"I imagine you would agree with Bob Marley, who said that one good thing about music, when it hits you, you feel no pain." Robert reinforces Negocio.

Negocio smiles. "True. No pain here. I'm alive in my Puerto Rico or as Raul Labrador once said, I'm proud of who I am, and I'm proud I grew up in Puerto Rico."

Negocio closes his eyes and leans back to enjoy the music. Having him cease his rat-a-tat chatter for a few moments is a welcome relief for Robert. He rests his ears while engaging his mind. With Negocio not talking, this is a perfect time for some mental meandering. Like most gig workers these days, he never has time for vacations. He cannot afford them. He simply takes short breaks between assignments. This is his first visit to Puerto Rico, probably his only visit. So why not enjoy this Caribbean escape?

As they noiselessly glide above the seaside street of Avenida Luis Munoz Rivera, Robert watches the Atlantic Ocean's waves slap the shore. Surging in and slipping out. Rushing and retreating. Flooding and flowing. Hypnotic. Relaxing. But, Robert is an analyzer. He never just sees. He witnesses.

Spellbound by the sea, his mind wanders - drifts in and out with the tide. With the water he momentarily slips away, happily escapes today for yesterday. He envisions the island as it once was, pristine and pure. He imagines how relieved and happy Christopher Columbus and his Spanish sailors must have been to see this lush island. After so many months at sea, finally land and safety. They must have rejoiced at finding fresh water, trees, grass, food and a protected bay. After months of stormy seas, Columbus dropped anchor and completed his second ocean crossing. Robert wonders if they thought they had found the paradise of Eden.

Still absorbing his music, Negocio remains silent. His eyes are closed. Hector is also enjoying a relaxing, semi-sleep swim in the soft guitar sounds and singing.

Massaging his wound from his Africa attack, Robert envies them their tranquility. He hopes he will also be able to enjoy a little serenity in this Puerto Rican paradise. Too much of the time, his mind is as turbulent and troubled as the storming seas Columbus crossed. So much of the reality he knows is disappearing. The world is changing too fast to understand, even for a cyber citizen like him, and he is a person who can be held responsible for changing it.

Abruptly, Robert's peacefulness ends. Zipping in from behind, a drone pops up next to his window. A small turret on its top rotates toward him. Is it a camera or a laser? Laser!

Instinctively, Robert leaps into the seat next to Negocio shielding him from the drone. Startled, Negocio squirms and slowly begins opening his eyes. A searing, bright light flashes. Zip, the threatening drone disappears, racing away ahead of a police drone.

Just as fast as he jumped next to Negocio, Robert hops back into his own seat. Quickly looking away from Negocio, he returns to studying the seashore scenery. He is embarrassed by his panic. Yet, he remains unsettled. Did he just witness, the graphene blocking a laser shot? In Puerto Rico for less than twenty-four hours and already under attack, twice. He does not consider this a good beginning.

After chasing away their menace, the San Juan police drone settles into position just outside Negocio's window. Awakening, Negocio waves toward the drone. A green light on the drone's side flickers as acknowledgement. On the opposite side a second police drone flies into escort position. Robert notes the drones' significant array of laser weapons. He determines they are sufficiently armed to provide formidable protection.

All is not peaceful in Puerto Rico.

POOR RICH PORT

Fully awake now, Negocio is also enjoying viewing the ocean, but he regards the kissing of sea and shore as a proud Puerto Rican, not as a Canadian tourist. He shatters the silence with his purely Puerto Rican observation. "You know Robert, Christopher Columbus didn't really discover America, he discovered Puerto Rico. We were here long before they were there. In 1493, the indigenous Tainos of this island met him with open arms and open hearts and he enslaved and raped them. History proves that some things never change when it comes to outsiders and our islands. America never treated us much better."

"Play Yo soy Boricua, pa'que tu lo sepas!" Negocio orders as the song, Lamento Borincanto ends. "This is another of my favorites. Tainos called this island Boricua, just so you know. It means, I'm Puerto Rican. Of course, I'm a proud Puerto Rican."

"Yes sir, I've heard that about you." Robert snidely remarks, before he puffs out his chest. "Well, I'm proud I'm Canadian. As actor Daniel Gillies once said, 'tell people you're a Canadian or a Kiwi when you travel and they'll adore you.' I appreciate adoration."

Where Calle Norzagaray replaces the Avenida Rivera, the ocean view is abruptly blocked by the stout stone walls of historic Castillo de San Cristobal and the tourists surrounding it. After hundreds of years, silent San Cristobal is still standing guard. Stoically, protecting San Juan. Of course, mankind goes nowhere without making war, Robert mulls. From the beginning of time until now, man is always fighting with himself. Clubs to cannon to cyber. Now digital death. Civilization is still so far from civilized.

Mankind will also always have poverty, he realizes as the proud, strong Castillo de San Cristobal gives way to a section of crumbling, slum housing. Squeezed into a low spot below the street's cliff and the rising Caribbean, surging seawaters surround and swamp the row of houses nearest the ocean. Higher up on the beach, the ramshackle houses stand on rotting wooden stilts, out of the water's reach, for the moment. Floating trash, rubbish and garbage swirls between the collapsing shacks. Blight blocking beauty.

"I see you're staring at La Perla, Robert. Hard to imagine something looking that bad is actually called the pearl. Ironic, isn't it? Still, looks can be deceiving. The La Perla neighborhood may not look like much, but the people living there refuse to live anywhere else, even with the rising sea threatening to wash it all away. When I tried to clean it up, I almost started a small war. My advice to you, though, is stay out of there. Most of the time, La Perla residents are no problem, but it's also a haven for drug dealers, smugglers and other criminals."

"La Perla looks like something from last century. I understand, of course, that you keep your oldest buildings for tourists. But, almost everything that I've seen here so far, looks out of date...behind the times."

"That's because it is Robert. Most of Puerto Rico is so far behind." Negocio sadly shakes his head. "And just think, Puerto Rico is Spanish for rich port. It's a poor rich port. Just look at those shacks. Look at those people sitting there with nothing to do. No work. No future. The majority of my people are just subsisting. They're Sists barely able to meet their day to day needs. I'm fighting to improve their lives and save Puerto Rico. Raise my people above those rising seas of poverty. I will do whatever is necessary."

"Blink your eyes and the present is past," Robert mumbles.

Negocio nods his head in agreement. "Yes, and I am afraid that Puerto Rico is starting the race from far behind. We will leap forward. I refuse to allow my nation to be a future failure."

Just past the Instituto de Neurobiologia, their auto-auto turns left onto Calle Del Cristo and enters the heart of Old San Juan.

"Here we are, Robert." While their auto-auto is rolling to a stop, Negocio is stepping out its door. "Now to reconnoiter and prepare before tourists flood the plaza."

Having fallen into this oddly shaped conveyance, Robert is in no hurry to now fall out. He navigates his exit through the auto-auto's multi-curved, access panel only when their transport is fully stopped. Silent and stalwart, Hector and Rubio follow him out to establish security. Their two accompanying police drones disappear into the flock of drones hovering above the plaza.

Robert finds Negocio impatiently waiting for him at the base of the Ponce de Leon Statue centered in San Jose Plaza. It quickly becomes apparent why he hit the pavement before their vehicle stopped. As soon as the popular Negocio is sighted, regular routines halt and a crowd of workers begins gathering.

Hector and Rubio hurry to form a buffer zone between him and his adoring public. Admirers shout his name and wave. Other devotees pose for selfies with him in the background. Excited and adoring, his worshipping throng swells forward.

Negocio smiles and waves and then motions with his hands for the crowd to step back. Thrilled to be near him, they ignore his request and hug him tighter. Robert begins to experience the uneasiness of claustrophobia. He struggles for breath, suffering an anxiety attack. Too many too close. Squeezing tighter and tighter. Just in time, San Juan police arrive to help restrain the crowd.

"There is simply no escaping the grip of social media, Robert. I don't announce my movements, but wherever and whenever I appear a crowd materializes. Forces me to move fast and often. Drives the police crazy, but I believe surprise is my best security."

With barrier tape and police in place, Robert and Negocio are no longer being squashed by his fans. But, that does not make them safe. As the San Juan police push the observers away, a fist fight erupts. Robert watches two men and a police officer knock an angry, screaming man to the pavement. He cannot hear what the man is shouting clearly, but to Robert, he appears to be threatening Negocio. The police shock him silent before Robert is certain.

Although no longer threatened by spectators, above and around them small aerodrones and biobots are swarming like flies. Standing much taller than Negocio, Robert finds them buzzing distressingly close to his head. After his visit from the drone during their trip, he is fearful. He swats at a bio-bee drone buzzing too close to his eyes. A second later he feels a sharp burn on his left hand. Immediately a fiery, welt appears. He has been bio-bee stung.

"I believe I just learned the painful lesson that I should never mess with your fan's drones." Robert shows Negocio his throbbing hand.

Negocio chuckles. "Oh well, welcome to the club. I've made the same blunder myself. Only it wasn't a fan's drone, it was my own. That one may have been mine too. I never know whether to swat or not."

"So it was a mistake?"

Negocio flexes his right hand. Occasionally, he still feels pain from the drone laser sting. "Oh, I didn't say that. I'm just telling you not to trust anybody or their drones."

Shadows from the increasing number of aerodrones speckle the blazing hot pavement. Although, he is covered above and surrounded below, Robert takes Negocio's warning to heart. He ducks and dodges instead of swinging and swatting at any of the growing swarm of drones and bio-bots.

"In these times of capricious loyalties, I've learned by painful experience that once I see a drone I can never turn my back on it." Negocio scans the cloud of flitting and flying electronics above him. "You never really know who is operating that drone or that drone or that purple drone over there. The operators are anonymous, hiding in the crowd. They could be friends, foes or enemy assassins. Ruthless reality of our time. So, I've just accepted life as a continual target. And, now that you're with me, you're a target, too. So, stay alert, and be prepared to duck or you'll deep-fry."

SAY QUANXI

Still early morning and yet, perspiration pours across Robert's face dripping onto his sweat-wet chest. Some of his perspiration is the result of Negocio's cheering speech, but the majority results from the soaring heat. He wonders how soon he will melt into a pudding puddle. He would welcome some Toronto snow right now.

Next to him Negocio stands cool and comfortable. Not a drop of sweat. But then again, he is standing in the shade of Robert's shadow. Robert considers his discomfort the cost of being a Canadian in the Caribbean.

"Right here, at seven tonight, I'm announcing my successful implementation of some geoeconomics by introducing our major Chinese partners." Negocio lowers his voice and moves closer to Robert. "They're part of the alliance that has been quietly financing my efforts to end our life as America's forsaken territory. Free of ridiculous US laws and restraints, and with Chinese help, very soon Puerto Rico will again mean rich port. I'm optimistically excited. Teaming with Chinese scientists and innovators will make Puerto Rico the creative center of the Caribbean."

"So you're selling Puerto Rico to the Chinese? No wonder so many people in the US are coming after you."

Negocio grimaces at Robert's comment. "Selling has such a nasty connotation, Robert. I prefer to use the Chinese term of Quanxi. In Chinese, Quanxi means connections or relationships, you know. But then again, so what if I do open up Puerto Rico to the Chinese? We owe America nothing. Nada. For more than one hundred years, America did nothing for Puerto Rico, except insult us, kick us around and bankrupt us. As a territory, our votes didn't count. Our Representatives in Congress were ignored."

Robert feebly attempts to calm his host. "Well, I'll admit that during my travels in the states, I've found most Americans to be

20

very ignorant about their own country. I doubt the majority of Americans even knew Puerto Rico was a US territory or, for that fact, even existed."

Anger flares in Negocio's eyes. He leans close to Robert and snarls. "Their ultimate insult was denying us statehood. We weren't wanted. Puerto Rico is not welcome. A slap in our face. A kick to our gut. So, since they don't want us...since Puerto Ricans aren't good enough to be Americans...I decided that we would not be the American lapdog to be kicked around anymore. I say, Independencia! And, on top of that do you know how deep in debt Puerto Rico is right now thanks to American dictates?"

"No I...well, I'm Canadian, so I..."

Negocio disregards Robert continuing his rant. "Well then, as a Canadian with the US trying to run you from south of your border you can understand why we could no longer leave our future in their hands. Mainland Americans' single greatest characteristic is that they are bewildered by the present and totally unprepared for the future. America is sinking into an era of arrogant ignorance. Don't you agree?"

Surprise silences Robert. He does not know how best to answer. He wobbles his head, neither agreeing nor disagreeing. "Well, uh..."

Speaking faster and faster, Negocio marches on with his angry monologue. "Besides, the Chinese are entrenched in Central and South America, now. You should know yourself that the Chinese established themselves through-out the Caribbean during the US racist rage period. Now that we're independent, it's finally our turn to benefit. America may not want us, but the Chinese certainly do. Besides industry, just think of our tourism potential. Millions of Chinese tourists visiting us. Wouldn't that be fantastic? They have the minds and the money. Lots of money. Why shouldn't they spend it here? Don't you agree?"

"Yes, I believe you make a valid point...I guess I..."

Without taking a breath, Negocio continues orating. "Sure, Quanxi is Chinese, but here we also have the saying, quien a buen árbol se arrima, buena sombra lo cobija. It's an old Spanish proverb that means if you want to succeed, you have to be close to successful people. If you hang around losers, you'll end up being a loser. Do you think we always want to be losers?"

"Well no…I wouldn't…I mean." Robert is increasingly confused. "Sorry?"

Embarrassed by his own ignorance, Robert stops stammering and begins surveying the square. Straightaway, he recognizes several security vulnerabilities. Not only is the plaza full of strangers, it is surrounded by unsecured buildings. It is an aged, concrete canyon that is perfect for an aerodrone attack or a laser shot from a window.

When Negocio stops to breathe, Robert cautiously inquires. "Sorry, but why are you making your announcement here where it's so open and accessible? Aren't you concerned about security?"

"Historical significance mi amigo. Historical significance. Our history means a lot to us. Ponce de Leon was the first governor of Puerto Rico. He established San Juan. But then, as you may remember from school, he left Puerto Rico to search for the fountain of youth."

"Yes, so?"

Pointing easterly, Negocio continues excitedly, "China's genome engineering genius, Shengwu Kexuejia, established a large genetic medicine operation in Catano across the Bahia de San Juan in a pharmaceutical plant the American government forced us to close. She's merging next-generation nanotechnology with advanced genomics creating an international genetics research and treatment center here. And one major area of her expertise is epigenetics. That's extending human life through genetic manipulation, or as you may call it…the fountain of youth."

"Yes, I've heard about epigenetics. But, I also understand that it's still in developmental stages." Teasing, Robert counters with his own theory. "I, on the other hand, am a Singularian. I hope to continually stay alive long enough to make it to the next life-prolonging innovation until I can upload my mind into a robot. I could be very comfortable as a robot…just call me Robby robot."

Negocio is too intense to consider Robert's jest. "Well become a robot if you wish, but I plan to remain human, thanks to Shengwu. Earlier this week, she told me that she has perfected her epigenetics…her fountain of youth."

Negocio jerks his thumb toward the statue. "So tonight, as the first president of Puerto Rico, I will officially announce that the fountain of youth has arrived in Puerto Rico and found Ponce de Leon."

"Well as comedian Red Buttons once joked about Ponce de Leon, who said when he discovered the Fountain of Youth, 'Where the hell are the paper cups? Never got a dinner!'" Robert chuckles at his witticism.

Ignoring Robert's poor joke and smiling broadly, Negocio spreads his arms as if embracing the city. "She's also providing the best genomic medical care available for Puerto Ricans. Imagine a nation of super-healthy, super-human, long-living Puerto Ricans. Just think, with Shengwu's epigenetic engineering, I may live to be one hundred and twenty or thirty or possibly, even one hundred and fifty. I'm excited about that. I just hope I'm still able to surf sixty or seventy years from now. I don't want to be just a doddering, one hundred and thirty year old man."

Robert smirks. "Hah, you remind me of the late Andy Rooney when he wrote that it's paradoxical that the idea of living a long life appeals to everyone, but the idea of getting old doesn't appeal to anyone."

Growling a harrumph, Negocio acknowledges Robert's remark before turning away and gesturing toward the ocean. "You can't see her research ships from here, but she also has crews of Puerto Ricans operating underwater drones searching for cone snails and other sea creatures for sources of conotoxins. So far, they haven't been too successful because climate change heat has killed so many of our coral reefs. But still, that's employment Puerto Rico didn't have six months ago. In addition, she's supplying major funding to our Instituto de Neurobiologia for additional research. Built the institute a new, highly-advanced, biotechnology lab."

Robert nods his head in approval. "I must say you and she are an impressive development team. You appear to be driving Puerto Rico forward at a record pace."

"On Puerto Rico's past I am building Puerto Rico's future." Negocio raises his right index finger to emphasize his point. "So yes, Puerto Rico is improving. But, it's requiring that I simultaneously introduce new paradigms of disruptive innovation, technological turmoil and change, which is difficult for some tradition bound Puerto Ricans to understand and accept. A few of my own people are resisting. They are not yet prepared to brave a new world."

Negocio turns and points north. "But our biggest problem is with our former territorial masters in the US. The idea of Puerto

Rico actually becoming something really scares some powerful people and businesses in America. Creates immediate opposition."

"Well, I've noticed that American's don't like to lose money or control." Robert interjects. "Especially when they are losing it to the Chinese."

"Oh, you're so right about that, Robert. So, when Shengwu approached me with her plan to transform San Juan into a center for genetic medicine two years ago, I realized we could only do it as an independent nation with our own laws. Otherwise, the Righteous Rightists in Washington would have shut us down with their anti-genetics laws. They did that before with our pharmaceutical companies. Then, when the federal government collapsed...well it made separating much easier. Declaring our independence became logical."

"Logical or convenient?" Robert's questions.

"Both..." Negocio attempts to wave away a dragonfly biobot flying uncomfortably close. "...it's the intrigue and sabotage occurring now that's my real problem. What they can no longer do legally, they're attempting to accomplish through treachery and violent intimidation. Some of my fellow Puerto Rican patriots have been threatened. Others have unexplainably disappeared."

Robert motions toward the crowd surrounding them. "But, with the majority of these people wild for you, I don't understand your concern."

Negocio waves toward the crowd. "Don't be fooled Robert. There are probably just as many people jeering me as cheering me in this crowd. You had to notice that one man that the police restrained. One reason is that many rich Americans invested money in Puerto Rico's failure. Money they will lose, if I succeed. Money I'm going to take from them, just like they always took it from us. So they send in disruptors to create problems."

The dragonfly drone buzzes across the top of Negocio's head. "With drones and with people, I must watch my back and my front. Just because someone looks friendly, doesn't mean they are. They may be smiling saboteurs or, worse yet, assassins."

"Well, on the trip here..." Robert begins to tell him about the auto-auto drone attack.

Negocio turns his head toward Robert and points at a dark scar on his temple. "This is a laser burn. Last week a drone shot a visual of me. Seconds later, it shot its laser at me. We're still searching for the drone's pilot."

"But, I don't guard people!" Alarmed, Robert interrupts him. "I can't guarantee your safety. I can give you some advice, but that's all. I do cyber security not human security."

Negocio chuckles as he raises his hand to wave away Robert's concern, "You're not here for me. I have my own security. I brought you here at the request of my Chinese partners to assist them with their cyber security problems."

Robert is skeptical. "You're joking. The Chinese have the best cyber security and the best hackers in the world. I don't think they need me."

"Ah, but they do Robert. Actually, Shengwu personally requested you. They want you to do what you do best. Track down the hacker, or hackers, that are already probing their systems…searching for weaknesses. They want you to eliminate them before they can successfully break through and input a virus or worm or hack in or whatever. The Chinese can't send their own people running around Puerto Rico and I can't either. But, you can go wherever you need to go."

Scarching the enthusiastic crowd, once again Robert sees only Negocio's adoring fans waving Puerto Rican freedom flags. "Why do you think the hackers are in Puerto Rico? They could be anywhere in the world. Hacking can originate a mile or ten thousand miles from here."

"Actually, I not only think they are in Puerto Rico, I believe I know exactly where they are in Puerto Rico…Fort Buchannan. My people and the Chinese have been analyzing their pattern of life, IP addresses and digital footprint, and they all point there."

"They didn't use an anonymous remailer or attempt to cover their tracks by routing through multiple devices…a botnet?"

"No, it was almost too easy. Too direct. It's as if they want us to know they are here…or there, actually." Negocio waves toward a woman calling his name."

"If you're so certain they're there, then go get them. Just look for the palest people there. They should be them."

"We would love to, but Fort Buchannan is still US federal territory. We don't want to antagonize the US any more than necessary until we grow stronger or the mainland government weakens more and completely collapses. And they know it too. They're teasing us…testing us. They're telling us that they know we can't touch them. So, that's why you're here."

Negocio squeezes Robert's shoulder. "You're the cheese in my rat trap."

"I beg your pardon." Robert frowns at Negocio's description of him as rat bait.

"We're hoping to use your achievements and fame to pull some of them out of their holes. Your reputation has preceded you, Robert. Especially since we publicized that you were coming. As soon as you arrived it was all over the hackers' social media sites of Internet Relay Chat, Cult of the Dead Cow and L0pht. Word spread faster than the six gigabites per second of KISS that you…the renowned Robert Goodfellow…the foremost trainer at the Black Hat anti-hacker conference…is in San Juan. You're a superstar hacker catcher and we want everybody to know that you are here. We want them to sneak out of their shady holes to gaze upon the sun - you."

"Well, I'm honored, certainly, but it sounds more like I'm the sacrificial goat tied to a post to attract tigers. And, as I recall, the goat is usually killed and eaten." Now nervous, Robert cautiously eyes an approaching woman. "You know, they may just decide that it's easier to waste me in the real world than to battle me in cyberspace. Nobody ever said hackers can't be killers. Digitals can be dangerous too."

"Oh come now, Rita didn't allow you to be killed and eaten by either of the two men tracking you last night. Did she? And now, we know exactly who those two are and where they are. So, without even trying, you gave us our first clue to finding these rats' nest. They came out. We spiked their Pina Coladas with nano-tracking particles and now…"

"You're far more certain your trap will work than I am." Robert searches the crowd for potential threats. "Me, I'm more inclined to believe John Steinbeck who wrote that man is the only kind of varmint that sets his own trap, baits it, and then steps in it. Personally, I've seen too many traps trap trappers."

Robert's quoting of John Steinbeck receives a derisive sneer from Negocio, so he attempts to explain again. "I don't think you understand sir. I'm more of a cerebral cyber-soldier and less of a fighting soldier. So, instead of this possibly becoming a physical confrontation, why don't you allow me to employ my newest hackback software. With my software, I can instantly initiate a counterstrike at the hacking source that wipes out their hardware and software and puts them out of business. A little deterrence by denial. Clean and quick and nonviolent."

"Well that's one way, but when I heard you speak at Black Hat you said the only and most effective way to stop a virus or hack attack is at the source. I remember you told the audience to just think of the cyber world as their own bodies and if they prevent the cold virus from entering their bodies, they won't get sick…"

"Yes, yes, I recognize my own lecture. I also say that once the cold virus is inside, you will be ill, and you will be ill for a while. So, prevent the insertion. Stop it before it starts. Close the entry point. It only requires one person to insert a deadly cyber virus capable of shutting down a nation and it only requires one capable cyberwarrior to stop them once they find them."

"Exactly! And that's why you're the man for this job." Reassuringly, Negocio pats Robert's arm. "Me saca *(Getting on my nerves)*. Don't be so fofo *(weak)*."

"What? I'm getting on your nerves?" Robert is insulted.

Negocio's mouth drops open in shock. "You speak Puerto Rican slang?"

"Oh no, not at all…" Robert lightly taps his right ear. "…but I am wearing a multi-language translator implant. I've understood everything you've said. So please, control your slurs."

"Well, then in English, yes I'm finding you annoying and don't be so weak."

Despite Negocio's insult, he continues feeling increasingly uneasy about his assignment of being the rat trap bait. Keeping an uneasy, vigilant watch on the surging crowd he continues his debate with Negocio. "I think it's important for you to know that I abhor violence…especially violence involving me. I see no gain from pain. But, on the other hand, I know many other methods for stopping the insertor and closing the entry point."

"Yes Robert, I expect you to use all your skills and your tools. But, I also understand that my Chinese associates desire that these hackers not only be stopped, but that they be eliminated. It's their belief that if you want to change an adversary's state of mind, then credible threats against cyberattack need to go beyond the cyber realm."

"Eliminate?" The term startles Robert. "Eliminate as in permanently erase? That seems a little harsh to me. Not actually in my job description."

"Acho, deja el gufeo! *(Dude, stop goofing around!)*" Exclaims Negocio, then he hesitates, as he remembers Robert's ability to understand his slang. He lightly pats Robert's arm again and apologizes. "Relax, I really don't mean that you should stop goofing around! You're just my bait. Remember? You worry about ending the cyber threats and leave ending the human threats to me."

GETTING THE BUSINESS

After several long minutes, a second BTI auto-auto silently glides to a stop behind Negocio's. Two Chinese men and three Chinese women exit into the square. As the police form a corridor through the curious throng, Negocio hurries to greet them. Warily, still watching the crowd, Robert follows a few steps behind him.

Impatiently, Negocio urges him to match his pace. "Stay with me Robert. I asked them to come here this morning just to meet you."

Excitedly, Negocio greets the group. "Welcome ladies and gentlemen, allow me to introduce you to Robert Goodfellow. As you requested, he is here to help you with your cyber security problems."

With a slight grimace, he continues, "I hope my pronunciation of your names does not offend you."

Smiling and nodding, a slim, Chinese woman in her mid-thirties steps forward to shake Robert's hand. She is bent to her left, limps and drags her right foot, as she advances. When she extends her right hand, Robert notices that her two middle fingers are the same length as her small finger - much shorter than her index finger. She is missing finger knuckles.

"Robert, allow me to introduce Shengwu Kexuejia. As I told you earlier, she's established a major medical and genome research facility here. Her clinic is already growing and expanding. Isn't that correct Shengwu?"

Before Shengwu can answer, Negocio quickly shifts Robert's attention to the taller, younger Chinese woman next to Shengwu. "Robert may I introduce Taiyang Neng. She is constructing our newest and largest solar power generation system in partnership with Fengli Fadianji here, who is building our connecting offshore wave and wind generator farms. With their help we'll finally be totally renewable energy self-sufficient and able to demolish our obsolete oil-fueled, electrical power plants."

29

Robert does not have a chance to speak before Negocio is introducing the remaining Chinese executives. "Diandong Qiche is the gentleman who provided us with our beautiful auto-auto glider and he is seeking a site to 3d print more BTI auto-auto ground gliders, as well as BTI autonomous aero carriages..."

"Yes, I consider BTI a mobility technologistic organization. We..." Diandong attempts to interrupt Negocio, but is silenced.

"...and Zhou Caoyao is researching our indigenous plants to produce natural medicines. She is coordinating her research with Shengwu and our Instituto." Negocio continues, ignoring Diandong.

Instead of attempting to shake all of their hands, Robert nods toward the group. They smile and return his nod. They are now associates.

Like Negocio and Robert earlier, they and the Chinese rapidly become the center of much public attention and interest. Visual recording and security aerodrones continually intermingle and hover above and around them while other personal aerodrones and biobots circle and disappear. But, two aerodrones persistently hover just outside the group. They are being watched intently by somebody. Robert wonders who.

Rather than be intimidated, Robert decides to hunt the hunters. With a prolonged blink of his left eye, he activates the piezoelectric sensors of his visual recording contact lens. Locking his eyes on the closest aerodrone, he rapidly advances toward it searching it for identifying symbols or marks. Except that this drone resembles the drone he spied outside Negocio's auto-auto, he notes nothing unusual. But, as he nears it, the drone emits an eardrum shattering, high-pitched squeal. He backs away covering his ears. Employing its sense-and-avoid technology, the drone also retreats.

"That was painful," Shengwu comments standing close behind him. "I've seen those types of aerodrones hovering around my facility. We chased them off using our anti-UAV Defense System and then followed them with some of our own drones. They loitered for a long time, but eventually we tracked them to Fort Buchannan."

"So they're Army?"

"Not certain. Could be. Could be some US Society Security goons." Shengwu eyes the drone hovering just beyond their reach. "Could be a private organization, too. Everybody operates drones."

"True." Robert turns to face Shengwu. "I must say that your English is perfect. Where did you learn?"

"California. I was born there and grew up outside of San Francisco." She proudly announces. "My father worked in Silicon Valley until Abaddon and his Society Security Deacons chased us out. He was the leading genome engineer on a US Department of Defense genetic engineering project called Experimental Life Forms or ELF. ELF was a super top secret US military genetics project synthesizing novel organisms to benefit mankind."

Hearing the words, super top secret, Robert steps between Shengwu and the drone to block it with his back. Although, he recognizes that he is probably too late. Every word, Shengwu tells him is being heard by someone somewhere.

Peeking around Robert at the hovering drone, Shengwu lowers her voice and steps closer to him. "Some SS Deacons arrested and tortured my father when he refused to use ELF to genetically engineer and create the army of mind-controlled monsters they wanted…an evil, mutant military. They called their program Christian Soldiers and demanded that my father genetically preprogram their minds to respond only to the orders of some royal Master."

"Wait." Robert raises his index finger to stop Shengwu. Now, he lowers his voice. "So, it's true. I saw rumors on the dark Internet about their so-called Christian soldier army. Army of God…at least their god…only their god, actually. But, I didn't believe it was possible. According to the rumors, they wanted it, as they say - marching as to war - against all other religions. What did your father do?"

Shengwu shakes her head. "After several brutal beatings, he agreed to return to his lab and work for them. Basically, they enslaved him to do what they could not do...had no ability to do. But, he never created anything for them, he just convinced them he was. Since they refuse to accept science, they had no understanding of his work. Righteous Rightists and SS Deacons are extremely ignorant people, you know... very naive. So, when they began to trust him and relaxed, he escaped to China. They've been desperately hunting for him, since. He is the key and holds the key to them staying in control of America."

"And what about you?" Robert notices Shengwu is cringing, as she tells him her story.

"Ironically, Abaddon's SS Deacons had already expelled me earlier. I had just graduated from UC Berkley and taken a job developing improved CRISPR-Cas9 gene editing methods for gene drives. I believe that if they had realized I am my father's daughter, they would have used me to force him to work for them. Luckily, I was already in China and beyond their reach."

Robert glances over his shoulder. The drone is still hovering behind him, closer than before. "Why are you telling me all of this now and here? This is dangerous."

"To combat possible hackers, you require entry inside all my communications, algorithms and data. Essentially then, you will be reading my mind and studying my thoughts, because my work is my existence...my life." Shengwu studies Robert's face for several moments. "We're partners now. So, I need to know that I can trust you, while you need to know what challenges may confront you and why those challenges exist. To understand that, you need to know who I am and why I ran."

"But, now you're back." Robert is incredulous. "Why?"

"Yes..." Shengwu wags her finger. "...back with a vengeance, you may say. Negocio and I hope to create a Puerto Rico populated with genomic enhanced Puerto Ricans. By expanding on the research my father taught me, my therapeutic cloning through organogenesis is proving highly successful. My gene therapy work is also producing impressive results. Puerto Rico's future superior beings are growing and flourishing right here in San Juan. I am very proud."

"Pardon?" Robert puzzles.

Shengwu smiles proudly. "Imagine a world without Multiple Sclerosis or Cystic Fibrosis or Huntington's Disease or Parkinson's Disease. With genomics and gene drives, I can eliminate them. Right here. Right now. Using genomic engineering, I can create a human without birth defects, like mine, and without genetic diseases. I can genetically engineer a healthy, super intelligent, disease resistant human. The only type of human capable of surviving in the future."

Robert's face brightens. "That's fantastic. You could benefit all of humanity. If you can end those problems, why, you'll fulfill

Hippocrates belief that wherever the art of medicine is loved, there is also a love of humanity."

Robert's praise encourages Shengwu. "It's not love of humanity, but the saving of humanity that drives me. As my Chinese cousins would say, it's my baoying. What I do in this life will have benefits in the next. So, I'm working to ensure there is a next or at least life on Earth after me. Do you realize that without human-directed evolution that the human race will probably not survive?"

After a few seconds of consideration, Robert attempts to laugh off Shengwu's dire prediction. "Oh come on now. That sounds overly pessimistic to me. I've a lot of life left in me."

Shunning his disbelief, Shengwu continues. "I believe future humans will require certain physical characteristics to flourish or maybe even survive on tomorrow's Earth. My father calls it rEvolution which he spells with a small r and then capital E for Evolution. It's a result of his ELF work."

Pausing, Shengwu meticulously examines Robert from head to heel. "Actually, I've been observing you for some time and I've determined that you possess many of those necessary physical and mental attributes mankind needs to evolve. You could be the prototype for a new improved human being."

"Prototype?" Robert asks apprehensively. "Do you mean clones? Like there would be a bunch of me?"

Silently, Shengwu smiles and nods in agreement.

"Oh, I don't think the world deserves to suffer like that. One of me is enough. Besides, I doubt that you could possibly duplicate my unique style and savoir faire." Robert jokes.

"Not clones as much as well…uh…new, improved, better humans that are a bit of you, Robert - the best parts of you - and the best parts of others. Genetic engineering of Biosystems using In vitro gametogenesis."

Robert grimaces. "So, they may still bear the burden of my appearance?"

"Well, I certainly don't want them to look like me." Shengwu wiggles her deformed fingers at Robert. "Nobody should suffer scoliosis, amniotic band syndrome and a touch of osteoarthritis, if they don't have to, and I am determined to see that future generations don't have to."

"Well true, but still, do you mean like in my image?" Robert places his right index finger on his chin.

Smiling smugly, Shengwu taps her forehead. "Why not? Mankind created its gods in its own image. Right? So, of course, since I am the creator…the Chuàngzuò zhě…who better to select and create mankind's future image, or as I believe, future gods than me?"

COFFEE RUN

Surprised by Shengwu's strange declaration, Robert retreats, just as Rita and Negocio arrive at his side.

"I'm certain that Robert is interested in learning more about your clinic." Negocio informs Shengwu, "But, Rita needs him right now, so I hope you'll excuse him. Besides, we all need to leave and return the plaza to the tourists until my announcement tonight."

"Perhaps a tour of my facility tomorrow morning, then?" Shengwu asks, offering her hand to Robert for a brief departure shake. "I have much to show you and you have much to learn, partner."

Shaking her hand, Robert nods in concurrence. "Tomorrow morning then. I look forward to it. Say, about nine?"

Beaming with delight, Shengwu nods in agreement. Attempting to break Shengwu's grip of Robert's hand, Rita begins pulling Robert away. "Let's walk and talk, Robert. I have some new information. Let's get some Puerto Rican coffee at the Cuartel de Ballaja coffee shop."

Rita guides Robert through the tourists and Negocio admirers toward Calle del Cristo. Like a pestering fly, the aerodrone Robert attempted to chase away trails after him. Weaving in and out of the crowd, a man and woman dressed as tourists also begin shadowing them. His attention on the aerodrone, Robert takes no notice of his human trackers. Rita discerns they are being followed and slows her pace. Behind the male and female tourists another couple completes their parade.

"I think you'll really like this coffee. It's distinctive. Grown here on the island."

"Coffee? I didn't know that Puerto Rico grew coffee. Is it a SPEA plantation?" Robert asks as he dodges a delivery boy weaving through the crowd riding a hoverboard.

"Who? What is SPEA?"

"Oh, you must have heard of the state of SPEA? Society Preserving Endangered Agriculture? The seasteaded independent state of SPEA? SPEA grows most of the world's commercial coffee, cacao and tea. It was on SPEA's coffee plantation in Ethiopia where I was shot." Robert touches his shoulder wound.

"No. No SPEA. Just three small plantations in our interior. Centuries old and family owned. They're mostly for tourists. But, they do sell some coffee locally." Rita forms an ok sign with her fingers. "Good, too. If you ask me."

"Plantations with humans? No robots? No guard drones?"

"Of course not. Don't be silly."

Robert acts as if he is wiping his brow with relief. "Good. I still wear scars from wrestling with some SPEA directed overland guard system robots. They call them DOGs. I call them brutal."

Rita stops and stares at Robert, inspecting his spindly body from head to heel. "Why would you pick a fight with a robot? I've seen you naked and I'm certain I can take you out myself, anytime I want."

"If you don't mind, I prefer to consider myself svelte. Maybe wiry. Certainly not spindly. Besides, what I miss in muscle I make up for with my mind." Robert flexes his left arm struggling to produce a decent bulge in his bicep. "I am a massive Metropolitan generation male. Am I not?".

"Oh yes, you're fearsome. You're a true cheche de la película *(guy who saves the day)*." Rita teases as she leads him along Calle Norzagaray and across the Cuartel de Ballaja courtyard into a small coffee shop.

Robert smiles. He knows Rita just jokingly called him a guy who saves the day in Puerto Rican slang, but he will keep his translating ability his secret. What she does not know may be a secret that helps him.

Finally, they are able to shed the aerodrone, which cannot follow them into the Cuartel. Like a dog waiting for its master to return, the aerodrone impatiently hovers and loiters outside, above the entrance.

Arriving inside, Robert discovers that Rita's favorite coffee shop is more than a secluded, quiet, air-conditioned retreat from the San Juan crowds and heat. The small shop is both a coffee roastery and a museum. Lining the walls of the small caffeine café is a variety of antique and obsolete coffee grinders and roasters that immediately capture his attention.

"Well, it's not Second Cup, but it'll do." Robert jokes.

"What? What is Second Cup?"

"Sorry, it's not important." Robert dismissively waves his hand. "Second Cup Coffee is just a Canadian specialty coffee retailer that I frequent when I'm home in Toronto. Not as good as Tim Horton's some say…maybe…but one of the best."

Her Puerto Rican pride offended, Rita snaps back. "Well, I doubt that your Second Cup serves iced lattes as good as the ones here. Don't slight them before you try them."

"Sorry Rita. No offense meant." Robert's culture-rooted politeness surfaces.

"Oh, I love Canadians!" Rita giggles. 'You guys are so polite. You say sorry all the time."

"Yes, we do seem to be profoundly polite. Definitely sorry about that." He stammers, embarrassed.

Shaking her head in bemused resignation at Robert's apology for apologizing, Rita steps to the counter. Robert catches a glimpse of Rita slipping a small packet to the barista. They both smile and nod in agreement. Without a word, the barista returns to business.

After ordering two iced lattes, Rita and Robert pass a man occupied with his wrist personal communication device. They seat themselves at the table farthest from the entrance. Rita sits with her back against the wall intently watching the door, while Robert casually studies the shop's antique coffee bean grinders and roasters.

The differences between these old roasters and the robotic, coffee production equipment he saw operating SPEA's Ethiopian coffee plantation astonishes Robert. The simplicity of it stumps him. He is so accustomed to computer-directed, robot-operated equipment that it is challenging for him to determine how the antique, manual roasters function. The metal gears and screw drives confuse him. After examining the obsolete machinery for several minutes, he realizes that his father was correct when he often described him as being a technology genius and either a digital dunce or a machinery moron. Unfortunately, his father was too often correct.

Soon after their iced lattes arrive, so do their stalkers. They spot Rita and Robert and then turn their attention to reading the menu. While the couple studies the selections, the barista serving them nods toward Rita. She returns her signal.

Robert slow blinks to activate his visual recording contact lens, as he silently observes their communications. He does not recognize the couple or understand Rita's intentions. But, he does know that in this type of situation, it is best if he stays out of the way and allows things to complete their course. He sits, sips his latte, watches and records.

Awaiting their drinks, Robert's shadowers take seats at a table near the doorway. The female sits facing Rita and Robert. She acts as if she is chatting with her male companion, but she is a bad actress. It is obvious that she is recording Robert recording her.

Covering his mouth with his left hand while idly fingering his cup with his right hand, Robert questions Rita. "So what is this news that you're going to tell me?"

"Can't really discuss it here and now. Not yet," Rita whispers toward her cup without acknowledging Robert.

With a large smile and a flourish, the barista delivers the couple their iced lattes. She waits and watches them taste and sip their drinks. Then she asks them if their lattes are what they expected. After they say their drinks taste good, she urges them to suck them down, so she can give them a free refill. The couple slurps their drinks, to keep the barista happy.

Blocking their view of Robert and Rita, the barista briefly chats with them. While urging them to enjoy their drinks, she asks them if they are enjoying San Juan and offers free tourism advice. Robert watches the woman twist and stretch struggling to see him around the barista's body barrier. She makes no effort to hide her true intentions. After showering the couple with several minutes of her attention, the barista approaches Robert and Rita.

"Would you like a refill?" The barista asks leaning close to Rita. Then with her back to the others, she whispers, "Wait about two minutes. They should be done by then."

"Yes, I think I'll have a refill," Rita answers, smiling and nodding. "What about you, Robert?"

"Oh, I think I'm good." He worries that the barista may have added more to his latte than espresso, milk and ice.

With a nod, the barista leaves to fill Rita's order. As she passes, the couple at the front table, she asks them if they want refills as well. The woman starts to respond then covers her mouth with her hand and closes her eyes. Her partner presses his hand against his stomach and begins sweating.

"Never mind." Rita calls to the barista. "I think we'll be going now."

As Robert and Rita walk past the increasingly queasy couple, Rita wishes them well, or unwell. Robert is not certain which.

"I hope you enjoy your visit here in our independent nation of Puerto Rico," she says with a slight smirk on her face, as she pays the barista.

"Oh well thank you." The woman responds with her hand spread across her mouth. "We've been enjoying our visit, so…"

"Excuse me." Standing, the man extends his right hand toward Robert while he presses his left hand against his gurgling gut. "I don't want to be too forward, but my wife and I noticed you in the plaza. You're Robert Goodfellow, aren't you?"

Robert briefly shakes the man's warm, wet hand. "Well yes, I am. Do I know you?"

"Oh no, we've never met. My wife and I are just big fans of your work. Watched a hologram of you speaking at the Black Hat conference not too long ago. Impressive…"

Rita tugs lightly on Robert's arm. "We really need to go now, mister superstar. A juyir, Crispín."

"Oh, ok then." Robert smiles at the man and his wife, as Rita pulls him toward the doorway. "It's good to meet you. Perhaps we'll run into each other again Mister uh…"

"Voleur. Lew and Lee Voleur. I certainly hope so, Mister Goodfellow. I certainly hope so."

Rita waves her hand while ushering Robert away.

"Well now, aren't you sorry about the way you doubted them?" Robert challenges Rita. "They're simply innocent tourists who recognized me and wanted to meet me. You forget that I'm a star. It was Joseph Joubert who said that innocence is always unsuspicious."

"Hah! It's you who are the innocent Robert, for I choose to believe Ernest Hemmingway who wrote that all things truly wicked start from innocence, and I believe your new friends Lew and Lee Voleur are truly wicked."

The second male and female couple from the plaza are awaiting them as Robert and Rita exit the coffee café and enter the Cuartel courtyard.

Rita quietly directs the two, as she points toward the Cuartel's public bathrooms. "They'll be coming out soon and I imagine they'll be running to those toilets. Stick with them and help them leave. They'll be very sick and possibly a little dizzy. Offer to accompany them to their rooms. In about an hour, they may pass out. Use it to our advantage."

Just as she predicted, the Voleurs stagger out of the coffee shop. Holding their stomachs with one hand and covering their mouths with their other hand, they stumble-run toward the bathrooms. Rita motions for her cohort couple to follow them.

"The fish took the Bait. Our job is done here. Step along Robert, we have much more trolling to do."

PINA COLADAS

Rita leads Robert through a side exit away from the aerodrone spy waiting and hovering above the main doorway. Hurriedly, she strides through a small garden park and into the crowd of tourists traveling Calle Beneficencia. Once hidden among the crowd, she and Robert slow to a casual walk into the bowels of Old San Juan.

Six blocks from the Cuartel, Rita stops and peers at a shaded shop window employing it as a mirror to see if they are being followed. Robert joins her. Both detect nobody suspicious. They continue to scrutinize the walkers behind them. Only a boy on a hover scooter stopping to enter the shop approaches them. Nobody else gives them any notice.

Assured that they are not being followed, Robert switches his attention to the merchandise inside the store. Filling the shop window from top to bottom are colored ceramic statues and painted wood carvings of the biblical three kings. Some of the figures are riding horses. Others are standing and holding gifts.

Intrigued and sweating hot, Robert begins entering the shop. "Rita, I'm going in here to investigate all of these three king sculptures and grab some cool air. I've never seen anything like this in Canada or the US."

"Of course not, you're in Puerto Rico now, not America. It's just another way we're different from America and why we didn't belong together." Lecturing, Rita follows him into the shop. "Here, we believe the Three Kings are a more spiritual and faithful representation of the birth of Jesus than some obscure, imaginary saint the Coca-Cola Company squeezed into a red suit and named Santa Claus."

She grasps a small painted carving and inspects it. "You're lucky to be in Puerto Rico right now. You'll be able to enjoy our biggest holiday with us. We start observing the Christmas holiday season at Thanksgiving and we will continue into January when we celebrate *Día de los Tres Reyes Magos, or as you would say,* Three Kings Day on Epiphany. It's the most important holiday in Puerto Rico, because it's our tradition to exchange presents on the eve of Epiphany…*La Vípera de Reyes*…rather than Christmas day. Also, it's a tradition for our children to gather grass or hay or straw in shoe-boxes and leave it out as food for the Three Kings' horses. We don't provide cookies and milk for Santa. Then we reward good kids with presents and candy. Bad kids end up with charcoal or sometimes dirt."

"Well, I admit that definitely sounds different from an American or even our Canadian Christmas. But, by what you're telling me, I think you've retained your traditions. Don't know why you're so bitter about it."

With a sigh, she replaces the carving. "Sadly, it's just another part of our culture America attempted to destroy. Over the years things have changed. Today, our children get their main presents on Christmas day, like you do. But, we still give a smaller, humbler and even more rewarding gift on Three Kings Day. We also have parades and festivals, family gatherings and parties."

"Actually to me, it appears you simply adopted the American meaning of Christmas…you know…conspicuous consumption. Spend money. Lots and lots of money. Spend it even when you don't have it. That's what I call the American way. The true meaning of Christmas in America." After cooling and completing his study of the shop and its merchandise, Robert wanders out of the store.

Back on the street, Rita's face brightens as she relates her childhood joys. "But, the biggest party is when Old San Juan throws its annual festival at the Luis Munoz Marin Park. It's really fun. There's live music, food and drink, and free gifts for some lucky kids. But, the highlight of my day is always when the Three Kings come walking into town."

"Did any of the Three Kings ever pass out from walking in this heat?" Robert asks as the street heat slams his face, "Is it always this hot in late November?"

"Así es la cosa *(It is how it is, whether we like it or not).* Puerto Rico is no different from the rest of the world. Every year, we're a little hotter. It's the endless fire. And yes, last year one of the Kings did faint during their walk. Although, as I remember, he may have fainted over rum drunk as well as being overheated." Rita adds with a chuckle as she strides ahead.

After walking several blocks, wiping his sweat-wet face, Robert begins lagging behind Rita. She leads him in and out and around downtown Old San Juan. He accepts that he is simply a lure that she is casting out to see if she can attract some more big fish. But, he wishes she was casting him in water instead of baking him on the paving stones. From the former home of Ponce de Leon, Casa Blanca, to the Departamento de Hacienda de Puerto Rico, Rita leads him past one pastel-painted building after another pastel-painted building, while expounding upon every inch of her city's centuries long history.

In the beginning, he enjoys following Rita. Her long, shapely, tanned legs encased in tight shorts are far more fascinating to him than the centuries-old buildings she is describing. But, heat, thirst and time begins to take its toll. Robert's attention wanders and his legs weaken. Rita's voice becomes a buzzing drone in his overheated brain. She is familiar with the heat. He is suffering. Sweat is burning his eyes. His throat aches for water.

He is so hot and parched that he considers grabbing and drinking one of the bowls of water dotting the sidewalk. "Why are these water bowls here, Rita?"

"For the cats." Rita points toward a large feline lounging in the shade next to the building. "San Juan is overrun by feral cats. The first sailors brought them."

Now that Rita has directed his attention to the first cat, he notices the shadows are teeming with cats and kittens. "Why?"

"In school we're taught that sailors brought three, four-legged animals to Puerto Rico; goats, cats, and rats. Goats for the sailors and cats for the rats. The sailors ate the goats and the cats ate the rats, which left the cats. Lots and lots of cats. Too many cats. There are more feral cats in San Juan and Puerto Rico than people. They're a plague."

As he continues to stumble along behind Rita, he envies the cats cooling in the shadows. After trudging along for several minutes, which seem like hours, Robert notices the scorching afternoon sun has driven almost all of the tourists off the streets. Only a few drones delivering packages and some street cleaning robots inhabit many of the blocks they walk. Even the felines are smart enough to have fled. Wandering about without a crowd exposes them. Which, he suspects, is exactly what Rita desires.

As Rita continues leading him on what he is certain is his death march. His fevered brain recalls the words of US Marine Corps General James Cartwright when he leaked the US involvement in Stuxnet, "You can't have something that's a secret be a deterrent. Because if you don't know it's there, it doesn't scare you."

"Rita, you do know that there are numerous better ways for being recognized in this city than walking yourself to death, don't you? Don't you?" Robert proposes as Rita continues ignoring him. "Why are we walking? Why don't we ride some Flyboards, hoverboards or hoverscooters? How about an electric unicycle? We'll still be able to see and be seen."

After repeatedly glancing over her shoulder, Rita beams and quickens her step. "Speed up, I see we're being followed again. At Calle Fortaleza, we'll turn right and duck into the Barrachina restaurant. I can identify them there. It's a major tourist attraction. Always has people. You'll like it. The Pina Colada was invented there."

"Is it cool in the Barrachina? I hope." Breathing heavily and drenched in his own sweat, Robert struggles to catch Rita.

"Yes, it's cool and their Pina Coladas are chilled. They also have ice water. Lots of cold ice water."

A turn here a twist there and they arrive. A blast of frosty air is a welcome relief to Robert as they enter the Barrachina lobby. Rita leads him through the hallway to the hostess. Answering the hostess' cheery greeting with a wave, she and Robert pass through and move to the far end of the bar. Rita positions herself so she has a clear view of the entrance and the other customers.

After chugging two large glasses of water and a Pina Colada, Robert is again able to communicate. "Ah I definitely needed that refresher, for it was Sophocles who said that if you were to offer a thirsty man all wisdom, you would not please him more than if you gave him a drink. So ok, now I've had my drink and now I seek wisdom. I've allowed you to drag me around this city for hours. Now spill it Rita. What is this information you promised me?"

Rita searches their area for nosey eavesdroppers or other active listeners. Nobody appears interested in them. She leans closer to Robert's ear.

"The two men who followed you last night are dead," Rita whispers.

"What! When? Where?"

"At six-thirty this morning, their nanobiological sensors we introduced signaled sudden cardiac arrest from myocardial ruptures."

"Both of them? At the same time?"

"Yes, both of them. About fifteen minutes apart is what I was told."

Pushing his second Pina Colada away, Robert eyes Rita suspiciously. "You poisoned them. Same as that couple…the Voleurs…in the coffee shop. You poisoned them."

Rita raises her hand showing her palm toward Robert. "Stop. Wait one minute. I didn't poison anybody. All we did was introduce nanobiological sensors and tracking devices into those two men and that couple. Now, we did add a few diarrhea inducing spices to weaken that couple in the coffee shop, so we could gather information about them. But, that's all Robert. Really."

Robert stares silently at Rita. He is not certain that he believes her. Nor is he certain that he trusts her. Why should he accept her story? She has misled him from the moment they met.

"Sorry Rita, I don't believe you and I'm leaving." Robert is halfway out of Barrachina before Rita reacts.

Blinded by his anger, he fails to notice the couple that tracked them into the restaurant jump to their feet when he passes their table. Like two wolves, they are on the attack. Robert is alone. He is vulnerable.

Standing outside Barrachina's entrance, he fingers his PCD signaling for a ride. Focusing his attention on his PCD, he does not hear the man and woman sneak up behind him. Seconds later, Robert is an unconscious lump on the sidewalk. He never knew what hit him.

RITA'S RUMORS

Blazing white sears Robert's eyes. Pain pounds through his skull. His stomach is churning. He is in agony.

"Wake up buttercup." Rita chirps far too loudly for Robert's buzzing brain.

He groans and covers his ears. Cautiously he rolls away from the burning light and buries his face in his pillow. He whimpers a few words that Rita cannot understand.

"What? I can't hear you."

"What happened?" Robert mumbles a little louder.

"Nanosecond electrical pulse. They hit you with this Nsep stun gun." Rita shows him a small cylinder that reminds him of his grandfather's flashlight. "Scrambled your brain instantly. A severe brain cramp. That's why you're aching so badly this morning."

Robert groans and buries his face deeper into his pillow. "I haven't hurt this bad since I woke under my bed after my graduation party at the University of British Columbia."

"Estás bueno! *(You're fine!)* Anyway, it's your own fault. I warned you." Rita wags her finger toward Robert. "You stormed out of Barrachina and stepped right into their trap."

With his arm covering his eyes, Robert rolls onto his back. Gently, he raises his arm above his face. Through his arm's protective shadow, he peers at Rita.

"Why?"

"Why what?"

"Why did they zap me?"

"Not sure. Kidnapping, I think. I found them struggling to cram you into a shared-use auto-auto. They couldn't squeeze your long legs inside. When they saw me, they dropped you and ran. Your head bounced on the street. Added to your headache a bit, I imagine."

"Where did they go?"

"Metropolitan Detention Center. San Juan police caught them three blocks away. The woman fought them, but the man surrendered peacefully. They're questioning them now."

Emitting several, loud, sympathy-seeking groans, Robert rises into a sitting position. He closes his eyes and massages his temples. His wrist PCD is stimulating his arm indicating it is time for him to prepare for his visit to Shengwu's facilities.

"Do you know who they are or where they're from?" He asks as he twists on the bed and places his feet on the floor.

"Not yet. But, we do know that the coffee café couple…your fawning devotees, the Voleurs…are members of a small, enhanced-genetics watchdog group. And, I don't think they're just interested in our sun and sights. According to our sources, it appears they're being financed by some pharmaceutical organization. So far, we haven't been able to learn much about their backers. Suspicious group. Real suspicious. Our team also found some evidence in their rooms indicating they have been surveilling Shengwu's facilities for several months. Collecting information about his patients."

Rita points at Robert. "We also uncovered some information concerning you."

"Really? What type of information?" Robert pushes himself into a standing position. He is weak and wobbly.

Rita hurries to his side to steady him. "It appears that you are on a hit list."

He waves her away. "A hit list? Me?"

Rita silently nods her head in the affirmative. Robert sags back onto the bed. He is no longer just sick. Now, he is alarmed and nervous. "But, they seemed so friendly and harmless."

"Well, of course they did. Obviously, that's their method for getting close to you." Rita asks, "Now, why do you think they want you?"

Rubbing the back of his sore neck, Robert confronts Rita. "Because, you set me up. That's why. So, I guess you and Negocio are very happy, then. Your plan is working just great. Although, I can tell you that I'm not at all enthused about my situation. Seems to be a lot of pain with little to gain."

Pointing proudly at a chair draped with Robert's new clothes, Rita ignores his disquiet and proclaims, "You won't be sweating today like you were yesterday. I printed a set of our best climate-control clothing for you. Just like I'm wearing. Keeps me cool and comfortable all day, no matter how hot it gets."

Hesitantly, Robert rises from the bed and shuffles, sorely, toward the chair holding his newly printed clothes. "You mistakenly think that you've hired some freedom fighter. Sorry, that I'm not. At best, I'm just a digital defender...a cyberspaceman."

Fingering and inspecting his new attire, he continues. "Please don't misunderstand. I do appreciate your help, Rita, and I definitely need these climate-control clothes, but you guys have the wrong guy. I hunt with cyber. This is not cyber. You know, I'm beginning to recognize myself in Rick Yancey's statement that we are the hunters---and we are also the bait. I don't like being the bait. Not excited about being the bait at all."

"Yes, just as we expected, you're definitely sucking the worms out of the woodwork." Rita flashes a satisfied smile, ignoring Robert's complaints. "But, now, it's almost time for you to strut your stuff at Shengwu's."

Dressing, Robert scowls and grumbles, "Before we go, will you at least tell me what caused those two men to die?"

"Not certain yet. They're still being examined at Hospital Del Maestro. But, it's something our doctors haven't seen before. I've been told that they've isolated their bodies in a type of biohazard containment room as a precaution."

"A precaution? Against what?"

"Against that heart fever superbug, possibly. We did some DNA phenotyping and were able to trace them to Tennessee...just outside of Knoxville. That's one of the areas being ravaged by it. People have been dying by the dozens. Faster than they can bury them. They seem to burn up inside. Some say that their blood boils."

"So why are they here?"

"Nobody knows, yet. They could have come down here hoping for a cure or they may have been banished down here as super-spreaders to infect as many of us as possible. Exterminate us."

"What!"

"Exterminism! Genocide by unstoppable super disease, Robert. It's inexpensive, effective and untraceable. Bioterrorism. It's the perfect murder weapon."

Shocked by Rita's accusation, Robert challenges her. "Now wait a second, you're not making any sense. Genocide? Nobody hates anybody that much."

Rita slowly shakes her head in disbelief at his naiveté. "Really? Do you think this is a new idea or the first time for the US? How many indigenous natives did American settlers and the US cavalry kill by infecting them with blankets containing small pox? The US devastated them with disease and then when they were too weak to fight they stole their land."

"Uhmm…?"

"Thousands. Thousands of innocent women and children. Americans purposely spread diseases that killed thousands...hundreds of thousands. Exterminated entire tribes. So, why do you think they aren't doing the same thing here? We are in a war, you know."

"War? War with whom?"

"War with America. It's an undeclared, clandestine and covert war, but it's a war nevertheless. They didn't want us to leave, because it embarrasses them. Yet, they still consider us and treat us as foreigners. Rebellious foreigners they don't like. They don't have the resources to openly attack us, and they certainly don't want to look any worse to the international community, but they can cripple us in other ways…like enabling another pandemic similar to the Zika virus. Back in twenty-sixteen and twenty-seventeen, the US Congress refused to fund our fight against Zika, so it crippled us. Keep us sick – keep us under control. That's their plan. Or they may just wipe us out. Exterminism!"

"Oh, don't be so paranoid, Rita. I was in the US before I traveled to SPEA's Venus and then Ethiopia. Puerto Rico may be independent now, but it is no different from everywhere else in the US."

Standing before a mirror, Robert primps and inspects himself. "War on the poor. That's what we're calling it in Canada. America's war on the poor. America's sovereign cities and Metrostates are prospering and growing. But, the Sists in America's countryside and rural small towns in the wastedlands are suffering. No medicines. No medical care. No training. No work. No future. And ironically, those impoverished souls are the same people that put this government into power. Sealed their own doom, you might say."

"Ok my Canadian friend, so why do you think they're down here? For our sun and surf?" Rita challenges.

Rubbing his temples, Robert frowns at his image in the mirror. His head is still vibrating and aching. "Unlike you, I don't know who they are…or were…yet. So, I'm not prepared to jump to any conclusions. So for the moment, I'll just rely upon the wisdom of Robert Burns. He wrote that suspicion is a heavy armor and with its weight it impedes more than it protects. So Rita, let's look for more evidence before we accuse."

"Ha! Está más perdido que un juey bizco *(You're more lost than a cross-eyed crab)*." Rita scoffs.

"What?" Robert fakes not understanding her insult.

"I said that you're more lost than a cross-eyed crab. Doubt me if you dare and at your own risk Goodfellow. Obviously, you didn't learn anything from your Nsep yesterday. Yes, I may be paranoid, but when I say that someone is out to get you – pay heed. My warnings are based upon fact. "

"In fact, the fact is that Negocio's and your plan is working." Robert grouses. "Working too well for me."

Finally groomed and dressed, Robert motions Rita that he is ready. "Let's go see Shengwu, so I can start doing something I'm actually good at doing. Let's kick some cyber butt."

STAMINA VITAE

From the distant past of old San Juan they travel into the futuristic present. Shengwu's facility consists of an advanced-science spa village encircling a clinic. Her facility rests across the Bahia de San Juan in the shadow of Old San Juan. A tall brick wall encloses the spa, protecting it from snooping and interference.

Robert quickly recognizes that the wall is constructed using special living engine bricks containing microbial fuel cells. He recalls reading that the cells give the bricks smart capabilities. Capabilities which enable them to make use of microbes to recycle wastewater, generate electricity and produce oxygen.

Hugging and hiding the wall is a mix of blooming Flamboyant Madagascar trees and Flame of the Woods saturating the landscape with vibrant reds and deep greens. But, Robert also notices that like the bricks, some of the tree leaves are actually artificial light-harvesting, leaf-like structures. Bushes composed of artificial inorganic leaves that capture solar energy and use it to change water into hydrogen fuel are intermingled with the actual living trees and bushes.

"A garden plot in a garden spot." Marvels Robert. "Behind these flowers, Shengwu has hidden her highly advanced medical technology well. Those artificial photosynthetic systems compose an excellent floral façade. I like the way this woman thinks. Appears the only reality she accepts is her reality."

Flitting and flying above and around the spa walls are dozens of small aerodrones. They form a geo-fence surrounding the facility's airspace. Spaced evenly atop the wall, Robert also notices the equipment of a multi-sensor drone warning system. Computer aimed lasers installed strategically complete Shengwu's drone shield. Considering all of her protection, Robert wonders how she can be experiencing hack attacks.

Swoosh. Their BTI auto-auto glides toward the entrance gates hidden in the lush landscape. As they approach, a dozen protestors jump from their revival tent shaded chairs and tables, and run to block the street in front of the facility entrance. While shouting for Robert and Rita to stop and turn around, they vigorously wave professionally printed placards and signs proclaiming, *Only God Shall Create Life* and *Genetic Engineering Is Satan's work.* Some of the protestors beat on their auto-auto with their signs. Others just shout sin at them.

They jump around with determination and dedication, but in the intense heat, they soon wither. Their protest is short lived. After less than two minutes, they are sweating profusely and wilting. Now silent and wet, they stagger back to their shading tent abandoning the street.

"Well, that wasn't much of a demonstration." Robert mockingly waves at the retreating protestors. "Appears they're heading back to their revival tent for a little reviving."

"Too hot for too little pay. We've investigated them. They're not Puerto Ricans."

"Who are they then?" Robert strains for a better view of the departed protestors.

"They're poorly paid protestors flown here from the mainland. Conservative Christian faith healers, I'm told. You know…they don't believe in science, evolution or modern medicine. Instead it's their notion that prayers or divine intervention or the ministrations of their individual healer can cure illness."

"Yes, I've met their type before." Robert smirks. "Gullible group. Of course being gullible is a requirement for their religion. But then, I believe all religion survives on gullibility. And, I expect that eventually, their gullibility will kill them. Ignore the laws of Science and you die from ignorance. They're sowing the seeds of their self-destruction…"

"…Anyway…" Rita returns Robert to their present situation. "…as you saw, they're basically harmless. They don't really bother anybody, so we allow them to stay here."

Robert disagrees. "I doubt they'll ever leave. Since they don't believe in science, I imagine they must consider Shengwu's genetic engineering an abomination that they must fight forever. Probably wouldn't like me either, since I believe in science not superstition. So, I doubt we would have much to discuss over a beer."

"Or a Pina Colada?" Rita teases.

Robert groans and massages his still aching head.

As they near the gates, the words *Stamina Vitae* engraved in a silver plate embedded in the wall catches Robert's eye. Shengwu's Latin name for her facility is deceptively simple. Meaning 'life threads' in English, it is illusory.

Stopping just outside the gates, a pair of security robots approach each side of their BTI from their stations in alcoves in the wall. The security-bots conduct identity scans of Robert's and Rita's faces and retinas. Completing their identification, the security-bots slide backward away from their auto-auto. The gates open.

"Proceed forward slowly and stop when your front spheroids contact the security stop. Sensors within the gates will scan your transport. You will be notified when to proceed." Directs the security-bot vocally to the passengers and electronically through their auto-auto's robotics-to-robotics communication system.

Their gate scan is quick. Cleared, their BTI receives directions to continue inside. The exterior circular pattern is repeated inside. Two dozen guest cottages encircle Shengwu's clinic. The clinic is a crystalline dome resembling a huge diamond in a sea of green-colored, energy-producing, artificial bionic leaves. Bionic-flower lined paths constructed of energy-producing tiles simultaneously separate and connect the cottages and the clinic.

Just inside the gate, their auto-auto stops again. They hear a hiss and then feel themselves descending. In moments, they are gliding through an underground parking garage toward Shengwu. She waves and smiles as they near.

"Welcome to Stamina Vitae, Robert." Shengwu vigorously shakes Robert's hand, before turning. "Hello Rita. Good to see that you're still watching him."

Pressing her uniquely fingered hand against a black fibrous square on a solid, metallic wall, a bio-chip embedded in Shengwu's wrist, activates a retinal scanner. She stares into the scanner until an electronic voice speaks, "Please state your name."

"Shengwu Kexuejia."

"Thank you. Your voice is recognized." A panel in the wall slides to the side opening a portal. "You may proceed."

"I have two guests. I entered their identity information earlier. I will enter their biologicals inside."

"Yes. Two additional humans may accompany you. Each must pass one second behind you and each other. They will be scanned as they enter."

As soon as they step inside, the panel closes behind them with a whisper. Perusing the chamber surrounding them, Robert realizes they are in a positive-air-pressure, clean-room. A cool, chemical sterilization mist floats from ports in the ceiling across the three of them. Warm drying air follows, creating a positive air flow that dries them while simultaneously shedding them of infectious organisms. Mist and air cleaning does not sufficiently decontaminate them.

Next, a panel opens on their left presenting them with three full-body, biohazard suits including oxygen filtering helmets. Rita and Shengwu slip into their suits with no problem. Robert is not so lucky. His suit is too short. He is only able to close his suit by slightly bending his knees and arching his back. He remembers seeing his elderly grandfather shuffling along in a similar stance.

After they complete dressing, the exit panel opens allowing them to enter the main clinic building. Shengwu and Rita casually stroll ahead while Robert shuffles behind. Shengwu leads them into her laboratory. They are the only humans in the room.

Communicating helmet to helmet, Shengwu explains her laboratory. "Along these three walls, are four enclosed gene analysis stations paired with genome editing stations and 3D bio-printers. These stations down here are connected directly to a specific patient genetic collection robot."

Sweeping her arm, Shengwu directs their attention around the room. "In fact, all of this is robotic. Robots and computers. I designed and supervised the production of my entire clinic. I only trust the accuracy and precision of robots. Humans are far too inaccurate for genome editing. One nano-slip in human genetic engineering can transform a man into a monster. So along with my robots, I have an Artificial Intelligence quantum laser-light computer operating my lab."

Leaning close and peering into one of the stations, Robert seeks to understand Shengwu's laboratory. "So your computer system is a closed system? How is anybody hacking it, if it's all inside this building?"

"No, that's my problem. Not all of my system is in house. My quantum laser-light computer is not here. It's chilling in the Pacific Ocean beneath the seasteaded SPEA capital city of Venus. Ever heard of it?"

"Oh yes, I'm familiar with Venus. Spent some time there, a while ago."

"Good. Very good." Shengwu joins Robert who is still observing the analysis and editing stations. "Information is the key component of my work. Algorithms. Too many highly involved and complicated algorithms for normal computers. So, I must transmit my data to the computer beneath Venus via SPEA's satellites. I'm working with some extremely intelligent lady named Pion there on Venus. She seems to interact directly with the computer or the computer is reacting to her. I'm not certain which. Sometimes I wonder if she may actually be a transhuman with a direct interface from her brain to the computer. I just know that she is a major reason for this clinic's success."

Chuckling, Robert straightens as much as he can within his suit. "Yes, I know Pion. And yes, she is indeed brilliant. She's not a transhuman, though. At least, I don't believe a chip has been implanted in her brain. Actually, she's a high functioning autistic, computer savant. An Asperger genius like Albert Einstein. Did you know that she is responsible for AIDAS...the principle reason the world is generally at peace right now?"

"AIDAS? I don't know anything about AIDAS."

"Few people do, actually. AIDAS is the acronym for artificial intelligence defense analysis system. It was a US defense system that Pion transformed into what I have come to call, the peace police or the prince of peace. AIDAS has already eliminated several of the world's trouble makers using its own form of peace enforcement."

"Peace enforcement?"

"Yes, it's a bit contradictory, I know." Robert turns so he can see Shengwu. "In the Canadian military, we're taught that peace enforcement refers to the use of military assets to enforce a peace against the will of the parties to a conflict. AIDAS, on the other hand, conducts peace enforcement by creating accidents through the Internet of Things."

"What?"

Robert grins mischievously. "Either you're peaceful or AIDAS may kill you with your toaster."

Shengwu suspiciously scrutinizes Robert. "Is this your subtle warning? Should I be nervous?"

"Started any wars recently?"

"No, of course not."

"Well, then you should be safe…unless you have a testy toaster." Robert reassures her with a grin.

Standing across the room, Rita is inspecting a single gene analysis and gene editing combination station separated from all of the other stations. Behind the station is an unmarked door. "Excuse me! Can you tell me about these stations?"

Hurriedly limping across to Rita, Shengwu slides between her and the stations, attempting to block her view. "This is a special project I am studying. It's still in the conception phase."

"What's in the room behind this door, Shengwu?" Rita reaches toward the door behind the station Shengwu is protecting.

"Just storage." Shengwu grabs Rita's elbow and ushers her toward the elevator. "Follow me Robert and I'll show you our patient reception and sample collection center."

"Secrecy is one of the shadier sides of private and public life." Robert considers Shengwu's actions suspicious. "The brilliant Canadian philosopher Ian Hacking taught me that. So what is behind the door Shengwu?"

"Well it could be where I hide my hopes and my dreams or it could be where I hide my dusty, old memories that I am embarrassed for you to see." Shengwu accesses her elevator. "I'll match your Canadian Ian Hacking with my Chinese Confucius who said, "it is more shameful to distrust our friends than to be deceived by them.' Sometimes a closet should be considered just a closet, Robert."

SEEKING QI

Smoothly and soundlessly, their elevator rises one or two floors. Robert is not certain about the distance. Then, after rising, the elevator pauses momentarily before sliding sideways. With a swish, the elevator door opens. Motioning for them to follow her, Shengwu leads them into a changing room where they remove their biohazard suits and store them in a sterilizing chamber.

"Ah, that's better." Robert stretches and straightens to his full height. "I was beginning to cramp."

"Yes, I apologize. When I entered the dimensions for your suit into my 3D printer, I obviously underestimated how tall you are. But, you're done with it. I don't think you'll need it again. The rest of your tour will be outside of the sanitary rooms. So, if you'll follow me please."

Pressing her palm against a scanner on the wall, Shengwu opens a panel into a long corridor. When she steps onto the corridor's power-floor-tiles, a lamp above her glows. Rita and Robert join her and the corridor brightens. The three of them proceed to the first set of opposing glass panels.

Standing in the center, Shengwu turns to face them and spreads her arms, so she is pointing to each side. "On my right are the rooms where my nurse robots collect our genetic samples from patients. On my left are the rooms where my nurse robots inject the engineered and edited genetic material back into the patients. You may observe that procedure through the one-way mirrors. We also visually record each step of each procedure. For safety, those recordings are filed with SPEA."

Robert and Rita step close to the first mirror-window opening into a genetic sampling room. At first glance, Robert thinks he is watching a patient receiving an MRI. He is only partially correct. The patients are being MRI scanned and sampled simultaneously, with the MRI targeting the area of the patient's body for sampling.

An attendant that Robert believes may be human stands near the MRI opening.

"So, you do have some humans involved in your process?" Robert asks, "Not just robots?"

"Yes, I do. I call them counselors. I don't allow them to do anything medical, but they provide the human touch and the human support that my patients require. They're my attempt to provide them with Qi. You know Qi?" Shengwu asks rhetorically a breath before she explains. "Qi is what my great grandmother in China called the vital energy that flows through the body and performs multiple functions in maintaining health. For Qi, I have the same counselor assigned to the same patient for both the patient's sampling and injection phases. But, they are never allowed to leave the human section of the clinic. In fact, you're the first humans other than me that have entered this observation corridor. Even my lead counselor Margarete is not allowed in here."

"I am privileged..." Rita remarks, stepping closer for a better view. "...to now observe this medical procedure from both inside and outside of the rooms."

"You were a patient Rita?" Surprised, Robert visually examines Rita searching for signs of her illness.

"She was one of my first patients. Weren't you, Rita?" Shengwu lifts her chin with her finger stubs and gently moves Rita's head from side to side. "And I must say, I believe you are looking extremely well, now. Are you experiencing any more problems?"

"No, my cancer is gone...completely gone." Rita grins.

A small smile on her face, Shengwu lightly pats Rita's cheek. "Rita suffered from what her doctor diagnosed as an inoperable Glioblastoma multiforme tumor. Since Glioblastoma multiforme tumors grow rapidly, invade nearby tissue, and contain cells that are very malignant, it is among the most devastating primary brain tumors that can strike adults. Even with proton cancer treatments, ninety-nine percent of people diagnosed with it die."

Shengwu's smile dissolves into sorrow. "Doctors found a similar tumor in my mother and started proton cancer treatments, but she only lived another seven weeks more. Because of US laws, they weren't allowed to treat her with genome engineering. I couldn't...Robert, they wouldn't even allow me...her daughter to try. All I was allowed to do was watch her die…just watch her suffer and die."

"But, not here, Robert. Here I am able to heal people and watch them live. Rita's doctors only gave her a slim chance of surviving her cancer, as well. But, here in Puerto Rico, with genome engineering, I changed that didn't I Rita?" Shengwu proudly announces.

"Yes, I am cancer free. Strong and healthy." Rita smiles and pirouettes. "Better living through genetic engineering. Esto es oro de la Palestina *(This is gold from Palestine).*"

"And this is what those science deniers want to stop." Shengwu points at the celebrating Rita. "And this is why I need you to eliminate them, Robert. If they had interfered or altered any of my communications with SPEA, Rita could be dead instead of dancing."

"Ah yes." Robert steps into one of his lectures. "I find it peculiar that today's science deniers choose to ignore the words of one of their famous religious leaders, Billy Graham, when he said, 'I'm thankful for the incredible advances in medicine that have taken place during my lifetime. I almost certainly wouldn't still be here if it weren't for them.'"

"Interesting comment, Robert. You'll need to keep that thought in mind to complete your work for me." Shengwu motions for them to follow her. "Let me show you the command center I assembled."

"So why here? Why not China? Why did you establish your clinic in Puerto Rico?" Robert questions, as he surveys Shengwu's ultramodern facility. "Especially with the anti-genetics, anti-science groups and SS Deacons so close and in control of America? The same groups that tossed you and your father out of America."

"Proximity, population and protection. I'm close to a major source of patients…America." Shengwu points north toward the US. "Many Americans need, want and, most important, can afford the genome treatments that Abaddon's US government refuses to permit. So here, I'm able to treat them while Negocio protects me with his independence and freedom from America's ruling bible bullies."

Shengwu touches her chest. "Besides, you forget. I'm American. Remember? California born and raised. China is just as foreign to me as it is to you. In fact in China, my father and I were considered US spies. But then again, they ran us out of the US because they thought we were Chinese spies. You could say, I was without a country until Negocio and Puerto Rico offered me a home. I owe him my life."

Stopping to view the interior of the last room, Shengwu rubs her hands together philosophizing. "I also believe a small nation like Puerto Rico with intelligent citizens starving and striving for success is better than a big nation filled with millions of unevolved, entitled and self-satisfied people."

She draws Robert's attention to the nurse-bots assisting the room's patient. "With today's world being operated by robots, computers and Artificial Intelligence there are far too many people left with nothing to do. I contend the world needs billions less. Uneducated, indolent individuals are dragging us all down. In the past, large populations equaled power, but today a large population equals poverty. Only negative population growth with eugenics planning will save humanity and the world. Well, anyway, that's my opinion and my design."

Shocked again by Shengwu's radical philosophy, Robert attempts to divert their conversation. "Well, I guess I'll have to agree to some extent. As I told Negocio, advanced and educated, small-population states like Singapore, Estonia, Sweden and Denmark do seem to be succeeding while large population nations of Russia, India and the US are divided and failing. That's certainly true."

"Using genetic engineering techniques my father taught me for good...for human-directed evolution, I'll produce just the right number of innovators, inventors and imaginers Puerto Rico needs to succeed." Robert hears Shengwu mumbling to herself before walking away from the room's window. "At least that's my blueprint for saving the future...and mankind."

At the end of the corridor, Shengwu leads Robert and Rita past a panel labeled *Lobby* and through another sliding door into a utilitarian, almost empty, room. In its center stands an adjustable-height desk with a pair of gestural interface gloves, a pair of data gloves and a holographic electroencephalographic algorithm receiver and transmitter or HEART hat laying on top. Stretching across the three walls facing the door are wall-sized, gesture-interface, display screens. Shengwu has created an immersive collaboration platform capable of interfacing, interacting, conferencing and collaborating visually with individuals around the globe.

"Well Robert, what do you think of my dynamic, infopresence workspace?" Shengwu sweeps her arm leading Robert's eyes around the room.

"Did you construct all of this for me?"

"Oh no." She chuckles as she walks to a spot on the wall close to the door. "This is my workspace. But, it's yours to share for as long as you need it. The gloves and HEART hat will give you the access to our system you'll require for your work."

She waves her hand before a sensor. An air-cushion, lounge couch appears out of the wall. "When you need to relax or think sitting down or even sleep, you can operate the workspace from here. I call this room my electronic brain cell. It's all alive."

Pointing at a bouquet of wilted Plumeria blossoms scattered atop Shengwu's couch, Rita broadly smiles. "Aw, I see your biggest, little fan has visited recently."

Blushing, Shengwu scoops up the flowers. "Yes, Peter is still my best boyfriend. He brought these flowers by this morning before Margarete took him to preschool. Every flower came with a little kiss. Just love that little guy. Love him so much."

"Oh yes, he is a sweetie." Rita grins. "How old is he, now?"

"He is about the same age, my son would have been, if he had lived." Although speaking at Robert and Rita, Shengwu is staring wishfully into her memories. "Here is a lesson for both of you. Hereditarily diseased people like me should not try to have children. Even in vitro fertilizing myself with the best sperm I could find…the donor looked a lot like you Robert…did not save my baby from my bad genes. When I held my poor, bent and disfigured innocent baby in my arms, I cried and I cried. His only mistake was me. Coming from me. He opened his eyes, looked at me, and then he died. I gave him the name, Bǐdé. Do you know what Bǐdé means, Robert?"

Although his inner ear translator interprets Chinese, Robert shakes his head. "No, no, I don't."

"Surprisingly, it's Chinese for Peter." Shengwu smiles at the flowers. "I found the Peter I lost, here. I don't ever want to lose him again. Ever."

Rita gently pulls the Plumeria from Shengwu's hand to end her daydreaming. "I'm jealous. I haven't received flowers for such a long time. Aren't they pretty Robert?"

"Oh yes, pretty." Uncomfortable, Robert follows Rita's lead and returns their conversation to Shengwu's workspace. "So, tell me how all of this works."

Shengwu claps her hands and the middle screen sparkles to life. Projected in virtual reality in front of the screen, far larger than life, is Pion. Robert immediately recognizes her expressionless face behind her expression recognition glasses. He is thrilled that she has returned to the unemotional, high-functioning autistic savant, he watched mentally combat an artificial intelligence quantum computer in Africa. From an isolated SPEA coffee plantation in Ethiopia, using only the power of her mind, she had prevented another US and Russian war. But her battle against AIDAS crushed her. She was rocking and stimming and buried within herself when he last saw her.

"Good morning Pion." Robert waves and sunnily smiles.

"You are wrong, Robert. It is night. You are late. I have been waiting for you." Pion's normally monotone, expressionless voice is abruptly elevated. "They are attacking us. You know. You must stop them!"

DEAD AND DYING

"How many more?"

"Six, Doctor Salud. Three couples." Infectious Disease Specialist Malo Tripa delivers his morning update to his senior colleague, Infectious Disease Internist Flojo Salud.

"Dead?"

"Two. A man and his wife. The other four are in intensive care and not stabilizing." Specialist Tripa continues.

"Ok. So, now we have four dead. The two men from the other night and the man and his wife from last night. Do you have their autopsy results?"

"Yes Doctor Salud, right here. According to the report, they immediately rejected typhus, typhoid and malaria. So it appears they suspected Ebola, since they conducted immunohistochemistry testing, a polymerase chain reaction test and a virus isolation on the four deceased, plus Antigen-capture enzyme-linked immunosorbent assay testing on the four critical patients." He replies, reading from his augmented reality glasses' diagnostic report screen.

"And...?"

"...And they can't identify it." Tripa blinks his eyes to update his AR glasses screen. "But, because of the test results, they're ruling out that new, extremely virulent Ebola super-virus that they're fighting in Africa. Also the serial development of ulcerating nodules they found in their upper respiratory tracts and lungs is not Ebola related. Neither are the aortic ruptures that ultimately killed those four people. Only the extremely high fevers and the fast progression of the illness is similar to Ebola."

Pacing nervously while tapping her fingers together, Doctor Salud considers all of her limited options. "Having eliminated everything else, I believe I was correct with my initial diagnosis last night. I think this is that new superbug devastating the wilds and wastedlands of Tennessee and Kentucky. I received a social media alert about it. They're calling it heart fever. My social media contacts think that it's already killed hundreds. Seems death is its first and only symptom. Other than that, nobody knows much about it. US government is suppressing all news."

Tripa nods his head in agreement. "If the government is squashing reports, that would explain why I found no mention of it when I searched all the online international medical information systems. Most unusual."

After accessing Tripa's reports through her own AR glasses, Doctor Salud judiciously reviews the test results again. "Whatever it is, this is beyond my knowledge. I don't know what to do for them. I just don't know. I'm at a total loss here. I don't know what else I can do. I've never seen anything that kills this fast."

Salud's wrist buzzes and she smiles with relief. "Earlier, I contacted Shengwu to see if she would help us. She just agreed. So, we'll need to transfer the patients to Stamina Vitae, immediately."

"Alright, I'll begin preparing the patients for transfer." Tripa alerts his orderly-robots. "They're in isolation now, so we'll need personal protective equipment and powered air-purifying respirators for both the patients and their attendants."

Doctor Salud shakes her head. "No, don't send human attendants. Too risky. Too much chance of spreading this…whatever it is. Use our autonomous medical transfer drones."

"Ok doctor, we'll use nurse-bots to transfer them, then we'll disinfect the bots and the drones, afterward."

"I want to transfer the four dead as well. Shengwu has agreed to look at them too. So, bio-bag them, tag them and ship them."

AETHON ARISES

The afternoon sun is raging when the protestors swarm into the street automatically halting the six autonomous medical transfer drones. Yelling and waving their signs, they give a good show for a short time. Then, they begin retreating into the shade. Except for one man. He grabs at his chest. Without a sound, he slams face first into the pavement. Dead.

Blood is pooling beneath the man's head as the protestors race back to assist him. Shouting "Abel, Abel", a woman lifts the man's head attempting to roll him onto his back. Two male protestors hastily join her. Together they turn the man over and begin dragging him toward their tent. Their hands drip of his blood.

As soon as the protestors clear the street, the medical transfer drones proceed. Just outside of the facility, the two security-bots approach, survey and inspect each of the drones. Cleared, the gates open and the drones slowly advance. One by one, they disappear beneath the ground into the facility's belly.

For their own safety, all the human counselors have been removed from the facility. With regret, Shengwu also ordered Margarete and Peter to stay away. But, Peter refused. During a quick drive by visit, he delivered his daily kisses along with a small Saint John the Baptist medal. As he proudly pinned the medal of Puerto Rico's patron saint to Shengwu's blouse, he informed her that now she is protected from all bad things. Shengwu lovingly fingers the medal as she awaits the medical transfers.

"I'm surprised at you, Shengwu." Robert remarks, pointing toward Peter's medal. "I didn't think a serious scientist like you would get sucked in by a local superstition."

Tetchily, Shengwu drops her hand to her side. "Superstition? No, I'm not placing any faith in this medal Robert. But, I do believe in the love of my best little boy pal Peter. When he pinned this on me this morning, he told me it will keep me safe so I can help people. We'll soon learn if he's correct."

Inside Stamina Vitae, nurse-bots shuttle the patients, with their life support systems attached, from the drones and up to genetic sampling rooms. The rooms are sterile with positive air flow. And as an extra precaution, Shengwu, Robert and Rita again don biohazard suits and helmets, even though they are observing from the separating corridor through the windows. With a satisfied sigh, Robert stretches to his full height in his newly printed biohazard suit. He extends his arms toward the ceiling and then bends and touches his shoe tops.

One by one, they watch nurse-bots slide the patients into their individual genetic sampling machines. The process is quick. It must be. Second by second, each barely living patient is failing closer to death. After less than five minutes, the required genetic samples arrive at the appropriate gene analysis station.

"Robert and Rita..." Shengwu taps them on their shoulders. "...we need to move to my workspace and interface with Pion. She'll tweak and twist SPEA's computer and decipher this puzzle."

"I just hope she can do it fast enough. None of these people look like they have time to spare." Rita hurries past Robert and Shengwu. "This is not terminal cancer where you have six months. This is just terminal. They may not have six hours."

As they enter the room, there is virtual reality Pion, wearing one of the HEART hats she designed. Her mind is flowing into her HEART and into the artificial intelligence quantum computer. They are one. Robert, Rita and Shengwu are spellbound watching her mentally manipulating her gesture-interface, display screens. A Brain ballet.

Expecting an answer at any moment, the Puerto Rico trio are waiting and sweating in their biohazard suits. With his nervous-energy, excited blood pounding like a drum in his ears, Robert realizes he cannot just stand, stare and wait. For relief, he decides to direct his attention to fulfilling his service contract - hunting hackers.

After removing his biohazard hood, Robert slides Shengwu's HEART hat onto his head. Turning away from the fidgeting Rita and Shengwu, he activates a separate display screen and prepares to begin sniffing through the facility's data stream. Interfacing his HEART hat with the Cloud through the chip located in his left forearm, he activates his personally developed packet sniffing program. With his packet sniffer, he captures the data packets flowing across Shengwu's network in a process similar to the obsolete wire-tapping of a telephone network.

Carefully and intensely, using his packet sniffer, he analyzes the facility's server logs, encrypted codes, transmitted data and messages sent and received between Stamina Vitae and SPEA. The code engulfs him like a river he is swimming. Searching to detect signs of intrusion, cyber-spying, cyberespionage, cyber-theft, malware or viruses reveals to him the facility's internal processes and activities in their entirety. But, he ignores everything that is normal in the data stream. He is seeking irregularities.

"Wait a second, now, that's interesting." Robert mumbles to himself and halts the code flow. Carefully, he studies a suspicious packet of code bobbing along in the data stream. It does not belong there. This packet is unique. Yet, he does not recognize the code as a virus or malware he knows.

Slow-blinking his eye contact-lens-recorder, he captures it and transmits it to his cyber analytics equipment for further study. He wonders if this strange packet is what Pion claims is attacking. The more he analyzes it, the more he begins to consider it a code packet designed for cyber-theft. Somebody is attempting to steal Shengwu's genome editing algorithms, not interfere, Robert determines.

Rita's rough shaking of Robert's shoulder yanks him out of his data stream study. "Pion's back with her results."

A solemn Pion straightens her expression-recognition glasses and stares at them, waiting for the trio to give her their complete attention. When the trio is fully focused, with a fatigued, measured voice, she describes her research results. "Glanders. Analysis of the eight samples indicates the presence of a mutated, antibiotic-resistant Glanders superbug. Glanders…"

"Rita raises her hand. "Uh, pardon me. Excuse me, but what is Glanders? I've never heard of it."

"As I was about to explain…" An annoyed expression crosses Pion's face.

Robert decides that her expression-recognition glasses are not making her any more personable than in Ethiopia. Pion is just as challenging in virtual reality as she is in reality. She still considers an interruption to be a personal insult.

"...Glanders is a contagious, acute, usually fatal disease of Equidae, or, as you would say, the horse family. It's caused by Burkholderia mallei, which is a human and animal pathogen. Glanders is characterized by serial development of ulcerating nodules that are most commonly found in the upper respiratory tract and lungs. Felidae, or members of the cat family, and other species are also susceptible, and infections are usually fatal. Glanders is a zoonotic disease, so it is highly infectious for humans from horses, with a ninety-five percent fatality rate in untreated septicemia cases."

"Sorry...uh...septicemia?" Rita cautiously asks.

Pion sighs impatiently. "Septicemia is an invasion of the bloodstream by virulent microorganisms and especially bacteria, along with their toxins from a local seat of infection accompanied especially by chills, fever, and prostration."

"So it's blood poisoning then. Why didn't you just say that?" Rita and Pion continue to frustrate and annoy each other.

"No. It is more. Septicemia is a dangerous infection of the blood, which may be spread through contact with the blood, nasal exudates or mucous of infected mammals. Without treatment, Glanders bloodstream infections are usually fatal within seven to ten days. Because it spreads so fast and has such a high fatality rate, Glanders is also considered a potential bioterrorism agent. It is currently not spread by airborne transmission. However, as the pathogen continues to mutate that could change."

Since Robert knows and understands Pion's autistic tendencies and need for emotionless accuracy, which Rita obviously does not, he decides to intercede with his own question once she has completed her statement. "So, Pion, have you discerned where this Glanders mutation originated?"

"Hello Robert. I cannot determine from the genetic samples provided where this particular Glanders mutation originated. However, I conducted research and learned that fatalities from something similar to this Glanders mutation have been reported in fifty-three separate rural wilds and wastedlands spread across the American states of Missouri, Kentucky, Tennessee, Arkansas, Alabama, Mississippi, Georgia and western South Carolina." Pion displays a map with the known areas of infection highlighted.

She replaces her map with ground level visuals of the infected locations. "They are incorrectly calling it heart fever. It is my theory that this highly contagious mutation is flourishing in these areas because their hot, humid, wet conditions favor its survival. Also, they are rural areas of poverty, with many unvaccinated horses and no major medical facilities. So, they are medicating themselves and each other, and spreading it."

A shaky visual of an excavator shoving dirt into a large trench filled with bodies appears. "My sources smuggled these visuals to me. They indicate that thousands of people have died from this during the past six to nine months and that thousands more are infected. The mortality rate is one hundred percent. Entire country communities have died. The US government is struggling to contain it, but once it starts, it spreads fast and can't be stopped. Now, the government is just attempting to squash all information about it."

After studying the sampling results herself, Shengwu poses her own question. "You say Glanders causes ulcerating nodules, but you do not indicate that aortic ruptures are a result of Glanders. Are the aortic ruptures from something else?"

"I am not a doctor, Shengwu." Pion tersely responds. "Lacking a better description, I am calling it a Glanders mutation because of its basic genetic structure. You are correct. My research concerning Glanders did not indicate that individuals infected by it normally die this fast or experience such high temperature fevers or suffer cardiac arrest due to aortic rupture. It may be a Glanders mutation. It may be something else. You may call it what you wish."

Robert, Rita and Shengwu stare silently at each other. Having no suggestion, Rita shrugs her shoulders. With her eyes, Shengwu motions toward Robert who is mentally searching the floor for an answer.

"Aethon! Call it Aethon." Robert finally proclaims, quite pleased with himself. "Aethon is Greek for burning and blazing and in Greek mythology Aethon was the lead horse of the four horses that pulled the chariot of the sun god Helios across the sky. Aethon is my name for this blazing-hot, horse-borne disease."

Shengwu and Rita nod their heads in resigned agreement, adopting the name Aethon.

"Very well, I shall code name the samples I have analyzed as Aethon and use that name for all subsequent related genome trials."

Pion announces, "Individual encrypted, genome engineering and editing algorithms are being transmitted to the appropriate editing instruments."

"Engineered and edited tissue should be ready for patient transplant within the hour." Shengwu declares, then she explains to Rita, who is staring at her confused. "What we are doing Rita is engineering the original Aethon genomes so they've become anti-Aethon. Now, when we transplant them back into their host patient they are carried on microscopic nanoparticles that act as nanotransporters. Basically, the nanotransporters haul the edited Aethon genomes directly to the Aethon infection. In theory…"

Still concerned about the intent of the suspicious code packet and what it could do to the genomic engineering algorithms, Robert interrupts Shengwu's explanation. "How secure is your data encryption, Shengwu? I noticed an irregular code packet during my analysis leading me to believe an advance persistent threat has been launched against your facility."

"We employ only the SPEA space satellite network along with asymmetric encryption with public and private keys. I think that is sufficient."

"When you are optimistic and life is going well is when you relax and are the most vulnerable to attack." Robert warns her.

"So, I'm not protected? Isn't SPEA's cyber security enough?"

"For the moment, perhaps. I don't think the hackers are close to zero day launch, so my discovery of that suspect packet may have forestalled its activation. But, I think you need to be very careful. If someone is sufficiently determined and creative, it's impossible to implement airtight controls over the transmission of digital information. Hackers can intercept your satellite network and access your data with the same cheap software and equipment they use to steal satellite television signals."

"Ok, if you say so. That's why you're here." She brushes off, Robert to continue her explanation to Rita. "…Uh, where was I…oh yes…in theory, the edited genomes should destroy the Aethon that is killing the patient without injuring any other tissue or organs. I just hope we've correctly engineered the anti-Aethon and we're not too late. If they had cancer instead of Aethon, I'd say some of them are in stage four."

Robert rubs his index finger along his nose, continuing to think about the strange packets. Knowing that the weakest link in every computer security system is the human user, he seeks to learn which door Shengwu opened allowing the hackers access. "Have you been accessing some different professional sites lately? I think you may have possibly picked up that strange packet at one of those. Hackers lurk in those sites like crocodiles at watering holes just waiting to pounce on unsuspecting visitors."

With her concentration elsewhere, Shengwu replaces her biohazard suit helmet never hearing Robert's question. "Now let's observe these transplants. From the bad, I will make the good."

The transplanting process is not easy to monitor with the patients encapsulated in a sanitary chamber. As the trio treks from room to room, each patient's vitals appear in a display viewable on their window. Robert notices the patients' temperatures are climbing past one hundred and six. Their blood pressures are highly elevated and pulse rates are pounding at one hundred and twenty or higher. They are racing toward death.

When they reach the end of the corridor, the transplants are complete. Nurse-bots begin retrieving the patients and shuttling them to their transport drones.

"Now, we'll see if we've engineered an effective genetic response." Shengwu revolves and studies the room windows lining the corridor. "But, we won't know for a while. They may require weeks to begin beating Aethon and rebounding. We just don't have the proper facilities to stabilize them here. We have to return them to the hospital for their recovery."

"Well, you know William Osler said that the good physician treats the disease; the great physician treats the patient who has the disease." Robert smugly grins. "So, you must be a great physician."

"Thanks for that insight and praise, but I'm a genome engineer. I modify DNA and RNA. I'm not a doctor. I leave the healing to the doctors."

FAITH HEALER HANDS

"Join me my brethren around our fallen brother Abel. We shall pray for his soul's deliverance from his earthly pain to the glory of heaven. For he has made the ultimate sacrifice in the service of our savior, Jesus Christ. He fell victim to the foul poison spewing forth from this abyss...this hall of Hell before us. He died so that you may live."

Standing at Abel's head, faith healer Fili Diaboli is leading his fellow Stamina Vitae protestors in a prayer of remembrance. Abel's bleeding body lies before him upon a brown-paper covered folding-table. Reaching forward, he covers Abel's pavement scraped and bloody face with his hands. Each of his fellow healers mirror him and place their hands upon the man's body. Diaboli closes his eyes and lifts his face skyward. His flock lower their heads and close their eyes.

In the hushed, intense heat, the prayers' sweat splatters upon Abel's body like salty rain. Plit. Plat. Plit. Plat. Plit. Plat. Then, finally, Diaboli speaks. In a deep commanding voice, he begins exorcising the dead man's disease demons.

"In the name of Jesus, under the power and authority of the Lord God Almighty, I command all forms of demonic illness to leave the body of Abel Kane now and go straight to the feet of Jesus Christ. Your assignment and influences are over. I rebuke all pain in the name of Jesus, and I command it to get out of his body right now. I rebuke all spirits of infirmity, nerve disorder, lung disorder, brain disorder, heart disease, AIDS, cancer, hypochondria, fatigue, anorexia, leukemia, arthritis, tumors, abnormal growths, diabetes and all other forms of sickness to leave Abel Kane's body now in the name of Jesus. Amen"

"Amen." The flock responds.

Reverentially, Diaboli and his flock end their prayer and step back from Abel's body. Near Abel's feet, a woman wobbles then drops to her knees with a groan. With a thump, she collapses onto the ground unconscious. Her shallow breathing is rapid and rattling. A stream of pink snot flows onto her chin. Sweat is bubbling from her fiery red skin.

Immediately, her fellow spiritualists surround her. Together, they gently lift her to carry her to another table. Drifting into consciousness, she groans again and begins wailing nonsensical words. On the table, she claws at her chest.

Diaboli takes her hands in his hands and pulls them away from her chest. "Gather around my children. Lay your hands upon Sister Ruth. Hold her in your hearts. We must pray together to drive the evil spirits from her body."

Ruth twists and writhes in agony, fighting against their restraining praying hands. She bucks upward and then falls against the table. Coughing and choking she battles to breathe.

Struggling to control her hands, Diaboli closes his eyes and begins reciting his prayer of healing. "Please fill me with your healing power. Cast out all that should not be inside of Ruth. I ask you to mend all that is broken, root out every sickness and disease, open all blocked arteries and veins, restore her internal organs, rebuild her damaged tissues, remove all inflammation and cleanse her of all infections, viruses and destructive forms of bacteria. Amen."

Ruth's eyes and mouth explode open. Silently screaming, she strains upward. Collapsing, she crashes against the table. She chokes a ragged breath. A sigh. Nothing more.

"She rests. I have healed her. For it is written in Exodus that I am the Lord who heals you." Diaboli triumphantly raises his arms.

"Praise the Lord!" Shout the gathered raising their hands in a heavenly salute. Their eyes close. They murmur personal prayers. Several sob.

From the dust, a feral cat Ruth befriended, leaps onto the table and licks the sweat from Ruth's cheek. The cat's mewing calls her fellow faithful's attention back to Ruth. Diaboli waves his hand at the cat attempting to shoo it away. Ignoring him, it continues tongue cleansing Ruth's face of sweat, snot and blood. Finally, a young girl gently lifts the concerned cat off Ruth, cradles it in her arms and carries it away. Whispering, "go away now", the girl releases the cat at the edge of the tent. It scampers to join a young boy playing in the nearby park.

"She is dead." Announces a young man staring at Ruth's open, blank eyes.

Reaching forward, Diaboli gently closes her eyes. "Your mother Ruth is at rest in the lap of our Lord, Obed. She shall suffer no more pain. She is in tranquility. So, let us remember the wisdom of Psalm one hundred and three that says, bless the Lord, o my soul, and forget not all his benefits: who forgives all your iniquities; who heals all your diseases."

"My children, cleanse, clothe and prepare our brother Abel and his sister Ruth to return in peace to their homes and families in Kentucky. I shall speak with our spiritual leaders and arrange for their homecoming." Diaboli directs as he walks out of the tent. "We require more Christian soldiers to continue our battle. Brother Abel and Sister Ruth have passed into heaven and the Jacobs brothers have yet to join us. I must return to my church and my flock to recruit more fighters for our faith. I shall raise a holy army for Jesus. A holy army that will destroy this ungodly, sin filled coven, like the tribe of Israel destroyed Jericho, with great sound and fury."

He turns to face his disciples and raises his arms above his head to inspire them to continue his fight while he is recruiting. "Remember as we are told in Deuteronomy, be strong and courageous, do not be afraid or tremble at them, for the Lord your God is the one who goes with you. He will not fail you or forsake you."

As he is ending his encouragement, the medical transport drones depart Stamina Vitae. Diaboli angrily shakes his fist toward them. "We must stop this profane sacrilege. Beginning now, you will no longer back down. You will stand your ground and halt all who seek to enter this den of depravity. For you are the warriors of God."

"Although, my body may be far away for many days, my spirit will be here with you." Diaboli grips the shoulder of Obed. "Brother Obed will be my eyes and my ears here, while I am summoning more Christian soldiers. Stand firm my children until I return with an army of the pure and just. For God and country we shall not stop fighting until we crush this demon and his ungodly chamber of incubi."

74

DEAD LIFE

"The dead will kill you."

"Why do you say that, Pion?"

"The dead are worse than the living, Robert. Aethon is more virulent and more infectious in the dead. Without the victim's immune system fighting against it Aethon multiplies exponentially and spreads throughout the body faster. Analyzing the samples from those sick patients, indicated Aethon was reproducing by dividing through binary fission every twenty minutes. In the dead bodies, every single Aethon organism is dividing into two after only ten minutes. One becomes two. Two becomes four. And in a few hours that first nasty pathogen explodes into millions making every bodily fluid highly contagious."

"Mortui viventes docent." Robert mumbles.

"Yes, the dead do teach the living." Pion nods in agreement. "You're correct, Robert."

Shengwu disappears into contemplation. Her wide-open eyes see nothing but her inner thoughts. She is calculating. Robert watches her face contort into a grimace. Apparently, the consequences of her considerations do not please her.

Frowning, Shengwu emerges from her cloud of thoughts. She exclaims excitedly. "Ok. Robert and Rita, we must take action. Now! Immediately! If Aethon spreads as fast as Pion says, we may already be too late. First, we must alert Negocio. If we don't get this under control, Aethon will devastate Puerto Rico. Second, quarantine Old San Juan. Lock it down. All of these people came from Old San Juan. So, we must keep it in the city. No more tourists in and no more tourists out. No, make that nobody in and nobody out."

Alarmed, Rita throws up her hand. "Stop. Wait. More than four hundred thousand people live in San Juan. Thousands of tourists, too. You can't tell thousands of tourists that they cannot leave. Especially since it's the holiday season. This is our busiest tourist season."

"Do you want a pandemic on top of as a possible epidemic?" Shengwu barks. "I'm especially worried about the tourists. The sick and dying are all tourists. They're not Puerto Ricans. But, they can spread it to Puerto Ricans."

Now concerned, Rita quizzes Pion. "Robert and I were in the same bar as all of those people with Aethon. Are we infected?"

"Did you touch them? Did they touch you? Did you have contact with any of their bodily fluids? Since Aethon is not yet transmitted through the air, unless you touched their blood, sweat, tears, mucous or feces, you should not be infected. But to be certain, you and Rita must receive genetic analysis to ensure you're clean." Pion's diagnostically logical response is not reassuring.

Robert flinches. "Is it necessary for you to drill into me with a needle? Can't you just look for symptoms?"

"No. I believe that by the time external symptoms appear, it is dangerously late. But, if you desire, you two can just take your chances, since you believe that you didn't come into contact with any of those who are infected and you don't have any symptoms so far." Shengwu remarks as she activates a separate computer.

"So far!" Rita extends her left index finger toward Shengwu. "So far?!"

"Truthfully, I'm not comfortable conducting genetic sampling on any healthy people until I have completely sterilized all of my equipment and rooms, and reviewed all of my current data. Also, before I engineer any additional anti-Aethon genomes, I need to see some improvement in the four people I've already treated. A cure in theory may not cure in reality."

"But, that may take days or weeks." Rita fretfully proclaims. "Hundreds more may get sick or even die by then."

"My facility is not capable of battling an epidemic. I cannot fight Aethon alone and one victim at a time, Rita. Genetic engineering and genome modification is an individual treatment not a mass treatment."

Pacing and thinking, Robert searches through his limited medical knowledge for a possible revelation. He discovers no inspiration. For, just as Shengwu confessed about herself earlier, he also is no doctor. He is a hacker tracker.

Rita is no help either. He notices that she is repeatedly placing the back of her hand against her forehead searching for a little heat indicating a fever. She seems to be making herself sick worrying about becoming sick. Robert is surprised. He did not expect someone capable of callously inducing dysentery in others to be a hypochondriac.

"I think I'm beginning to feel warm." Rita presses her right palm against her cheek and reaches for Robert's left hand. "Feel my forehead and tell me if you think I'm hot."

Recoiling, Robert yanks his hand out of Rita's reach. "I don't think that's a good idea. Remember, Aethon travels through bodily excretions. Don't want no strange sweat on me."

"Strange sweat! We've shared a lot more than sweat." Rita again reaches for Robert's hand.

"True, but you weren't dying then." Robert teases, keeping his hand just out of her reach.

Rita scowls at him. She does not appreciate his jest. Turning away from Robert, she wipes her fingertips against her forehead. Her fingers are dry, but she remains concerned that she is discovering Aethon symptoms.

"Actually, Robert is correct Rita. Aethon is extremely transmissible. I believe we should avoid human contact to avoid contamination." Shengwu adjusts her bio-hazmat suit. "We can't go anywhere in these, but I'm not leaving here without some protection. None of us know just how far this Aethon has spread or how many people are infected. We must be cautious."

"And what do you suggest? I don't plan to spend the rest of my life in here." Rita growls, as she twists to adjust her uncomfortably confining hazmat suit.

From behind, the voice of Pion interrupts their squabble. "Shengwu, I suggest immunization through genome editing or, perhaps, by turning off some t-cell inhibitors with immunotherapy. As soon as you have sanitized a sampling room to your satisfaction, submit individual samples for analysis."

"A room should be sanitized soon. But, what will sampling the three of us accomplish Pion?" Shengwu is curious concerning her plan.

"By combining the genetic data obtained through the earlier samples of the ill and dead individuals, and your individual samples, logically it should be possible to develop an immunotherapy. Developing an algorithm editing your individual genomes should make it capable for your bodies' own immune systems to self-inoculate you to protect you against the current Aethon strains. Depending upon genetic similarities, it may be possible to develop a genetic poison pill or a vaccine for others."

"I want to go first. I volunteer." Rita shoots her arm into the sky and then immediately lowers it, embarrassed.

Chuckling, Robert points toward Rita. "I think you should definitely sample Rita first. You know it was Hippocrates who said that it's far more important to know what person the disease has than what disease the person has. And Aethon definitely has her even if she doesn't have Aethon."

Rita sullenly scowls at Robert. With her fingertips, she again searches her forehead for Aethon sweat.

Without acknowledging Robert's attempt at humor, Shengwu guides Rita forward. "Sampling room one is sanitized, as is its related equipment. I'll have some nurse-bots meet you in the waiting room and assist you. Relax Rita, you're going to be ok. I will see to it."

Shengwu ushers Rita into the waiting room. After she disappears, a few minutes pass before Robert watches her and a nurse-bot enter gene sampling room one. She is wearing a hospital gown. Experienced by her prior cancer treatment, Rita does not hesitate and climbs directly onto the sampling platform. She disappears into the scanner. Less than a minute later, she reappears with a wide smile and hops off the platform. After she leaves the room, the robot sanitizes it.

"Your turn, Robert." Shengwu grasps his arm and directs him toward the waiting room.

Trading his hot hazmat suit for a light and cool hospital gown brings a long sigh of relief. As he steps out of his dressing room a nurse-bot rolls to his side. Together they enter the sampling room. An intense chemical odor stings Robert's nose and eyes. The chemical smell is painfully potent on the sampling platform and in the sampling station. Robert closes his eyes as they begin watering. The chemical is actually an anesthetic powerful enough that he does not detect sliding inside the machine or the sampling needle inserting and retracting. Only when the nurse-robot announces that his testing is done, does he realize that he is out of the sampling tube.

Outside the sampling chamber, a nurse-bot awaits with a newly printed set of hospital scrubs and slippers. "These provide for your comfort and safety."

Ignoring the robot, he searches the chamber for his own clothes. They have disappeared. Reluctantly, he slips on the scrubs. But, after stretching and twisting and bending, Robert nods his head in approval. The scrubs are comfortable. Shengwu has finally learned how to print his size.

When he returns to Shengwu's workspace, Robert finds Rita intently watching Pion working in her lab on Venus. Pion is oblivious to Rita, as she and her AI computer intently analyze Rita's RNA threads of life. She is consumed in her search for a genetic code cure. She is seeking a technique to restrict the ability of Aethon to replicate so it self-destructs.

"She told me she is modifying Aethon's replicating polymerase so it fights against itself. Something about swapping out one amino acid in the polymerase for another, resulting in a checkmate effect on the virus. Do you know what that means?" Rita is confused and concerned.

"It means she is attempting to outsmart Mother Nature..." Robert remarks, as he retrieves his HEART hat. "...and if anyone can do it, Pion will."

"While we wait, I'll work." Adjusting his headgear, he returns to digitally sniffing and analyzing the packets in the data stream flowing between Stamina Vitae and Venus.

Using the visual of the suspicious data packet he recorded earlier, Robert examines Shengwu's latest communicated data stream. His search quickly succeeds. Among the packets of their recently transmitted genome sample data, he finds a duplicate suspicious packet. Line by line, he separates the packet into its elements. Cyber-espionage, he concludes. Somebody is attempting to steal Shengwu's genome sampling information and his genome editing directions.

Reaching into his bag of cyber-security tricks stored in the Cloud, Robert accesses his hack back program. With a few mental commands, he transplants his genetic programming packet into Shengwu's data stream. Dangling it like a fat, juicy worm before a hungry, bottom-feeding catfish, he waits and watches. The hackers are watching, too and strike swiftly. Perfect. As soon as their program invades Shengwu's data stream, Robert's program attaches itself to it. The cyberspies came to steal something and Robert generously feeds it to them. There is no escape from his Trojan horse. Robert injects his virus into their virus.

"And now we wait and we watch and we listen." Robert chuckles quietly.

"Why are you so happy?" Shengwu interrupts Robert's gloating.

"Oh, let's just say I believe I just shot a rocket down the throat of a shark. If I did it correctly and my genetic programming works, they should be screaming in agony in a few minutes as their systems suffer melt downs. I only wish I was there to watch and enjoy. My hack back program includes my special signature that makes them remember me. As they self-destruct, their computers scream a sound that breaks glass and shatters eardrums."

"So, you've eliminated them? No more hack attacks?" Shengwu asks excitedly.

Robert is cautious. "Possibly, but probably not. It depends on who they are, who they are working for, and what they're attempting to achieve. I'll be surprised if they don't continue trying. That would be unusual. So, I've introduced my computer virus killer into your system."

In an attempt to reassure Shengwu, Robert taps his forearm in front of his transmission chip. "The program I've injected into your system is provided with the eyes and brains of my AI computer. It's called genetic programming. It's alive and it will evolve to continue hunting down and killing any virus invading your system. It operates by itself. My AI will alert me whenever an unusual packet appears. And, I do expect that there will be more packets assaulting your system and challenging my virus killer. I doubt that these packets are from just one small, independent group that decided they don't like you. They need a reason and a sponsor to be here. Who are your competitors?"

"Competitors? I don't..."

Robert slowly nods his head. "Oh yes, I'm certain that you have competitors. You just may not know who they are. In my opinion, the programming packets I discovered in your transmission stream are seeking information. Somebody wants to know what you're doing and how you're doing it. Whoever they are, they want you to succeed, so they can steal your expertise. They're depending on you. They need you. They cannot afford to destroy you. They're thieves. Pirates."

"Oh no Robert, that is bad. Very bad. You must eliminate them. No one must steal our algorithms. It would be a catastrophe, Robert. A catastrophe! Do you understand?"

"Well no, I'm not certain that I do."

"One tiny mistake- that's all it would take. One little error by somebody reproducing a stolen genome editing algorithm could mean the difference between creating a genome that kills Aethon and creating a genome that is a super and unstoppable Aethon. A plague that could wipe out millions or more."

CAT SCRATCH FEVER

"Momma! Momma!" Screams five year old Peter as he runs crying into his house. Blood drips from a bite on his right hand and claw marks on his right arm.

"Peter! What happened? Your hand. What happened to your hand?" Peter's mother, Margarete, grabs his hand and rubs away his blood with her fingers.

"Ow, momma. Ow! You're hurting me." The small boy cries struggling to pull his hand free.

Pulling and tugging, Margarete drags Peter to their lavatory sink where she tenderly and carefully washes away his blood. She dabs his wounds dry with a towel. The bite in his hand is deep. Several drops of blood ooze to the top of his wounds. Peter begins whimpering.

"Here Peter, mommy will kiss it away. Mommy will make it all better." Lovingly, she kisses each of his scratches and his bite. Peter's sticky blood spots her lips. With her tongue, she licks it away and swallows.

"It still hurts momma. It still hurts."

"I know honey. I know. Let me put some medicine on it and a bandage. Ok?" Margarete begins franticly searching the drawers of her medicine cabinet for medical supplies.

"I don't know why that kitty bit me. I just petted it and hugged it. I was nice mommy. But, the kitty bit me. Why mommy?"

"I don't know Peter. Some cats are just mean. Or maybe it was sick." Halting her searching, Margaret examines his hand and arm again. "Peter, was the kitty sick? Did the kitty look sick?"

Scared, Peter begins sobbing and shaking. "I don't know, mommy. The kitty came from the tent people."

"Peter, I think we should go to the clinic. That kitty cat may have rabies. I want a doctor to look at you. Ok, baby?"

82

"No mommy! No! No! The doctor will hurt me. Give me a shot. No mommy." Peter struggles to pull away then falls to the floor curling into a ball and refusing to move. "I want to see Wu! Wu knows what to do, mommy."

"Please Peter, help me out here. Cooperate. I don't have time for your nonsense, now." Touching her wrist, Margarete summons transportation. "I know you like Wu, but she's not a medical doctor. You need real medicine."

Fifteen minutes later, Margarete and Peter are registered and huddling together in the clinic's crowded waiting room. Autonomous medical robots and robotic nursing assistants slide from person to person gathering samples and statistics. To reassure young children like Peter, and equally apprehensive adults, the robots are anthropomorphized. Their heads are constructed to resemble non-threatening characters from children's entertainment or cuddly teddy bears.

"Hello. Hola. How may I assist you today? Cómo puedo ayudarte hoy?" A teddy bear masked autonomous medical robot inquires of Margarete.

Pulling Peter's right hand toward the robot, Margarete explains, "My son was bitten and scratched by a stray cat. I'm afraid the cat may have rabies."

"You are requesting a medical image analysis for rabies. Is that correct?" The mechanical mouth in the medical robot's teddy bear opens and closes not quite matching the words.

"Yes, a rabies test on my son Peter."

"Are any additional analyses for other infections required?" Inquires the robot.

"No, just rabies. Rabies only. I don't know anything else that it could be."

"One test for rabies is ordered. For our records please state your complete name, your address, your occupation, your place of employment and the patient's complete name."

Seeking some privacy in the crowded room, Margarete leans close to the robot to answer. "My complete name is Margarete Consejero. My address is Calle Plaza Toa Baja. I am a patient counselor at Stamina Vitae. The patient is my son Peter Consejero. Is that sufficient?"

A sanitized shelf slides out of the center of the robot toward Margarete. "Infrared spectroscopic examination of the wound is required. Place the patient's injured area on the extended examination panel with the wound up."

Holding him by his elbow, Margarete gently positions Peter's hand atop the examination panel. Peter whimpers and attempts to withdraw his hand, but cannot escape his mother's strong grip. Above the shelf an arm with a golf ball sized sphere appears from the robot extending and lowering its spherical head close to Peter's bite wound. From the sphere a spectroscope glows faintly for five seconds above his bite before going dark and rotating away. With a click, the sphere rotates to a new position, locks into place and begins spray coating Peter's bite and claw wounds with antiseptic, artificial skin tissue. His wounds disappear beneath the artificial skin.

The examination and medicating complete, the panel slides from beneath Peter's hand and retracts within the robot, as it begins reporting results. "Spectroscopic diagnostics indicate no presence of rabies. The examination detected the presence of a gram-negative bipolar aerobic bacterium not rabies. The antibiotic sulfamonomethoxine with trimethoprim was administered to the injured areas via the artificial skin application."

"So, he will be ok then?" Margarete lightly strokes her fingertips across Peter's repaired hand and arm.

"Future health cannot be determined from this examination. The application of medication and the artificial skin tissue is to decrease pain and prevent additional infection. Return for a second examination and treatment for recurring illness. This session is complete." With no additional discussion, the autonomous medical robot's teddy bear head mechanically smiles and slides away from Margarete and Peter to examine the next patients.

Slightly disappointed and still concerned, Margarete leads Peter through the crowd of other patients and out of the clinic. She is relieved that he is not suffering rabies, but she worries that the unidentified bacterium the robot reported is serious. But, she cannot request an examination of an unnamed bacterium. From working with Shengwu, she knows that without human curiosity, medical robots analyze only the conditions they are ordered to analyze.

Without a name to correlate with a condition in its database, the medical robot is useless.

An auto-auto share vehicle sits available outside the clinic. They hurriedly climb inside to escape the heat. In seconds, they are returning home.

"Mommy..." Peter murmurs as he lays his head on her lap.

"What, honey?"

"...I don't feel good. I feel hot."

"Close your eyes and take a little rest, so the medicine can do its job. You'll feel better after a little nap."

"Mommy? Can we go and see Wu tomorrow?"

"I don't know, Peter. Maybe. Now rest."

Margarete stares at her hand. After brushing Peter's hair and his forehead, her palm is wet from her son's sweat. He is feverish. She is perspiring herself. She is scared.

GENOME GENERATION

"The genome editing directions for Rita are complete and have been transmitted." Pion announces with a frown furrowing her face. "She can receive her engineered genomes, now."

Noting Pion's puckered brow, Shengwu asks with concern. "Is there a problem?"

"Yes, there is a problem. Aethon mutates quickly, so I don't know how long an individual's immunity will last." Pion nods toward Rita. "Also, Rita's Spanish-Taino Carib based Puerto Rican genomes are different enough from your Chinese-Anglo genomes and Robert's African–French Canadian genomes to require different genome editing algorithms for each one of you. Based upon my calculations, I do not believe a universal vaccine created by editing genomes can be developed based on the samples you transmitted earlier or the samples from you three."

"Well Pion, you know we mixed-breed mongrels are survivors." Robert jokes, "Sometimes ugly, but hard to kill."

Shengwu paces in front of Pion's VR image, vigorously rubbing her hands together. She reminds Robert of someone desperately shining a lamp wishing to summon a magical genie. Except that Robert knows the magic genie Shengwu seeks to stop Aethon will not appear in a puff of smoke to grant three wishes. It may never appear.

"May I get my edited genome injection now?" Rita impatiently and nervously begs.

Silently waving her hand, Shengwu sends her away. With a sigh of relief, Rita happily departs to receive her genome injection.

"Have you ever heard of Kisameet clay, Shengwu?" Robert quietly ventures.

"What?"

"Kisameet clay. It's only found in British Columbia. It's an old natural remedy used for centuries by the indigenous people on the central coast of British Columbia. They treated various medical problems from skin ailments to internal infections with it."

"So what? What does Canadian Kisameet clay have to do with Aethon in Puerto Rico? Aethon is not a skin ailment." Shengwu snaps.

Robert ignores Shengwu's pique. "So, a team of researchers from the University of British Columbia in Vancouver found that Kisameet clay is effective fighting a selection of bacteria known as the ESKAPE group, which includes pathogens such as MRSA. Those same bacteria can also cause dangerous conditions like pneumonia and septicemia. Septicemia is involved in Aethon. Remember?"

"Yes, of course I remember, but what do you expect me to do, order some Kisameet clay from Canada? What is your point?" Thrusting both hands at Robert, Shengwu barks, "Get to the point!"

"Well I suppose that is a possibility, but my point, Shengwu, is that Kisameet clay is natural, yet complex. It is earth. Soil that consists of different minerals and an advanced microbial community. Its unique mix of chemical, physical and microbial properties is what allows for the antimicrobial activity and makes it more effective than any manufactured medicine. So, instead of attacking Aethon directly, person by person, let's see if we can find a type of Kisameet clay here in Puerto Rico. Something natural."

Shengwu pauses to consider Robert's proposal. "Actually that's a good idea Robert, except my research crews are out in the Caribbean searching for cone snails to extract their pain killing venom."

Robert snaps his fingers and then taps his temple with his right index finger before pointing it at Shengwu. "Isn't one of your team members studying this kind of thing?"

"Well yes, Zhou Caoyao is researching Puerto Rico's indigenous plants. Hopes to produce natural medicines. She is working in the El Yunque National Forest. That's Puerto Rico's rain forest."

"Whoa. Wait. Did you say rain forest?" Robert steps back from Shengwu. "No thanks, rain forests are not healthy for me. Too many people have tried to kill me in rain forests. When does she come into the city? I'm safe and secure in cities."

"Relax Robert, you'll be safe. Most of El Yunque is filled with tourists. Besides, there isn't that much left of that rain forest. Heat and drought has killed a lot of it. Anyway, she's renting a house in Guavate about fifty kilometers outside San Juan. It's an easy glider ride. I traveled there and visited Zhou, myself."

"Guavate, eh? Fifty kilometers outside of San Juan isn't too bad." Robert nods his head and lightly strokes his chin. "I believe I can handle that."

Rita snickers, as she reappears from her treatment. "Ooooh. I don't know. Could be very scary for a metroman like you, Robert. Shengwu didn't tell you that Guavate is just a small town and, oh my goodness, it's in the Carite Forest in our mountainous Cayey region. Huirle como el diablo a la cruz *(to run from it like the devil from the cross)*, Robert."

Robert flinches when his translation implant tells him Rita just advised him to avoid it at all costs. He grins to hide his distress, so she will not discover that he understands her Puerto Rican slang.

Ignoring Rita's teasing of Robert, Shengwu continues. "Anyway, last I remember, she is researching some plant called guanabana out there. It's reported to have natural healing properties. And, if it will help you any, I believe she regularly returns to San Juan to use the new lab in the Instituto de Neurobiologia."

"Then, by all means, I think we should visit Zhou, immediately. With genetic manipulation, she may be able to develop an answer to Aethon through nature. Discover some Kisameet clay here in Puerto Rico. It's a long shot, but…"

Raising her hand, Shengwu halts Robert. "You're leaving only after both you and Rita complete your treatments with my edited genomes. After your edited genes replacement is completed, you'll be spray coated with a clear germ and bacteria shield. It's like a second skin. We will also spray the hair on your head. All of your hair will be a little sticky until it sifts through onto your skin. It's just like getting a thick spray tan."

"Well, I'm not too familiar with spray tans." Robert chuckles and raises his dark skinned hand in front of Shengwu. "But, I look forward to your spray anyway. For as Thomas Fuller once said, 'He who cures a disease may be the skillfullest, but he that prevents it is the safest physician.' So spray away Shengwu. Spray away."

"Yes, well, be that as it may, first the treatment and then the spraying." Impatiently, Shengwu points toward the door exiting into the waiting room. "And the spraying will certainly occur in a booth without me."

In the treatment room, Robert soon realizes that insertion of replacement edited genes is basically the reverse of the sampling procedure. He is in and out of the treatment room in less than five minutes. It is all routine. But, he is less assured concerning the spraying step.

Naked and nervous, Robert activates the germ and bacteria coating shower. The spray tickles Robert in places where he is usually not tickled. It is not unpleasant, but it is far stickier than Shengwu indicated. After his coating is complete, he struggles to open his eye lids and separate his fingers. Using his adhered fingers, he pries his lips apart with a pop. Walking starts painfully and tentatively, as his tender body parts reluctantly free themselves from each other. Dressing in a freshly printed set of hospital scrubs is equally painful and difficult.

Gingerly rearranging his adhering genitalia, as he leaves the spray room, Robert angrily mutters, "I doubt that Rita suffered this type of pain and aggravation."

"You're correct. It's strictly a male problem. But, the stickiness will ease soon, as will the pain." Shengwu surprises Robert outside the spray room and ushers him toward another room. "However, now I've decided that I want you and Rita to also wear my flexible polymer membranes. I have a newly printed set for you in here."

"Membranes? In this heat? You've injected me with edited genomes, sanitized me and sprayed me. Isn't that enough?"

"No. Not as far as I'm concerned. Not with a deadly superbug like Aethon. Besides, my membranes are different. They're composed of an array of aligned carbon nanotubes that block biological agents while still allowing you to sweat. You'll wear the membranes beneath the clothing Rita printed for you."

"And what about you?"

"I won't be accompanying you. With my body and knees, I can barely walk on flat, level surfaces. I would be more of a handicap than a help in a rain forest. Besides, I have responsibilities here. I need to conduct more research with Pion to gain a better understanding of Aethon's genetic configuration. Also, I plan to immunize Negocio and Puerto Rico's other leaders. Police too. I must protect my protectors."

MEDICINE IS MONEY

"No Shengwu! Quarantining San Juan, shutting it down and locking out new tourists is not possible, especially now. This is the holiday season…our busiest time. Tourists are coming and going and spread throughout the island."

Agitated, Negocio impatiently paces back and forth in front of Shengwu. The actions Shengwu is demanding of him pose more than a problem. They are a catastrophe. His new nation is already fighting to stay afloat in a deep, red sea of debt. Survival of San Juan and his struggling state depends on tourism and tourist money. He is certain Puerto Rico will not endure if he wastes money rounding up and ejecting tourists and then barring more tourists from entering.

Negocio stops pacing to gaze out his office window at the tourists filling the street below. "Besides, how do I do it? How do I separate and isolate San Juan from the rest of Puerto Rico or all of Puerto Rico from the rest of the world?"

"I do not know President. I only know about the dead people that I've seen and the sick people that I've treated using engineered genomes."

"And how are those people that you treated? Are they getting better?"

"At this time and as far as I know, they are stable. At least that is what Doctor Salud reported to me just before I arrived. But, it's only been a day and being stable now does not mean that they will improve."

"And have any additional deaths from your so called Aethon fever been reported?"

"Well no, I haven't heard of any, but it's only been a few hours since…"

"No more dead and the sick are stable?" Scowling, Negocio challenges Shengwu. "So why are you panicking? Why are you calling this an epidemic? Be careful Shengwu, epidemic is a very,

very scary word. Very scary. Too scary to be just tossed around. Especially, here in a tourist resort. Puerto Rico needs every tourist and every tourist dollar to stay alive."

Shengwu lowers her head and stares at the floor in silence. She is distressed by Negocio's refusal to comprehend and share her concern. But, she knows the danger is real. She cannot escape Pion's description of Aethon and her warnings about its virulence and ability to mutate and spread.

Fingering her hair, she searches for an argument that will convince Negocio. "You are correct. There may be no Aethon epidemic here...yet. But, that doesn't mean we're safe. There may be many more sick and dying victims of Aethon in San Juan or in a different Puerto Rican city. Just because we don't know about them doesn't mean they aren't there."

"But Shengwu, you have no evidence that they are there...or here...either."

Shengwu attempts another course of persuasion. "President, through my tests of the patients from Hospital Del Maestro, I am certain that all eight of them suffer from Aethon. Also, all eight told Doctor Salud while they were still conscious that they attended the same nightclub. A nightclub filled with many other people. People who are possibly scattered around San Juan or Puerto Rico now."

"So where did it...this Aethon as you call it...come from Shengwu? Mosquitos, like malaria and Zika? I know it didn't materialize out of nowhere. How did it get here?"

"I'm not certain President, but at least two of the dead are brothers. I've learned they came from an area of Tennessee where Pion told me something like this Aethon is ravaging the countryside. Now, those two died here. But, only after they had been here for a while, possibly spreading this killer to more people than the six other victims, I saw. Or any of those six may have spread it. So, we don't know how many infected and sick people are in San Juan."

Negocio continues considering the tourists. "From Tennessee? I don't think we have many tourists visit from Tennessee. Isn't Tennessee where most of the Sists are on drugs? Was there meth, heroin, fentanyl or opioids in their body? Why do you think they came here?"

"I've been pondering the same question myself. So, on a hunch, I compared samples of their DNA with DNA samples from my former patients. I discovered that the two deceased brothers are named Jacobs and are cousins of a woman named Rachael from Maryland who I treated for Parkinson's disease. She is fully recovered and living in Baltimore. But, they're related, so…"

"…so they came here because they know of you, then?" Negocio scratches his head in thought. "But, why were they following Robert?"

"I no longer think they were following Robert. I think they were pursuing Rita, not Robert. I found in my records that Rita and their cousin Rachael received treatment at the same time, and I believe they became friends."

"Ok Shengwu, so they were following Rita that night. Why?"

"Not certain. But, I have a theory…" Shengwu silently waves her index finger in the air, as if she forgot what she is planning to say.

Impatiently, Negocio motions with his hands for her to continue. "So…?"

After a few moments of thought, Shengwu returns to her analysis. "…I think they realized they were sick and were seeking help from Rita. But, she wouldn't allow them to get close, because she thought they were after Robert. She is protecting him. Remember?"

"Yes Shengwu, I assigned her, so of course I remember," Negocio testily snaps. "But, I don't understand why they didn't approach you directly. If they knew they were sick why did they not go straight to your clinic?"

"I asked myself that same question. So, I reviewed everything I had and could find about Rachael and the Jacobs brothers." Shengwu smiles and nods her head. "And that's when her cousins' actions began to make sense. I believe they wanted Rita to sneak them into my clinic; past that group of protestors at the entrance gate. They were seeking my help, but they couldn't come in my front door because they would have been seen by the protestors. Turns out some of the protestors are people from the brothers' home town and members of their church."

Negocio is hearing, but is not listening to Shengwu. He is inside his mind processing what he is being told, searching for advantages not problems. Tapping his forehead with his index finger, he is visualizing the possible opportunities arising from

93

Shengwu's story. Negocio is optimistic that benefits exist in everything. The secret is to discover them.

Finally, after reflecting in silence, Negocio decides to share his thoughts. "If I understand you correctly, you're thinking that these brothers…the Jacobs…traveled all the way from Tennessee based solely on the hope that you could help them because you healed their cousin Rachael. Am I correct?"

"Yes, I suppose."

"Could you have healed them, if they had arrived in time? Isn't that what you told me?" Negocio says, developing a plan.

"I think it depends upon the individual and how sick they are. After all, healing Aethon victims is not my area of expertise. Pion and SPEA's super-fast, laser computer are the true experts. Besides, Genome engineering is not a one cure fits all situation. Each person must…"

Excited, Negocio interrupts. "That's perfect Shengwu. We have an old saying here in Puerto Rico, no hay mal que por bien no venga or in English, something good comes out of every evil. Hundreds or thousands of people are sick on the mainland. Desperate people. People who can't receive your treatment in the US because the federal government isn't allowing genome engineering. People like the Jacobs, who are willing to travel hundreds of miles to see you just hoping that you can save them. People who are willing to abandon their faith, their friends and their families, because they heard from their cousin that you may be their salvation."

"Well that's my theory, but…"

"No, that's reality." Negocio faces Shengwu to capture her attention. "When we first met, you told me that you want to heal humanity. Remember? You said you want to improve mankind. In memory of your mother and your son, you want to cure diseases and make humans capable of surviving in the future. Remember?"

Shengwu nods. "Yes, of course, I remember."

"Well, now is your opportunity to cure the incurable or at least save some very sick people. You'll become the healer that you told me you want to be. If this Aethon is as dangerous as you have been telling me then it's your responsibility to do your best to stop this scourge." Negocio is happiest when peddling his persuasion.

Negocio's statements distress Shengwu. "But, for me to treat someone with Aethon they must come to my clinic. That could mean hundreds or possibly thousands of infected and infectious Aethon victims flooding into San Juan. They could contaminate all of Puerto Rico and possibly create a killer epidemic. Thousands could die."

With both hands, Negocio points at Shengwu. "You know what this Aethon looks like and you know what to expect. Now, if those…no…when those individuals you've already treated recover, they're certain to announce it through social media. If the word isn't already spreading. Just the fact that those Jacobs brothers came to San Juan tells me the word is out about you and your clinic. So instead of allowing Aethon carriers to wander around Puerto Rico lost and possibly infecting others, we prepare for them. Coordinate them. Control them. We can't stop an Aethon epidemic from overrunning Tennessee or Kentucky, but perhaps here we can manage it."

"How can you be so certain? I'm not." Shengwu counters.

Negocio waves his hand across his desk energizing its computer monitor. "No te panikees. I've got it covered with these Center for Disease Control epidemic control directions right here. The CDC is disbanded now, but I still believe in its instructions. Let me read you some of it. I think it is common sense. For example these directions begin, *good outbreak control relies on applying a package of interventions, namely case management, surveillance and contact tracing, a good laboratory service, safe burials and social mobilization. Community engagement is key to successfully controlling outbreaks. Raising awareness of risk factors for infection and protective measures that individuals can take is an effective way to reduce human transmission.* See Shengwu, straight forward. Nothing new."

Shengwu slowly shakes her head from side to side. "No, no, no, it is not that simple or easy. You can't treat Aethon like it's a common cold outbreak. It's a killer. A killer. A type of Aethon is reported to be responsible for thousands of deaths in Tennessee and Kentucky. And you know, we already have people here who have died from Aethon."

"Ah yes those people who died. Glad you mentioned that. There are CDC directions for taking care of them here too." Negocio bends over his desk and reads. *"Outbreak containment measures, including prompt and safe burial of the dead, identifying people who may have been in contact with someone infected and monitoring their health, the importance of separating the healthy from the sick to prevent further spread, and the importance of good hygiene, maintaining a clean environment...*"

Vigorously shaking her head no, Shengwu dissents. "No! You don't understand. My clinic is small and is at full capacity now. Aethon is not easily treated, either. Engineering genomes is a complicated and difficult operation. Then after the genome replacement, you need hospital facilities and medical staff and robotic nurses and medical supplies. All of which is expensive and in short supply."

"I understand your reluctance Shengwu, but, as I said before, you must realize that Aethon victims are coming. If the Jacobs brothers came then there are definitely more on their way...or already here. You can't stop them. I can't stop them. And obviously, officials in America are definitely not stopping them. They probably want them to leave. I don't know, but they may be making them leave. Putting them on the airplanes or on ships. Buying them tickets. Makes for less problems for them. We cannot outrun this Tsunami. All we can hope to do is manage the flow of victims to contain the disease and provide their treatment. I will manage. You will treat." A proper politician, Negocio capably merges rumor and speculation.

"No! I will not abandon my other patients and my other research projects. I am..."

"No! You are correct Shengwu. You will not abandon your other patients and research. I'm still depending on you to transform Puerto Rico into the creative center of the Caribbean. However, yes! You will treat any Aethon victim that arrives at your clinic."

Frowning, Shengwu indicates she still doubts the President's plan.

Negocio straightens to his full height attempting to induce her into agreeing. "Pope Francis said many years ago that a little bit of mercy makes the world less cold and more just. Now, I'm not a real religious man, but I do believe it is your duty...no...it is our duty to humanity. We are Puerto Ricans. We may be a poor people, but we are not a cold, callous, hate-filled people like they have become on the mainland. We must help."

Shengwu nods in agreement. Her sense of altruism overwhelms her fears of an epidemic. She may not be a doctor, but she is still a healer. Her life is Life.

"Yes, it's the right thing to do and possibly profitable, too." Once again Negocio is in quest of the diamond among the coal. If there is any way he can help Puerto Rico, he will find it. "Because, you will charge for your treatment. You will charge as much as the patients can pay. Then we will appeal to the UN and the World Bank for assistance. Charities too. Charities are very sympathetic and generous toward small nations fighting medical emergencies. Medicine is money. La piña está agria. Puerto Rico needs it. You're going to make it."

"And you will coordinate it?" Shengwu continues to be wary of Negocio's promises.

"No, we…you and me…we'll coordinate it, as a team with our state police, La Uniformada, and our health department, Departamento de Salud. Remember, you're in the newly independent nation of Puerto Rico. We're on this island all by ourselves now, so either we do it or it doesn't get done. But, we must begin before we can finish."

"Then sir, to begin, I will need to implant you, your staff and as many police and health department workers as possible with genomes edited to resist Aethon. Then all of you must be trained to recognize and safely handle Aethon sufferers. They cannot be allowed to freely wander San Juan and Puerto Rico."

"True Shengwu. Good point, we cannot allow them to mingle with Puerto Rican citizens and healthy tourists and possibly infect others. But, we also don't need any bad publicity or fear like Zika caused us back in 2015 and 2016. We must ensure that we appear self-sacrificing and compassionate to the rest of the world. Yet, we have to be smart about this, so we don't create alarm here among our own citizens."

"Yes sir, it's important we remember that small things make big impacts."

Negocio returns to watching the tourists outside his window. "Yes, I agree. So, once you have…very discreetly…implanted the police and the health department workers, you'll train them to recognize Aethon sufferers…inconspicuously, of course. There's really only two external entrances into San Juan - the airport and the cruise ship port, so that's where we'll station them. I'll establish a Puerto Rico customs. I'll call them the Arrivals Greeters. Keep it friendly and non-threatening. They can survey, assist and escort."

Again Shengwu vigorously shakes her head no, challenging Negocio's instructions. "I don't know how to train people to recognize Aethon sufferers. I'm a genome engineer. My work requires analysis and engineered editing of an individual's RNA using SPEA's laser computer. As I told you before, it's an individual by individual process."

"Then change your process, Shengwu. Dios aprieta pero no ahoga! God will squeeze, but will not choke you!" Frustrated, Negocio slaps his hands together shocking Shengwu. "Invent! Innovate! It is not what you know, but what you do with what you know that is important, Shengwu. Put that cyber genius Robert Goodfellow to work. He should be good for something other than catching hackers."

"Well, I suppose…"

Delighted with himself and his plan, Negocio smiles broadly at Shengwu. "Anything else?"

"The protestors. They cannot remain outside of my facility. They'll intimidate and interfere with patients seeking treatment, like they did with the Jacobs brothers. If people are too afraid of them to…"

"I'll see what I can do, but they're not breaking any laws. Removing them may raise too many questions. People will be curious. So, we'll see. Is that all?"

"No that is not all. There is one principle that you must not forget in your planning. Aethon spreads fast and kills quickly. Thousands could die. If you don't contain and control it, like you promise, Aethon will devastate Puerto Rico. How many dead neighbors can you bury by yourself?"

FORSAKEN – FORGOTTEN

"You've been compromised. You have humiliated us. Both of you are an embarrassment."

"Yes, Deacon. I understand." Explaining his failure to complete his assigned mission to his superiors in Washington D.C. from San Juan's Metropolitan Detention Center is certainly not something Albern Dumm expected to occur when he and his partner, Faul Dusslig arrived in Puerto Rico six days ago. But now, this is exactly his uncomfortable situation. Sitting in the center's secure conference room, he meekly avoids eye contact with the scowl of his crusade commander.

"No Albern, I don't think that you do understand. Not only did you and Dusslig not accomplish your assignment, but now Goodfellow, Shengwu and the Puerto Rican government are aware of your presence." Society Security Elder Deacon Mack Evoil glares at Albern through his holographic display. "Your incompetence has exposed us. You were ordered to be discreet…to not bring any attention to our recovery effort. You failed, miserably."

"Yes sir, but once Faul and I are released, we will finish your assignment. We remain your obedient servants."

"No. You and Faul are done. You are liabilities, now. I've already dispatched your replacements. Willy Wanker, Billy Bollocks and Pour LeNuls should arrive in San Juan tonight."

"But sir…"

"Pardon me? Are you challenging me?" Evoil glowers at Albern. The heat of his anger sears the air from Washington D.C. to San Juan.

"No sir, I would never do that, but I thought our mandate was to apprehend Robert and deliver him to you, not hurt him. Willy, Billy and Pour are brutal Order of Sicarii enforcers. They may kill him."

"You're correct. They can be brutal, but they're effective. I doubt that they will fail me, as Faul and you did. But to ease your conscience, I've instructed them to take whatever actions that are necessary to secure mister Goodfellow and ensure his cooperation. They should not kill him...unless necessary."

An uneasy, queasiness engulfs Albern. Not a violent man himself, he considers Evoil's brutal tactics atrociously cruel. "But of what use will he be to you, if he is too injured to assist? Robert is not a violent person. Why do you want to hurt him?"

"That...Albern...is personal." Evoil scowls. "Goodfellow is not as innocent as you think. Not only has he obstructed our partners' cyber-surveillance efforts, but he destroyed their equipment, as well. His interference cannot go unpunished."

Evoil grinds his fist into his forehead, as if trying to scrub away pain. "But more importantly, he owes me a debt from Africa. A debt that I plan to ensure he pays...with interest. For as it is written in the book of Matthew; 'ye have heard that it hath been said, an eye for an eye, and a tooth for a tooth.'"

Evoil's words alarm Albern. When he and Faul agreed to travel to San Juan and kidnap Robert, they considered it their sacred duty. After all, Evoil had convinced them that Robert was in league with these treasonous Puerto Rican rebels and the atheistic Chinese. But, their plan was only to kidnap him and deliver him unto Evoil, not kill him.

Albern dares to object. "I cannot condone such cruelty against Robert. He has done nothing to warrant such vindictive and callous treatment, Deacon Evoil."

Glowering, Evoil shakes his finger at Albern as he rains down upon him hell fire. "Do not dare to interfere! That is not your decision, nor do you truly understand our situation, Brother Dumm! Robert Goodfellow is not yet expendable. But, he is only my means to an end. I know that he is working with Shengwu. So, through him, I can gain access to her and her father Yisheng. Yisheng created and then stole ELF."

"ELF?" Albern is unaware of the ELF connection.

"ELF and Yisheng must be found and returned to serve our Lord." SS Deacon Evoil swells his chest and points his finger at Albern. "For ELF is described in the teachings from Jeremiah when he says, 'You are my war-club, my weapon of war; and with you I shatter nations, and with you I destroy kingdoms.' ELF is our weapon, Albern, our war club, delivered unto us by God to create the Earthly Christian kingdom of our Lord."

"But, that cannot be. ELF is immoral genetics." Bewildered, Albern challenges him. "Deacon Evoil, you told us yourself that genetics is evil."

Softening his voice, Evoil attempts to neutralize Albern's ELF concerns by providing a different motive. "Yes, in the hands of non-believers, genetics is the work of Satan. But, we are believers. Goodfellow is also our conduit to those non-believers of SPEA. They are doing the devil's work and must be stopped. Through him we shall destroy all our enemies. If that means he must die, then when the time is right, it will be God's will."

No longer understanding Evoil and fearing that there is no reasoning with him, Albern decides he only desires that Faul and he be allowed to return home. "When shall we be released?"

"That's between you, your lawyer and the Puerto Rican authorities. We are no longer involved and disavow any connections with you. Any additional appearance or participation by you two will be dealt with punitively. As far as we are concerned, you failed us and you no longer exist." Blip. Evoil disintegrates into a blank, black screen.

Staring angrily at the black screen, Brother Albern quietly vows, "O Lord, God of vengeance, God of vengeance, shine forth!"

SICK SIGNS

Watching the lengthening line of frightened Puerto Ricans pushing and shoving and fighting their way through the entrance of Stamina Vitae, Robert recalls the words Scottish poet Robert Burns once wrote, "The best laid schemes o' mice an' men gang aft agley", or as he remembers it from his English literature class, the best laid schemes of mice and men often go awry. Clearly, Negocio's plan to have Shengwu inconspicuously implant his staff and as many police and health department workers as possible with genomes edited to resist Aethon has gone way awry.

An implanted and protected police officer or health department worker is never discreet and will never be silent. Certainly not in Puerto Rico where the family is still an extended system encompassing not only those related by blood and marriage, but also godparents and informally adopted children. So, they will demand the same protection for those they love – their families. Their families tell their friends. Their friends tell their friends. And, in a surprisingly short amount time, every Puerto Rican is queuing up for implanting.

The news spreads as fast as the digital signals of social media carrying it. In a matter of minutes, three million Puerto Ricans are terrified of something named Aethon. Something, they have never known before, but they instantly fear, and there is only one place where they know they can be made safe – Stamina Vitae.

Now, Robert understands why Rita pleaded that he come and assist Shengwu at her clinic, instead of aiding Zhou. She was not exaggerating when she exclaimed to him, "We're being overrun! Margarete is not here. We need you now." In less than forty-eight hours, San Juan has changed from peaceful to panic. Instead of facing a pandemic, Negocio and Shengwu now face pandemonium. Only seven in the morning and fear-filled families pack the street.

Robert's auto-auto halts as seven protestors sluggishly wander onto the pavement in front of him. As usual, they wave their signs, shout some biblical quotes and pound on the front of the vehicle. Also, as usual, he smiles and waves at them. But, they are not as aggressive this morning as in the past, Robert notices. They are just robotically going through their motions. Perhaps they are beat by the heat or perhaps they recognize him and realize that their protests will not stop him. After all, they did not discourage any of the hundreds awaiting treatment

After the protestors shout their last sermon at him and begin lethargically wandering to their tent, Robert climbs out of the mulish vehicle. It refuses to proceed with humans blocking the path in front of it. Locked in hover, its electronic voice brays that it is 'unsafe to continue' – 'unsafe to continue'. Robert is forced to hike the remaining half mile to Shengwu's facility's gates. He is an intruder and not greeted with appreciation. Instead, his walk to Stamina Vitae becomes a gauntlet run.

Fearful of contagion, Robert notices that the throng has adopted an official uniform consisting of paper masks, latex gloves and apprehensive looks from foreboding filled eyes. Afraid that the person next to them may be infected, family members cluster closely together to establish a safe space. They glare at the other groups near them, snarling at anyone who breaches their invisible safety boundaries.

"Hey! Mira pescao *(look here, you fish)*! Where do you think you're going? The back of the line is behind me! " A mother attempting to corral three arguing children shouts at Robert as he walks past them and their improvised shelter.

Unprepared for the woman's verbal attack, he meekly responds, "I work here."

"Then why are you out here?" The mother thunders at him, as she struggles to restrain her battling boys. "Wait your turn. Like the rest of us!"

"But, I'm needed inside."

"Yeah, I need to get inside too mister. We've been waiting here for seventeen hours."

Screaming and bawling, her two boys tumble to the pavement in a wrestling fight. While she is momentarily distracted by her children, Robert slips past her deeper into the crowd of other anxious and angry waiters. They are no more accommodating or understanding. In their opinion, he is a foreigner, an intruder, someone who may be infected and infectious.

They form an outraged and distrustful human wall determined to defend their safe spaces and positions. An elbow rams into his ribs. A leg thrusts forward tripping him. He stumbles, but does not fall. A slap here, a smack there, and too many insults to count. One after another he takes their shots.

Bruised, battered and rattled, Robert finally staggers through the gate and into the facility. But being inside the gate is no reprieve. Shengwu's carefully planned and constructed bio-energy producing garden is now a trampled and trashed, overcrowded, makeshift camp of apprehensive families.

Cautiously, he picks his path to the clinic building entrance, avoiding as many unhappy campers as possible. But, he cannot avoid the strong stench of urine, feces and rotting food that assaults his sinuses. Feral cats and dogs scavenge through the discarded food wrappers and bags. Hordes of flies and gnats swarm from the ground with each step. Obviously, many of these people have been waiting far too long.

Remembering how Pion emphasized that Aethon spreads through human excrements, Robert proceeds cautiously. He steps vigilantly. Nobody, he passes appears ill with Aethon, but he is not taking chances. He has no desire to test Shengwu's preventative sprays and clothes.

Only by shoving his way through a loud, bickering crowd does Robert finally battle his way inside the clinic building. Squeezing through the entrance, he wedges into a reception room crammed wall to wall with hot human flesh. Crying children, arguing adults and the strong stink of sweat slams him like a fist.

Head and shoulders taller than most of the crowd, Robert searches for a familiar face. He spies Rita, who is quarreling with a young mother holding a loudly wailing baby. She is struggling to soothe both.

Robert waves to attract her attention. "Still no sign of Margarete?"

"You certainly took your sweet time getting here." Ignoring his question, Rita shrilly assails Robert as he wades through the sea of humanity toward her. Then she mumbles so Robert cannot hear, "Más lento que una caravana de cobos."

Two women next to Rita listen, laugh and point at Robert, confusing him. "What did you say Rita?"

"I told them you're slower than a caravan of small crabs." Rita jerks her thumb over her shoulder. "Shengwu is waiting for you in her immersive collaboration workspace. This entrance behind me will respond to your bio print."

Inside her collaboration workspace, Robert discovers Shengwu discussing her deteriorating situation with Pion. "I cannot examine and treat this many people. My equipment is being overused and beginning to malfunction. I'm concerned about the accuracy. Any gene editing mistake will have serious consequences."

"I am experiencing severe problems here, as well, Shengwu. We are dangerously overextending and stressing our resources. You have to stop. Stop now!" Pion appears to be reaching her shut-down stress level.

"Stop! I fear if I don't test and treat these people, they will riot. Wreck my clinic. They may…" Mumbling, Shengwu slumps onto her rest couch. "I need help. I can't do this by myself. I need my head counselor Margarete. With a look and her soothing words, she could pacify their Aethon fears. Establish a triage to separate the well from the sick."

"But, they don't have Aethon and they are obstructions. Possibly intimidating somebody who is infected and infectious, and spreading it to others because they cannot fight through this crowd of healthy hypochondriacs." Looking extremely exhausted, Pion leans forward. Her left eye twitches as her hand quivers. "These people are not sick!"

"But, they are sick! Sick with fear." Robert bursts into their discussion. "I just fought my way through several hundred…no maybe a thousand terrified people. And there are more coming. More coming every day. They are scared. Scared to death. You cannot abandon them."

"What is your solution then?" Shengwu irritably retorts.

"Reassurance. We must make these people feel safe." Robert hesitates. "No, actually we need to make everybody in Puerto Rico feel safe. If they aren't infected with Aethon, then others should know it. Freedom from fear is the best medicine we can provide."

"And how do we accomplish that?" Shengwu asks unconvinced.

"We investigate, invent and improvise." The prospect of a challenging new mission excites Robert. Catching hackers is beginning to bore him. It is a fight he has won many times before.

"I hope your execution is as clever as your enthusiasm…" Rita interjects as she charges into the room. "…because I could really use some help out there. I just separated two mothers intent on beating each other to be the next family examined. I can't do this any longer. I need help! Where is Margarete?"

"Well, I need your help too, Rita. I also need a source of graphene and the best and latest 4D printer, because the bio-analyzer I am planning must adapt as fast as Aethon mutates."

"Which device do you have planned Robert?" Pion inquires from Venus.

Employing the HEART hat translation of his thoughts into Shengwu's virtual reality system, Robert begins constructing his mind's creation. "I see a wearable patch capable of monitoring the body's biochemical and electrical signals. My patch will contain a flexible suite of sensors connected to a small motherboard, all manufactured via a screen printing process on a thin graphene sheet that can be applied directly to skin."

Floating in space in front of Robert materializes a three-dimensional, skin-thin, spotted, white oval. He rotates and flips the oval, viewing and studying it from every angle. Nodding his head while stroking his chin, Robert silently approves his initial design. Then, the oval spins from Robert's control. To his surprise, he watches it unexpectedly change color.

"I recommend you incorporate the graphene-based DNA probe transistor developed in the late teens by the University of California of San Diego researchers." Pion suggests, as she manipulates Robert's oval. "Their graphene-based biosensor chip detects DNA mutations in real time."

Sleepy Shengwu shakes awake. "DNA mutations like Aethon? Will it detect Aethon?"

Smiling, Robert shakes his head affirmatively. "Great idea Pion. I had forgotten about the UCSD biosensor. I should've known that you'd remember. You never forget anything. Yes Shengwu, together I am confident that we can do it. It may not detect Aethon perfectly, but it will be a beginning. Certainly better than the nothing we have now, anyway."

"Sorry, but I do not understand." Rita rather meekly inquires. She has abandoned the waiting, fighting crowd for a few moments of peace. "How will this work better than Shengwu's equipment?"

"They won't work better, Rita. They won't work as well. They're just a possible alternative, if we fabricate them correctly." Robert explains, "Possibly, these graphene-based sensors may deliver Aethon test results easily, in real time, and inexpensively. They're for warning. That's all. Early detection and screening. Keep people from being terrified…of each other. Potentially, we can use something as simple as the standard breath testing technique perfected by Hossam Haick in Israel or we may use DNA to…"

Pion continues Robert's description. "…we will combine dynamic DNA nanotechnology with high resolution electronic sensing and integrate wireless electronic devices to detect the presence of a genetic mutation known as a single nucleotide polymorphism or in this case, Aethon."

"Thanks Pion, but your explanation did not help me at all." Rita snidely retorts.

"Your ignorance is not my concern. You are a most inadequate replacement for Margarete. Margarete learned quickly and did not question the obvious." Pion snipes at Rita before returning to Robert. "Robert are you prepared to proceed?"

"Think of it this way, Rita." Robert attempts to cool the antagonism between the two women. "Shengwu, Pion and I are working to develop a type of simple Aethon detection badge, so people will immediately recognize infections. Something simple. Easy to understand. Say with changing colors, for example. Yet, it must be convincing."

"Convincing?" Rita ponders the idea. "Because it really won't work?"

Robert grins knowingly. "Certainly. It must work. But, the public requires medical theater, a lot of show, to believe. Nurses. Doctors. White gowns and big Latin words. The less they understand, the more certain they are that they're being cured."

"...Green you're clean. Red you are dead. That's all they need to know." Pion states dryly before inquiring acerbically. "Do you require additional explanation Rita? Again?"

After she shouts the curse, vete pa'l carajo *(go to Hell)*, at Pion, Rita storms out and returns to the bedlam of the clinic's greeting room. As she leaves, Robert believes he hears her indignantly grumbling a threat to strangle Pion, if she ever has the opportunity. He chuckles knowing that she is not the first nor will she be the last to issue that threat.

Robert is surprised by Pion's animosity toward Rita. She has rarely displayed such emotions since he has known her. He wonders if she could be jealous of Rita's friendship with Shengwu. No, he doubts it. He is not certain she possesses that emotion. She must just be fatigued, he imagines. Which, if he is correct, means that soon, she may be too tired to be effective. So, Robert decides to refocus Pion's attention to developing Aethon detectors.

"Ok Pion, as I recall the UCSD developed graphene-based DNA probe transistor operates by directly incorporating DNA itself into the graphene sensor. They used a process known as a DNA strand displacement, where a DNA double helix has one of its strands swapped out and replaced with a complementary strand. So Shengwu, we're relying on you to provide the DNA we need."

Robert's instructions to Shengwu stimulate only silence. Instead of listening, Shengwu is peering at her personal communication device. She is obviously extremely alarmed.

"Shengwu? What is wrong?" Robert quietly walks to her side.

"Margarete. I still cannot locate Margarete. I am concerned. I haven't seen her and Peter for three days. This is not normal. Not normal." Shengwu shakes her head and rubs her brow. "You know Peter always stops by before he goes to school, and usually after school too. We talk. He tells me about his day. He brings me flowers. He gives me his best hugs."

"How have you attempted to contact her, Shengwu?"

"With everything that I have...standard telecoms and all of the social medias, but I cannot go to their house. Not now. I cannot leave here. No, not with all of these people."

"Well that may be all that you have, but it's not all that I have." Robert offers as he slips a HEART hat onto his head. "Are you willing to let me breach her privacy to learn if she and Peter are ok?"

"Well, I don't…"

"Whoops, too late, I'm already in. Can't beat remote administration tools when you want to hack a known associate. Now let's see what we can see with the cameras in her PCDs, webcams and other devices." One after another, Robert energizes Margarete's digital eyes and begins searching.

Fretfully pacing, Shengwu silently studies the floor behind Robert.

"Oh, I don't like this. Shengwu, I believe you should contact the FREMS paramedicos. Have a medical team dispatched to her home immediately."

"What! What do you see? Show me! Show me!"

"Well now, they may just be sleeping, so don't go crazy on me." Reluctantly, Robert displays a shadowy visual of Margarete lying on a small bed clutching Peter to her chest.

"Margarete. Peter." Shengwu sobs. Tears streak her cheeks. "Oh no. Margarete! Margarete! Peter…"

Robert is routing Shengwu's cry through Margarete's equipment and into her room. He can hear her calling them. Peter hears her, too. Slowly the little boy stirs.

"Wu?" Peter weakly lifts his head and pleads. "Help me Wu. I don't feel good. Mommy won't wake up. Wu? Wu?"

"I hear you Peter. I hear you." Shengwu desperately reaches toward Peter's virtual reality image. She is in agony. She stretches forward frantically struggling to help the little boy. Her hand futilely paws through his augmented reality image.

Placing his hand on Shengwu's shoulder, Robert attempts to soothe her. "I've alerted the San Juan FREMS. Someone should be there to help them very soon, Shengwu. Tell Peter, so he won't be frightened."

Instinctively leaning close to their AR images, Shengwu softly encourages Peter. "Don't be afraid amiguito. Some people are coming to help you and your mother. Peter, can you wake your mother?"

"No Wu, momma is sick. Momma told me to let her sleep."

"Margarete. Margarete wake up." Shengwu gently calls. "Margarete?"

With a groan, Margarete stirs. She smiles ever so slightly, but does not open her eyes. Peter whispers to her and then kisses her cheek.

Gradually, reluctantly, she climbs into consciousness. "Wu? Wu is that you?"

"Yes Margarete it's me. Help is on the way. Can you…" Sirens and pounding on Margarete's door interrupt Shengwu.

Robert and Shengwu watch the emergency medical team rush into the bedroom. Enveloped in anti-bacterial suits, the team are huge, faceless, hulking monsters. Peter panics. Screaming, he dives off the bed and scrambles beneath it. Margarete is too weak to move. She calls out to Peter, coaxing him back.

Shengwu softly beckons him, "Mi pequeño amigo please come out. They only want to help you. For me Peter? For me? Please?"

Hesitantly, Peter peeks at the medical team. A female paramedico lures him forward. On the other side of the bed, FREM team members transfer Margarete to a robotic aero-gurney. She appeals for Peter to come and hold her hand. Seeing his mother leaving, he hurries to walk by her side. Hand in hand they disappear from Shengwu and Robert's view.

Sobbing Shengwu leans forward her trembling hands on her knees. Tears of relief stream across her face. "Thank you Robert. Thank you. Little Peter. Margarete. They are my family. My family. My only family."

DOUBLE TROUBLE

Despair. Pion's holographic face is a picture of anguish and gloom. With her silent, haggard stare, Pion delivers her deathly diagnosis before saying a single word. Sobbing, Shengwu collapses against Robert's side. Robert inhales deeply, a choke of dread catches in his throat.

"Advanced Aethon." Pion finally states unemotionally. "Peter is in extremely critical condition. He is small and his Aethon is more virulent. Margarete is in serious condition."

"Have you edited their genomes Pion? When can we transplant their genomes?" Robert anxiously asks as he assists Shengwu to her rest couch.

"Margarete's genomes should be edited and ready for transplanting now. Is she prepped for implant?" Pion peers toward Robert. "If she is ready, then the transplant may begin immediately."

"Yes, Margarete is ready." Shengwu calls from her perch on the couch. "But, what about Peter?"

Silent, Pion looks down, gathering her data and her thoughts before delivering her diagnosis. "Two strains of Aethon are alive and growing in Peter. He and Margarete are both suffering from one strain of it. It's the same strain of Aethon found in those Americans. But, Peter is also infected with a second, similar, but definitely stronger strain of Aethon. This second strain found in Peter is a mutation of the first. It is my theory that this second strain mutated as a result of Peter receiving some form of medication, an antibiotic perhaps. As soon as the antibiotic was injected, some of his Aethon mutated into a slightly different genetic configuration."

Having recovered her poise, Shengwu rises from the couch and approaches Pion's hologram. "How distinctly different are the two Aethon strains infecting Peter?"

Pion grimaces and hesitates before continuing. "Significantly. Actually, radically different in some genetic ways. I fear generating an effective edited genome is…"

"Is what Pion?" Shengwu impatiently asks, "Is what?"

"Impossible." Pion states coldly - emotionless.

Shengwu emphatically shakes her head no. "No, I refuse to accept that. Nothing is impossible. You forget. I'm a genome engineer. I modify DNA and RNA. I developed the gene editing algorithms combatting Aethon. I make medical miracles happen. Now, I just need some time. I'll just reconstruct…"

"How much time do you estimate Peter has, Pion?" Robert interrupts Shengwu.

Pion reluctantly responds to Robert's question. "Time? I refuse to guess Peter's day of death. The same edited genomes will be transplanted into Peter that are being transplanted into Margarete. I anticipate some stabilization. I cannot predict the edited genomes' impact upon Peter's mutated Aethon. He is already weak and struggling."

"I will not allow him to die." Shengwu vows as she slides on her HEART hat to begin mentally manipulating genetic algorithms. "If there is a way for my little Peter to live, I will find it."

Formulas fly through the air. Shengwu summons them into place. She reads them. She considers them. She groans. She wipes them away. One after another, faster and faster, she decodes, decides and dismisses. She is frenetic in her search and increasingly frustrated in her failure.

Robert watches her in amazement. He tries, but is not capable of even completing a reading of any of her formulas before she waves it off. With each new disappointment, her groans swell louder. She is growing increasingly exasperated.

"Shengwu! Peter is preparing to receive his edited genome transplant in room two." Pion announces loudly to crash Shengwu's crazed crusade.

Shengwu snaps her fingers ending her contemplations. Her screen flickers to black. She is on the move. "Robert, come with me. Peter needs us. He's too young to be going through this alone."

Robert hesitates. "Shouldn't we suit up? Isn't Peter contagious?"

112

As she hurries through the door, Shengwu points toward their suits hanging in the corner. "Your suit is over there. I don't have time. Peter doesn't have time. He needs me now."

When Robert, fully encased in his hazmat suit, enters room two, he finds Peter terrified and squalling. Rivers of tears are flooding across his fever-flushed cheeks. Although weak, he is struggling against the nurse-robot and refusing to lie down to receive his implant. He is miserable.

Shengwu is kneeling by Peter's side attempting to calm him. "Peter. Peter. I'm here. Wu is here, Peter."

Shengwu repeats and repeats again her soothing serenade. Peter is crying too loudly to hear her. After many minutes, finally he hears her. Peter throws his arms around Shengwu's neck - hugging her close - burying his face deep into her shoulder. "Wu!"

"Yes Peter, Wu is here. I'm right here my little love." Shengwu gently runs her fingers through his sweaty hair then kisses his burning forehead. "You have to lie down now Peter, so I can give you some medicine. Will you lie down, if I hold your hand? I will stay right here, Peter. I won't leave you. Ok? So, will you lie down for me Peter?"

Peter tightens his grip. Shengwu coughs. Peter is choking her. Straining to force him to release his strangulating hug, Shengwu pleads with Peter. "Please, Peter, let go. Lie down, so I can give you some medicine. You need this medicine. Please Peter."

Gently, Robert pries Peter's small hands apart. Together, he and Shengwu force Peter backward onto the patient table. With Robert holding Peter's right hand in his gloved hand and Shengwu holding his left hand, the patient table slowly slides ahead. As the anesthetic air takes effect, Peter drops their hands. He disappears inside.

Bending and stretching, Shengwu peers inside to scrutinize her equipment's treatment of her seriously, sick companion. Softly, she clutches his small foot. She needs to know he knows she is with him.

Peter is still sedated when the patient table returns him to Shengwu. Sliding her arms beneath his limp body, she presses him against her breast. Her tears sprinkle upon his sweat-wet hair. As she gently rocks Peter, Shengwu kisses the top of his wet hair. A smile creeps across his face.

Not wanting to wake him, Shengwu whispers her fears to Robert. "I'm afraid Robert...very...very afraid. I don't know if I can save Peter. He is so weak and his Aethon is so strong. I found nothing in my algorithms. I'm beginning to think that beating Aethon may be impossible."

Robert chokes back his own tears. Shengwu's torment is tearing at him. "You cannot surrender to Aethon, Shengwu. Too many people are depending on you. Peter is depending on you. You must keep searching. You need to remember that Audrey Hepburn once said that nothing is impossible, the word itself says I'm possible!"

"Then you need to make it possible Robert. You've become my last hope - you and Zhou." Sobbing, Shengwu is in heartrending agony. "Promise me Robert. Promise me that you will not stop looking until you find an answer to this Aethon epidemic. It must be stopped. Promise me for Peter's sake. Promise me Robert."

PICK YOUR POISON

"Step it up Robert. We're losing daylight and we're losing time. Remember, we're not in Canada. Being nearer the equator, we have less time in our day to waste. I must examine this area to our right before dark. Neither of us wants to stumble around out here in these trees on this mountainside at night." Scrambling through the brush up the side of El Yunque's El Toro Mountain, Zhou hurries Robert forward. He is slowing her frantic search for a natural treatment to stop or at least slow the Aethon epidemic.

Sucking desperately for oxygen, Robert yanks on a tree heaving himself upward. Slipping and sliding atop the leaves, ferns and moss cluttering the rain forest floor, his right foot skids backward, throwing him down. His knee slams against a stump. He slumps onto the steep, stony mountain side.

In the rain forest heat, Robert is boiling in his own sweat. Encased in both Shengwu's protective membrane and Rita's special garments, he is self-basting and roasting himself. After shedding Zhou's digital sampling bag, he rolls onto his back. Above him the trees and clouds swirl and dance him dizzy. He closes his eyes. Thump. Thump. Thump. His heart pounds his blood into his brain.

"Why did I volunteer to come out here?" Robert moans, as his stomach's contents climb up his throat. "I don't belong here. I should be working in a clean, cool lab. That's where I belong. I have to finish those badges. I have to stop those cyber thieves. They don't stop. I can't stop…oh, my aching head."

Prostrate on the forest floor, his raging pulse slowing, he remembers the real reason why he is stumbling through this rain forest. He promised Shengwu. Visions of Margarete and Peter fighting to survive flood his mind's eye. He also sees Shengwu collapsing into tears clutching Peter in her arms as he battles a mutated, stronger strain of Aethon.

All night at the facility, Robert and Rita attempted to console her and offer sympathy, but she remained inconsolable - almost suicidal. Only when Robert repeatedly swore that he would team with Zhou and immediately begin assisting her search for a natural remedy did Shengwu step back from the brink. Watching Shengwu cuddle little Peter, as he burned with fever, crushed his heart. Her pain became his pain.

"You aren't looking too good." Zhou observes after she clambers down the slope to his side.

"Yes, well I'm not feeling too good, either." Robert gasps, as he unbuttons his shirt searching for relief.

"What is this covering you are wearing? You look like a burnt sausage."

Robert runs his fingers across his chest. "Shengwu designed and printed this to protect me from possible Aethon infection. Like she was my mother, she demanded that both Rita and I wear them before she would allow us to leave her facility."

"Well, you're not with Shengwu now, Robert, you're with me. Have you been encased in this outfit the last two days?"

"Yes, but we were working in the Instituto de Neurobiologia lab in San Juan analyzing those Aethon victim genetic samples, so I wanted this extra infection protection."

"Ok. I understand that, but you're not there now. You're in the middle of a rain forest with me...only me...and there's no way I can haul you out of here if you collapse from a heat stroke. So, get rid of that suffocating cocoon."

"Gladly. It's strangling me like a starving boa constrictor. Shengwu promised me that her special nanotube cloth would breathe. Well, she is wrong. It's not breathing...and neither am I...almost."

"Well take a few minutes to recuperate Robert, but don't linger. Our time is quickly disappearing. If we don't discover something soon for little Peter and his mother, we'll lose them. I'm afraid we'll lose Shengwu too. She was mentally collapsing when I visited her last night and I think she is just physically exhausted, as well. She is not sleeping. She is not eating. She is either with Peter and Margarete or working at her workspace. If we can't give her some positive news soon...well we just need to find something...and soon."

Zhou does not stay with Robert. Nimble as a mountain goat, she scampers up the steep slope leaving him to care for himself. Alone, with relief, he happily peels off Shengwu's second skin. Resting naked, except for his undershorts, his sweat covered body chills in the feeble breeze whispering through the thick trees.

Hiding in the shrubs near him a Coqui frog cheerily chirps. Above him two red-throated hummingbirds flitter and circle. They are the first real biological hummingbirds Robert has ever seen. He observes that they are smaller and less colorful than the biomimetic hummingbirds he owns in Toronto. Also, they are not as friendly. When he extends his hand the twin birds flash away.

"Ok, fly away you biological Trochiliformes. I can print a dozen of you in my lab that are prettier and smarter." Robert grouses at the empty air. "Wish I could print an Aethon cure that easy."

Although he appreciates the peaceful nature show while momentarily reviving in the cool, he knows that Zhou requires his help. He is her research assistant robot. Her normal robotic assistant cannot operate in this thick undergrowth and on these steep slopes of the El Yunque rainforest without trampling and crushing the endangered vegetation. Lugging her digital sampling bag and portable spectrometer is now Robert's chore.

It is difficult for robot-proponent Robert to admit it, but some tasks still remain that only humans can accomplish. Although, as he massages his cramping legs, he wonders if he is the best human to replace her robot for this work. He rarely walks outside on anything that is not paved and clearly marked. Being in nature is simply not natural for him.

Unable to see Zhou on the mountain above him, he worries that he may lose her in the brush, if he does not hustle. If he loses her then he is lost. She knows where they are and how they got here. He trusts her far more than he trusts his GPS in this trackless, overgrown section of the rain forest where the thick leaves and tangled limbs block his GPS signals.

After redressing in Rita's 3D printed cooling clothes, Robert wrestles into Zhou's digital sampling pack. Grabbing his discarded protective clothing, he starts struggling up the mountainside toward where he last spied Zhou.

Tripping and slipping and banging against the brush, Robert plows his way upward through the thick, tangled undergrowth leaving a trail of sweat, blood, bruised vegetation and anguish, muttering. "Ah, but these are the sacrifices I make in the name of science and to save mankind."

In his haste, Robert is carelessly clumsy. Too tall for wandering through El Yunque's thick, leafy canopy, he is constantly bending and twisting to avoid a face full of foliage. But, he does not duck low enough as he claws his way through a grove of Palo Bronco trees. It is a mistake he will never forget. Pulling himself ahead, he yanks a spindly Palo Bronco tree onto himself. As the bottom of the tree's leaves slap his arms and cheeks, needle-like, stinging hairs sear his skin. His arm burns as if ablaze.

"Augh!" Robert screams alerting Zhou to his distress.

"Don't touch your face or arms! You'll only hurt worse, if you touch them." Zhou yells from above him. "Rinse your affected areas with your water. It will help ease the sting. But, no matter what, you're going to hurt for at least the next half hour. And stay away from those stinging nettles to your left and the Dumbcane plants directly ahead of you. They're even more painful."

Shaking his fiery arms, Robert surveys the jungle entangling him. "I'm afraid to move. How can plants with such beautiful blooms be so dreadful?"

"Oh, I disagree Robert. It's their sting and poison that makes them useful. We won't discover an Aethon antibiotic in a petunia. Or in guanabana either, as I've already discovered. But in these plants' poison may hide the potion we seek."

"Really? Which plant? They all look equally poison to me."

Zhou raises a large green leaf in her gloved hand to show Robert. "I am particularly interested in this Dumbcane plant, because its leaves contain needle-like *calcium oxalate* crystals and *proteolytic enzymes.* Very potent. Eating its leaves can cause temporary paralysis of the mouth, tongue, throat and vocal cords. Also, if you accidentally rub it into your eyes the crystals from the leaf can cause temporary vision loss and swelling of the eyelid."

"And that's good for you?"

"Well, it's a start. Actually, I am searching for something more lethal. It requires a killer to kill a killer. Aethon is a superbug that is simply mutating too quickly to tackle with hope and half measures. To stop Aethon, it must be eradicated...eliminated completely."

Carefully backing away from the Palo Bronco tree, Robert searches for a safer path up the mountainside to Zhou. "Aha! I see you follow the old saying that what doesn't kill you will make you better or in this case, what doesn't kill you may heal you, eh."

"Robert, be certain that you record the exact location of the Palo Bronco tree that bit you. If the samples I've taken from it and the soil around its roots indicate that it can be genetically altered to be useful, we will need to know where to find it again."

After recording the location, Robert cautiously advances toward Zhou through a growth of ferns. "Are these plants safe?"

"Why are you asking me Robert? I thought you were a digital genius." Zhou snaps, annoyed with his interruptions of her work. "You're wearing the world's knowledge embedded in your wrist. Use it. And while you're accessing the genus of those ferns, which by the way aren't going to bite you, look up the rare Manzanillo or Manchineel tree. There aren't too many of them in Puerto Rico, so I could really use at least a general vicinity."

After reaching Zhou and finding a small hole in the leaves, a few accurately directed thoughts activates Robert's wrist computer and the heads-up display of his smart contact lens. First, he records the GPS coordinates for their current location and the plant and soil specimens found there. Then, he searches for Zhou's Manchineel tree.

His quest is quickly answered. "We need to go to the beach Zhou. Manchineel trees prefer sandy, wet soil. Very few of them grow inland."

Zhou biosensor scans her plant samples with her portable spectrometer then loads them into the digital sampling bag riding Robert's back. "Ok. I have all of the samples that I need from here. It's time to return to the Instituto anyway."

Robert is not listening. He is studying the description of the Manchineel. "Zhou, do you realize how dangerous these trees are? According to this you should definitely not eat the fruit. Not touch the tree trunk or any branches either, and do not pick up any of its shiny, tropic-green leaves. They also say that it's best if you don't stand under or even near the tree for any length of time whatsoever. And if you're near the tree do not touch your eyes. Everything about this tree is poison, even the air around it. This is one deadly plant. Are you certain that you want to mess with a Manchineel?"

"Yes, even more so now." Zhou's eyes sparkle excitedly. "I believe its poison holds some real promise. The more poisonous the better."

"Ok then." Robert quips, as he cautiously begins descending the mountain. "Obviously, you're a disciple of sixteenth century physician Paracelsus who said that poison is in everything, and no thing is without poison. The dosage makes it either a poison or a remedy."

"Very insightful of you Robert. However, I doubt that even with all your memorized brilliance that you know Manchineel's scientific name is *Hippomane mancinella,* which translates to the little apple that makes horses mad." Zhou gracefully skitters across the forest floor.

As Zhou and Robert concentrate on carefully exiting the rain forest, they fail to notice the arrival of two, green-throated, mango hummingbirds. They are an extraordinary bird, rarely seen, especially in Puerto Rico. They are too unusual to be here. If Robert spots them, he immediately identifies them as two biomimetic birds. But, he does not notice them, nor does he realize that he inadvertently summoned them with his Manchineel tree query.

Fearing he may fall, Robert is focusing on his footsteps. With a whisper, one of the birds hovers into position five feet above his head. The other bird flutters into the same position above Zhou. Tiny spies, the hummingbirds listen, watch and record, seeking to know what they know.

After some thought about Zhou's statement, Robert excitedly snaps his fingers. "Which could potentially make Manchineel the perfect candidate to fight Aethon! Correct?"

"Oh, there's no fooling you, is there?" Looking at the ground and choosing her steps carefully, Zhou descends El Yunque. "Now why don't you apply your genius to locating some Manchineel for us? If the Manchineel doesn't provide some positive results, then I fear that I won't find any magical cure for Aethon here in Puerto Rico. We need an antibiotic or vaccine or something right now. The people are scared. They're desperate...beginning to panic. Shengwu cannot win this battle by herself. Her clinic is too small and genome engineering is too slow."

Silently, Robert mentally searches through all the data about the Manchineel he can find until he uncovers a probable location.

"Are you ready to travel to the La Parguera Nature Reserve on the southwest coast? Manchineels often live among mangroves and La Parguera is Puerto Rico's biggest mangrove forest."

"I believe you meant to ask if we are ready to travel. Didn't you Robert? Because we're both going and I certainly hope you're better piloting a boat than you are trekking through these trees. I have no desire for you to drown me."

"Then I suggest that you invest in the best life jacket available." Robert jokes as he slips and lands on his back in the brush.

"Luckily, I know how to swim." Zhou continues as she steps across the prostate Robert.

SHENGWU VOWS

Torrents of sweat pour across Peter's face and puddle on his hospital bed. A feeble moan escapes him. His breathing is shallow and ragged. He writhes in agony. Aethon is clawing deep into his frail body, shredding him. Peter is fighting for his life and losing.

"Oh Peter. Peter. My sweet, little, baby boy. I'm so sorry." Sobbing, Shengwu softly whispers to Peter while stroking his small hand. "Sooner. If only I had known sooner."

Gradually, a fragile, crinkle-smile flickers across Peter's face. With puffs of breath, he whimpers. "Wu? Wu?"

"Yes Peter, I'm here. I'm right here." She gently cups Peter's fever-hot hand. His tiny fingers tickle her palm.

Choking, Shengwu kisses Peter's burning forehead. "I fear I failed you in this life, but I promise you…I promise you Peter that I will not fail you in your next. Soon, you'll never be sick again…and I promise that you'll live a long, long life. You just can't do it in this body."

From a bag by her feet, she retrieves her HEART hat. Gently and lovingly, she slips her HEART hat onto Peter's head. Peter whimpers, but is too weak to do anything more. Shengwu lightly brushes his damp hair from his fever-hot forehead.

"Now listen closely Peter. My sweet, little Peter, I'm not going to hurt you. I would never hurt you. But, I need to tickle your brain. It may sting. Just a little sting, so you'll react. Then when you react, my hat will record your thoughts. Actually, not really your thoughts. My hat captures the teeny, tiny little electrical impulses in your brain's cells creating your thoughts. Your character and personality generate those thoughts and your reactions. Ok?"

Shengwu squeezes Peter's hand. "Are you ready, Peter? Just a little sting."

Peter flinches as Shengwu runs her finger along the side of the HEART hat activating it. He utters not a sound. Then, after thirty seconds, an elfin grin creases his pale face. His eyes flutter open."

"Wu." He whispers with joy in his feeble voice when he sees his best friend.

"Oh Peter! Yes, it's me. Look at me Peter. Look at me." Shengwu is thrilled.

Concentrating Peter's vision on her focuses his attention and emotions on her. She is mining his mind and gathering gold. All of his thoughts flowing into the HEART hat's memory concern his relationships and love for her. She is capturing his heart in her HEART.

Peter's eyes slowly close. He drifts away. Not quite asleep. Not quite awake. Drifting in a dream stream somewhere in between.

"Peter, listen to me. Listen to my voice. Remember my voice Peter. Remember what I tell you." Shengwu pauses, waiting for Peter to react before continuing. "I love you Peter. Wu loves you. You love Wu. Peter and Wu love each other."

Momentarily floating near the surface of consciousness, Peter stirs in his hospital bed. With his eyes closed, he mimics Shengwu in a faint whisper. "Peter loves Wu."

Peter slips into silence. For a few moments, Shengwu watches Peter's chest rise and fall with shallow breaths. "Hell is for us, the living, when a so loved child dies. You are taking so much of my heart away with you."

With a wave of her finger, Shengwu de-activates her HEART hat. Gingerly, she slips the HEART hat from his head and places it in her lap. With a push of her finger she opens a small slot in the center of the top of the hat and retrieves a miniature memory chip.

Shengwu displays the chip to nearly comatose Peter. "Now, I've made you immortal. All of you is right here. All of your learning and laughter and love is right here, ready for imprinting in your future you."

VOLEUR VISIT

The silence is unsettling. It is not normal. No protestors are rushing into the street to stop Robert from entering Shengwu's facility. Instead, it is a bio-hazmat-suited San Juan police officer who hails and halts his auto-auto. He orders him to exit his glider for Aethon screening.

Robert is pleased and eager to comply. Obviously, while he was stumbling through El Yunque with Zhou, Shengwu implemented the plan and the equipment Pion and he designed. He puffs with pride seeing the officer wearing one of his green-is-clean Aethon patches.

As the police officer samples his breath and scans him with his spectrometer biosensor, Robert hunts for the missing protestors. They are nowhere to be seen. Their large revival tent is gone. Where it stood, Robert watches three hazmat-suited animal control officers running through the weeds chasing wild, feral cats. Bounding and weaving, the quick cats are easily eluding the frustrated officers. One officer stumbles and crashes to the ground. When the officer does not move, two kittens jump from the grass landing atop the officer where they playfully wrestle with each other. The two kittens scamper back into the grass as soon as the officer breathes.

"Sir, my biosensor is not detecting the presence of Aethon. By order of President Negocio, entry is restricted to Aethon sufferers seeking treatment." The officer leans past Robert to glance inside the glider, seeing nobody he continues his questioning. "Why do you wish to enter Stamina Vitae?"

"Well officer, I was just moved into Stamina Vitae and I also work there. As a matter of fact, I assisted in developing your Aethon biosensor and your Aethon detection patch." Robert responds smugly. "By the way, where is my patch?"

Unimpressed, the police officer hands him his patch. "Here sir, wear this at all times where it can be clearly seen. It is required."

124

Looking toward the area where he saw the protestors less than eight hours ago, Robert seeks an explanation for their unexpected disappearance. "Where's that religious group? They were in their tent when I left this morning."

"Five dead, six quarantined and four near-dead are receiving treatment in this clinic." The officer declares with no emotion, while nodding his head toward Stamina Vitae.

"Five dead? When did that happen?"

Nervously looking first over his left shoulder and then over his right shoulder, he lowers his voice and leans close to Robert. "It was their stench. Two of them had been dead so long - don't know how long - that they were beginning to stink. Starting to rot too, I hear. Some people in those houses over there complained. When they investigated they discovered Aethon."

"In the people from the tent or in those houses?"

"Hunh? What?" The officer is distracted, watching a green hummingbird hover above them. He points past Robert. "Look over your head. That's the prettiest bird, I've ever seen."

A quick glance skyward and Robert realizes he is being watched by a biomimetic drone, but he chooses to ignore it. He does not want to have to explain that it is a bionic bird to the officer. "Yes, it is pretty. Now, tell me where they found the Aethon."

"Oh yes. Both. They found Aethon in both. But only a few cases in that neighborhood. Nowhere else, so far. Why?"

Not wanting to alarm him about the possibility of an epidemic, Robert assumes nonchalance. "Oh, just interested. It's part of my work here. Which, by the way, I need to start doing. So, may I proceed now?"

With his eyes still riveted to the hummingbird drone, the officer waves Robert toward his auto-auto. "Yes sir, of course. Just remember to always wear your detection patch."

As Robert is boarding his auto-auto, another glider carrying four frantic Americans arrives. His body blocking the street, the officer forces them to halt. Immediately, they assault him with threats and curses. The nearest glider rider throws a bottle at him. Jumping to the side, so the bottle misses him, clears their way. The glider rolls past the officer and Robert toward Stamina Vitae.

"They're all bullies. Don't care about anybody, but themselves." The officer complains to Robert while watching them disappear around a curve. "I don't think anybody can cure them of all that ails them. They're just sick."

Robert energizes the glider, waves to the officer and advances. Just beyond the officer's sight, a couple step from the shrubs into the street forcing Robert's auto-auto to a sudden halt. Are they lost Aethon sufferers? No mistake. It is a planned disruption. The man and woman march toward his vehicle. As they near, Robert recognizes them as the couple from the coffee café - Lew and Lee Voleur.

"Lower the front left window." Robert commands the auto-auto.

Before Robert can speak, Lew Voleur steps to the opened window and leans inside pointing toward him what Robert immediately identifies as an Nsep stun gun. In a deep, threatening hiss, he issues a menacing recommendation. "Mister Goodfellow, I suggest Lee and I be allowed to join you. We have important business to discuss."

Recoiling from the pain his last encounter with an Nsep caused, Robert quickly complies. Lee slides into the seat next to him while Lew climbs into the other seat. Lee is also sporting an Nsep.

"I really don't think you need those." Robert nervously grins toward Lee. "Why…why don't you put them away? I'm quite willing to discuss whatever you would like to discuss."

"Change your destination to Area de Descanso one, Robert. It's not far and the three of us will enjoy a private walk-talk on the beach." Lew orders while continuing to point his Nsep toward the side of Robert's head.

Ten minutes later, Robert is standing between Lee and Lew watching the waters of Ensenada de Boca Vieja. The beach is scarcely populated with nobody in their area. They are hiding in plain sight. Above them the biomimetic hummingbird is again circling.

"So how are you two? You're both looking much better today than the last time we saw each other." Robert attempts humor to relieve the tension. Simultaneously, he is also talking to stall until Negocio's promised physical protection arrives. At least, he thinks he remembers Negocio indicating he would provide him with protection.

As he fingers his Nsep, it is clear that Lew is not amused by his jest. "You may consider poisoning us funny, but we didn't enjoy it. I am still not eating…or drinking…especially not drinking coffee…and I loved coffee. Ruined it for me. Thank you very much."

"Well that is unfortunate, but a little bionic bird tells me we're not out here to discuss your health or enjoy the sea breeze. What is it you want?" Robert continues his effort to keep the situation peaceful.

"We're here to discuss your continuation of good health." Lew waves his Nsep in front of Robert's nose. Lee reaches across Robert and pulls the Nsep from Lew's hand.

"Well thank you Lee. I appreciate your concern for my health. But, I especially value you assuming possession of those." He points at the two Nseps she is now holding, but aiming away from him. "Don't know how many Nsep shots my brain can bear. Stunned once already. One brain baking is too many. Perhaps that's why I'm not aware as to how I can help you. So, how can I help you?"

Lee rejects Lew's intimidation tactics attempting calm persuasion of Robert. "Our needs are actually very simple Robert. We want you to continue doing what you're doing, but enable access for us. Just us."

Perplexed, Robert silently stares out into the sea watching a passenger ship approach San Juan's docks. "Sorry, I'm not certain I understand. You want me to continue intercepting and stopping hacking attacks on Shengwu, except for you? That's impossible. Not only can't I do it, I won't do it. Shengwu convinced me that any error when using her genome editing algorithms can be catastrophic."

Adamant, Robert locks eyes with Lew. "No. I will not help you steal her genome editing information. Far too dangerous. Could be a disaster. A world-wide disaster."

Unexpectedly Lew agrees, surprising Robert. "You're absolutely correct. We arrived at the same conclusion after studying some of her algorithms. Besides, we do not favor human genetic tampering. We believe man making man is wrong. So, we were quite happy when you crashed our competitor's hacking system…"

"Competitors?" Robert snickers. "They're very amateurish competitors."

Bursting in, Lee interrupts. "Don't underestimate them. They're dangerous, Robert. They're mercenary contractors working for big pharma, and they're not at all happy with your destruction of their equipment and your interference. You're doing the one thing they never allow. You're costing them money and they don't like to lose money...a lot of money. So, their plan is to eliminate you, which will eliminate your block."

"Big pharma? Which big pharma?" Robert doubts Lee's wild warnings.

"It's a cabal...several international companies." Lew expounds, "Big pharma is funding both those religious fanatics protesting outside Shengwu's facility, as well as those mercenary contractors. It's all about revenue and profits. Big pharma needs Shengwu and all genomics to fail, actually kill somebody, so genomics are illegal internationally. They can't afford for genomics to eradicate diseases, because then nobody will need to buy their medicines and the entire health care system will collapse. They are deadly serious about stopping Shengwu...and now...you. The two of you are threats that they are quite eager to eradicate."

Warily, Robert slides backward away from Lew.

Lew pauses, steps forward, leans in close to Robert and lowers his voice, as if sharing a secret. "And you wouldn't be the first person they've made disappear...not by a long shot, especially now that big pharma and the US government are depending on each other for Economic survival. We're talking billions of dollars, Robert. So, Abaddon allows them to do whatever they want as long as they continue funneling funds to his government. Anything...to anybody."

"Yes, that's not new knowledge. Economics rules the world and the US is in a financial crisis. But, you're sounding a bit overly dramatic to me. Are you actually telling me that big pharma sent somebody here to kill me and Shengwu?" Robert smirks.

"Big pharma or the government or both working together. Yes." Lew continues his shielded warning. "We've heard that there are people...sent here...down here now...professionals...so..."

"...so, be careful Robert. Be on guard. Expect their attack." Lee cautions, "Be prepared for them. According to social media, they're coming after you. Now, you help us and we'll help you with them. Help you'll need, because they're not planning to be nearly as pleasant and courteous as we are my friend."

Robert sneers. "Oh yes, definitely, I count you two as my best buddies. Can't have enough friends like you two."

Lew grabs back the conversation. "Anyway, genome engineering is too difficult and too tricky and too specialized. We abandoned that idea. It's just not possible for us and definitely not profitable."

"Ahem." Lee frowns at Lew as soon as he mentions profits. "Lew misspoke, Robert. Now we're far more interested in your work with Zhou, not Shengwu. Her work is now extremely important and, for several reasons, our primary interest. See, we represent an independent pharmaceutical organization. We know medicines. We don't know human genomes. Have you ever heard of Terra Sigillata?"

Robert's lip curls in contempt. "Oh yes, I've heard of Terra Sigillata. You're pharmaceutical counterfeiters."

"We are not!" Lew indignantly roars. "Counterfeiters sell fake drugs...dangerous drugs...killing drugs. Terra Sigillata is no counterfeiter. Terra Sigillata sells real pharmaceuticals, true pharmaceuticals, desperately-needed pharmaceuticals on the gray market. You're from Canada, so I know you've heard of the pharmaceutical gray market. Haven't you?"

"Yes, of course, I have. The gray pharmaceutical market is basically the market created by selling legal goods outside of a manufacturer's authorized trading channels. Canadians have been selling drugs on the gray market for decades. But, just because you claim Terra Sigillata is legitimate and operates in the gray market, doesn't mean that I believe you..." Robert indignantly responds. "...because, I don't!

Again Lee attempts to calm the situation. "True, Mister Goodfellow. You're correct. Terra Sigillata has sold what you might call counterfeit drugs. We prefer to say they're duplications. They're just not the same as the pharmaceuticals sold by the big pharma companies. But, they are drugs that the public demands. They are drugs that the public can afford. And, our drugs still help people...still make them feel better."

"Or are you profiteering by pushing placebos that fool them into thinking they are getting better instead of dying?" Robert argues.

Lew pounds his finger against Robert's chest. "Listen to me you smug bug. You really have no choice. This is do or die. Either you cooperate with us to do something about this Aethon bug or many more people are going to die. And as far as I'm concerned, if you don't help us, you will be one of them."

"Back off Lew!" Lee barks at him with a scolding scowl.

Insulted, Lew glares at Lee for several seconds before turning and stalking away from the pair. Robert exhales loudly, relieved to watch him march away. He enjoys a few seconds of silence.

"Please excuse Lew, Robert." Lee apologizes. "Three members of his family living outside Horse Cave Kentucky suddenly died last year. All of their horses died, too. Strange thing is, it was right after the Bureau of Land Management injected their horses with an experimental sterilization drug. Actually, the Bureau injected horses all around that part of Kentucky."

Lee rubs her index finger and thumb together. "Paid everybody good money for their horses, too. Money those people desperately needed. Told them that the drug wouldn't hurt their horses, just sterilize them. Said, if the drug worked there, then they'd use it to humanely get control of the thousands of abandoned and wild horses running loose all over America. Too many discarded horses is a big problem, I hear. I also hear that the Bureau is injecting the drug into Mustangs and wild horses in the west, now."

With tears welling in her eyes, Lee chokes. "Nobody knew why they died then, but Lew now is certain it was from this new, virus-super-bug you're calling Aethon."

"Well now, his rage is beginning to make a little more sense." Robert glances toward Lew. "He's still crazy, but at least..."

Lee lovingly gazes toward Lew. "He's not a bad man, Robert, and Terra Sigillata is actually not an evil company. He's simply being ripped apart by what he sees happening with his kinfolk. In the US now, nobody cares about poor country folk or anybody that's poor, anymore. They just call them Sists and neglect them. No money. No doctors. No medicine. Big pharma and doctors can't make enough money serving poor people out in the country, so they've just abandoned them. Now they're dying. Like his family. Thousands just dying."

Robert watches Lew pacing a tight circle on the beach a short distance from them. Head down, staring at the sand, he paces compulsively, carefully stepping into his own shoe prints. "Well that's terrible, but I don't understand what he expects me to do about it. Their deaths certainly aren't my fault."

"Yes, he knows that, but he also knows you. He's absorbed everything he can find about you. You're almost a hero to him or at least you were until the coffee shop incident. Then…"

"Whoa, wait a second," Protests Robert. "I had nothing to do with the coffee shop events. That was Rita and her friends of the Independent Puerto Rico movement."

"That's good to know, Robert. Well, at least, it's good for you. It's not so good for Rita, now. Learning that little bit of information will just make him angrier and more determined."

"Determined to…?"

"Not certain, but…" Lee motions with her eyes toward Lew. "…just understand that he may not look it, but he is prepared and very capable of fatally harming Rita, Shengwu, Zhou or anybody else, if you don't cooperate and give him what he needs…and soon."

Now, petulantly kicking at trash and flotsam washed up onto the beach, the short, round, bald Lew does not impress Robert as being a killer. He remains uncertain if he should seriously fear Lee's warnings about him. After all, with Rita working and living inside Shengwu's facility in the cottage next to his, she should be beyond Lew's reach. He is also dubious of their warnings about a bunch of sinister, vengeful big pharma contract killers threatening him. At this moment, neither Lee's nor Lew's threats nor their dire warnings of death are convincing Robert. But he also recognizes that desperate people will do desperate things. He just cannot gauge how desperate these two really are.

"Look Lee, I'm having difficulty believing all of your ominous warnings and deathly threats. I've been combatting hackers for some time now and surviving. So unless you or Lew have more persuasive information, I'm returning to Shengwu's." Robert turns on his heel to leave the beach.

"Wait!" Lee grabs his arm yanking him to a halt. "Robert, I know that you may not believe me, but this is not about stopping hackers anymore. Working with us may be the only way for you to protect Puerto Rico and save three million innocent Puerto Ricans from the ravages of Aethon. It's up to you. You can cooperate with us or you can be responsible for the excruciating deaths of thousands of children. Do you actually want their innocent deaths on your conscience?"

"What!" Robert wrestles free of Lee. "What ridiculous tale of terror are you attempting to force feed me now?"

Lew's voice rises from behind them. He has rejoined them. "You may call us unbelievable and our claims, nonsense. But whether you choose to trust us or not, a boat loaded with Aethon infected Sists will arrive in Puerto Rico soon. In fact, that ship we just watched pass may have been it...and there are more coming."

"And just how do you know this Lew?" Robert's doubts continue.

Insulted by Robert doubting him, Lew emphatically jabs his finger at him. "We know because we're there, Robert! My relatives and our Terra Sigillata workers are there. Big Pharma and the federal government were willing to just ignore the Aethon victims until they started stumbling into the sovereign cities and Metrostates...threatening the Urbanites and creating a panic. Immediately, the Urbanites' panic caused big pharma's drug sales to skyrocket. Scared Urbanites are paying big money for anything big pharma promises will prevent Aethon. People are paying thousands of dollars for useless cold medicines and rioting when they can't get it. But, as you know, right now, there is nothing, no medicine that will stop Aethon."

Lee interrupts Lew, attempting to calm him. "Life in the wastedlands of West Virginia, Kentucky and Tennessee is cheap...medicine is not. So, our people working in those territories are reporting government round-ups of anyone suspected of Aethon infection or considered at risk of infection. Then they're hiding them and reporting that they've been healed by big pharma's newest, high-priced medicine. They're selling billions of dollars of worthless medications, not by healing anybody, but by making the people disappear. Meanwhile Aethon is still out there infecting and killing entire families."

"Oh Lee! Tell him what Abaddon's Society Security Deacons are actually doing," Lew growls. "Here's what's really happening, Robert. After months of burying the thousands of Sists who have died from Aethon, South Carolina, Arkansas, Tennessee and Kentucky are bankrupt. So, under Abaddon's guidance, recently established state medical militias are cleansing the countryside. Sick or not, if one of these medical militias capture you in a contaminated sector, you and everybody in your family are hauled to a quarantine camp."

"Pardon me?" Robert asks, "What's a quarantine camp?"

Squeezing her eyes shut, Lee grimaces and shakes her head. "A quarantine camp is a filthy, crowded, poisonous, hell-on-earth. If you don't have Aethon or some other disease when they hurl you into one, you'll probably catch it there. Forcing people into the camps is just spreading Aethon and making it more resistant to medication."

"How can you do that to your own people?" Robert declares outraged. "It's inhumane. Criminal."

Lee nods in agreement. "You're correct Robert. It is an atrocity. It's also the new US policy of exterminism…eliminating their problems through death. In America, humans no longer matter, money is all that matters. The Righteous Rightists leaders tried benign neglect…just letting Aethon victims die out in the rural wastedlands. They're also encouraging suicide. They call it decency dying."

Lew interrupts. "But, those programs aren't working fast enough. When some Aethon carriers escaped the camps and fled to the cities they decided to get rid of them. That's why the Deacons and militias are beginning to ship them to Puerto Rico. Not only are they clearing them out of the states, simultaneously they're hoping to devastate your disloyal, independent Puerto Rico. Turning Puerto Rico into an island of the damned. They see it as a win-win situation. Abaddon crushes rebellious Puerto Rico by cleansing America. Big pharma supports the action too, because they're still raking in billions from scared Urbanites who don't know about the camps."

Robert shakes his head in disbelief. He had been wrong and Rita had been correct when she insisted that the US government is responsible for the appearance of Aethon in Puerto Rico. Ship loads of Aethon victims will quickly bury Negocio's government by overwhelming his medical facilities and then spreading Aethon to more Puerto Ricans. Negocio can't turn them away and he knows

Shengwu can't handle a flood of more Aethon victims. She is already struggling to cope with the number of Aethon cases storming into her facility now.

Lew awakes Robert from his thoughts. "So now you understand why you must provide us with your research findings. The only way you can save Puerto Rico is to enable us to start fighting Aethon at its origin, back in the states. We're depending on you Robert. If you don't help us, Aethon will burn like a raging wildfire across Puerto Rico and America's countryside slaughtering hundreds or thousands of innocent people whose only crime is they're poor and ignored. Like my family. For all of us, this situation is desperate. You have to admit that."

Stroking his forehead, Robert considers his options. As hard as he tries, he still cannot eliminate his deep doubts about Lew and Lee. Their stories are just too wild. Exterminism? Genocide? They do not seem logical or reasonable. He continues to wonder how much of their expressed concern is actually about personal profit instead of people. And really, why would big pharma and the US government plot to kill him?

He challenges them. "Philosopher Benjamin Disraeli once said that desperation is sometimes as powerful an inspirer as genius. But Disraeli wasn't searching for something that is not even known to exist. Sorry, but despite all of your ominous warnings about thousands dying and people wishing to kill me, I'm not convinced. Besides, I think you are seeking information from the wrong person. Zhou is the genius not me. I'm just her field assistant. You should be talking to her or one of her technical aides at the Instituto."

One hundred yards or so down the beach, two men step out of the trees. As soon as they spot Robert and the Voleurs, they turn away and huddle together. Lee leans forward squinting her eyes for a better look. Instinctively, she distrusts them. They walk and talk and dress in too-loud, touristy patterned clothes to be innocuous Puerto Ricans seeking fun on the beach.

Oblivious to the two men, Lew continues arguing to persuade Robert. "Zhou's the scientist, true. But, you're the communicator. You can tell us what we need to know without her or anybody else becoming aware that we're corresponding. Confidentiality is a necessity, especially if she discovers something. If big pharma or the government discover that we're working together, it will be bad for all of us."

Lew lowers his voice to a hiss. "Rita and Zhou especially, because they don't suspect. They're the most vulnerable. They will kill. Believe me. They've killed before. Your death, Rita's and Zhou's deaths or a million deaths are unimportant to big pharma and the government. Only profit is important. So if you find a cure, especially an inexpensive cure never tell them. Never let them know. A cheap cure they do not control is a catastrophe for them. They will destroy you, Rita, Zhou and everybody who knows about the cure."

As Lee is studying the two suspicious strangers, they launch two small drones. The drones rise quickly and circle the men. For a moment, they appear to be harmlessly flying new toys. But, Lee never relaxes. She senses that something is wrong.

Her eyes glued to the two men and their drones, Lee backs toward Robert. Standing next to him, she whispers her warning. "Get out of here Robert. Fast! Lew and I will stay behind to deal with these two. Now move!"

Not knowing why Lee says run, but taking full advantage of his opportunity to escape, Robert bolts for the trees with Lew shouting after him. "Don't forget! Stay in contact. We're depending on you. Zhou's and Rita's lives are..."

Thinking he hears a drone buzzing overhead, Robert dives onto the ground. Crouching behind some bushes, under the cover of the trees, he peeks back at the beach. As if fighting wasps, Lew and Lee are throwing sand and swatting at two drones zipping around, laser-stinging them.

For a moment, Robert smirks. Watching Lew and Lee jump, squirm and howl with each laser sting gives him a momentary feeling of satisfying retribution for Lew threatening him with an Nsep. But his period of vindication is short, ending when he hears the approaching men shouting threats at Lew and Lee. He quickly determines from their demands that these are not Negocio's men coming to protect him. They are attacking the Voleurs because they want him. They are armed and dangerous. Up and out. He races to the safety of the auto-auto and Stamina Vitae.

NEGENTROPY

"Shengwu is missing!" A distraught Rita confronts Robert when he pushes into Stamina Vitae through a fear-filled, feverish, chaotic crowd. "She vanished after returning from visiting Margarete and Peter. I'm worried Robert. Very worried. She is so upset. I'm afraid she may do something crazy."

Having just escaped some mysterious assailants and the Voleurs, Robert is more excited to find Rita safe, than he is concerned about Shengwu. Even distressed and flustered, she looks good to him. He envelops her in his long arms with a crushing hug. "Are you ok?"

"Of course I'm ok. Why shouldn't I be?" Embarrassed, Rita pushes away from Robert. Stares, snickers and snide insults from the unruly multitude awaiting treatment aggravate her.

"Acho, deja el gufeo *(Dude, stop goofing around)*!" She snaps at him with a puzzled glare, as she shifts and rearranges her hazmat clothing.

Stung by Rita yelling at him, Robert drops his hands and retreats. He hesitates, unsure if he should tell her about the Voleurs and the threats against her being his reason for his joy at seeing her. No, not yet, he decides. Not with the room crammed with ailing people.

For the first time since arriving, Robert takes time to scrutinize the impatient, belligerent people jamming the room. Within seconds, he realizes that most are not Puerto Ricans. Like the hundreds camping and waiting in the courtyard, they are Americans. Fat, loud, obnoxious and demanding American Sists sniping and snarling at each other to be the next to receive Shengwu's treatment.

Recognizing their nasal whining, Robert identifies them as the Aethon sufferers from Tennessee and Kentucky. Possibly they are the Sists that Lew and Lee warned him were coming. By force of their numbers, their aggressive manners and their heavy weight, they have squashed the few ailing Puerto Ricans into a small corner of the room. They are also bullying Rita, overwhelming her with their continuous complaints. Robert concludes he can only help her by reassuring her that Shengwu is sane and safe. He must find Shengwu.

"Uh…well…I'm sorry Rita. I misunderstood," Robert sheepishly apologizes. "Now where did you last see Shengwu?"

"Well, I haven't actually seen her. I mean. I did see her…via the security system. Not in person, mind you." Rita offers a sanitary swab to a mother holding a squalling, vomiting child. "She came in through the parking garage entrance. Tears in her eyes. I could see her shaking and sobbing. Then she disappeared. Never saw her on this level and now I can't locate her."

"Ok, you continue to work with these people while I hunt for her." With a press of his hand, Robert accesses the non-public area to conduct a quick search.

In Shengwu's work room, Robert discovers no evidence of Shengwu having recently been there. However, he does notice that holographic Pion is present and working. He considers it odd to find her image active in the empty room. Normally, she only transmits when she is collaborating with Shengwu or him. But, Shengwu is not in this room.

Pion mumbles something, as if collaborating with someone he cannot see. Robert waits, but nobody appears, yet Pion continues conversing with an invisible cohort. After observing her intently working, Robert decides it is wise not to interrupt her and proceeds to the lower level laboratory.

Shengwu's laboratory is silent except for the whisper of the positive air purifying machines' breathing. Only her genome testing and editing equipment is active. Surveying the lab, Robert notices that, for the first time he knows, Shengwu's special- project genome equipment bay is operating, as well. When he first arrived, she told him this equipment was only for her special project. It was not working then, but now it is. Robert is suspicious. Only she can operate this equipment, so she must be near.

Standing next to her equipment, Robert calls for Shengwu. He silently listens for a response. Believing he hears two voices talking on the other side of the closed door behind her special equipment, he waits silently. When he thinks he hears the conversation stop, Robert shouts for Shengwu again.

A rattle and a bang, and the door swings open revealing Shengwu while simultaneously providing Robert a peek into the hidden room at her back. Inside, Robert spies an older Chinese man scampering out of sight. He only gains a glimpse of him before Shengwu yanks the door closed blocking his view.

"Yes Robert, how may I help you?" Shengwu asks as she locks the door with her right hand print. With her left hand, she swipes the remains of tears away from her red, swollen eyes.

Robert points toward the door. "Who was that man in that room?"

Startled by Robert's question, Shengwu is silent for a moment before she attempts to divert his curiosity. "A man? There is nobody in there."

"No. I'm certain that I saw an elderly Chinese man inside that room."

Shengwu again denies Robert. "Oh, you may have seen the hologram de-energizing. That's all. Just a hologram Robert."

"But, I'm certain…"

Pushing past Robert, Shengwu hurriedly limps toward the elevator. "Well, you're wrong. Now, come along. Rita requires our assistance."

Ignoring her, Robert continues staring at the door, convinced that what he saw is a human, not a hologram. He does not accept her disavowals. She is acting peculiar and that makes him all the more curious about what Shengwu may be hiding inside that room. He is also intrigued by the unusual activity of her special-project genome editing equipment. But, as he leans forward attempting to gain a better view of her equipment's operation, Shengwu summons him again.

"Come Robert! Rita needs us!"

As soon as Shengwu steps into her reception room and sees the quarreling, disorderly mass of sick and dying Aethon sufferers awaiting her - relying on her - her mask of rock-hard composure and self-control melts. She crumples into a chair outside the noisy, frantic crowd and drops her head into her hands. Robert is unsure if she is suffering exhaustion or defeat, or both. Studying her face and her shaking hands, Robert agrees with Rita's earlier diagnosis that Shengwu is so deep in despair as to be suicidal.

Her eyes flooding her cheeks with tears, Shengwu lifts her head to peer at the boisterous Americans overflowing her office. "I cannot do it Robert. I cannot. I cannot save all of these people. I may not be able to save any of them. There's too many of them. Too many. And more come every day. It's a hopeless fight. I'm losing it. I'm really losing it."

Gently placing his hand on her shoulder, Robert attempts to console her. "You can't blame yourself. You and Pion are doing your best. You're saving people. Some people. Peter and Margarete? What about them? They're getting better, aren't they?"

Shengwu trembles. Her shoulder shakes beneath Robert's comforting hand. She chokes. "My little Peter is dying. I'm doing all I can do to keep him with us, but I don't think I can save his body from Aethon…two types of Aethon. It's too much…too much for a little boy."

"Oh, I'm so sorry. I thought he was doing better." Robert squeezes her shuddering shoulder. "How is Margarete?"

Sighing, Shengwu slowly shakes her head. "She is stable. My last analysis indicates that her edited genomes may be beginning to overcome her Aethon. I think she may recover, but it's going to require time…lots of time. And worse, last night I lost two more of my first group of genome transplants. The others are still struggling."

Robert searches the room for any of the religious protestors. "I was told by a health guard that you're caring for some Aethon infected protestors, but I don't see any of them."

"Only one, a young boy named Obed, comes in here. He isn't infected. He refuses genome preventative treatment, but he actually helps me some." Shengwu points across the room toward a pale, willow of a fellow assisting an elderly man. "That's him there."

Shengwu is dispirited. "The others are at the hospital. But, I'm not optimistic that any of the other faith healers will recover. Even while I'm desperately trying to save them from dying, they're praying for me to rot in hell. They almost seem to be willing their bodies to reject my edited genomes. I think they'd rather die than allow science to save them. Why are religious fanatics so self-destructive?"

"I don't know, but why do you think your genome editing is failing the others?" Robert whispers, hoping none of the people waiting for treatment hear and panic.

Closing her eyes, Shengwu traces the bridge of her nose with her index finger. She is searching herself for an answer. "I'm not certain, but I fear that once Aethon establishes itself inside a person's body that it begins to mutate into other forms. Survives through constant change. So, you chase it, but never capture it. You can't trap it and kill it. Once in a person's body, it seems we can't kill Aethon or other diseases it may spawn. That's why Aethon has to be stopped before it gets started."

"Like you did with Rita and me?" Robert tugs at Shengwu's tight anti-Aethon wrap. After mingling and mixing with the infected people surrounding him in the waiting room, he is thankful that he redressed before departing El Yunque.

"Yes, but more. You are only two people, and you're only protected from Aethon." Shengwu's thoughts float away from her overflowing waiting room. "So what if we cannot find a way to stop Aethon? What next? What if I'm correct and Aethon is mutating. Every year millions of people become infected with some new bacteria or virus that are resistant to anything and everything we can throw at them. Viruses and bacteria are evolving, but mankind is not."

A fever-faced, young boy vomits and collapses onto a woman sitting on the floor. She violently heaves the boy off her lap and onto the floor. His mother feebly tugs at the boy attempting to cradle him. She is too weak to comfort her dying son. She cannot love him one last time.

Waving her arm, Shengwu directs Robert's attention to the people in her waiting room. "Just look at these people. Look at us. We're a failing human species. Soon we will disappear like the Neanderthals and Denisovans. We're losing the survival race, Robert. The human body must change as fast as the diseases attacking it, but we won't naturally. So, our only chance for species survival is to create a type of invulnerability by genetically engineering human evolution. I'm exploring that process now. My father..."

"Father?" Robert interrupts.

Shengwu stops and quickly redirects her conversation. "So Robert, have you and Zhou discovered anything that can possibly help our bodies block Aethon? We need it immediately."

"Uh well, not yet, but we're continuing our quest." Finally, his opportunity to secure Rita arrives. "Zhou and I are planning to search on the other side of the island tomorrow near La Parguera and we need Rita to guide us. I hope you can spare her."

Robert is being honest with Shengwu about desiring Rita to guide them. He and Zhou will be searching a mangrove swamp area that neither of them know. They are already lost. But, he is not planning to tell her that he is also attempting to shield Rita from the Voleurs.

Shengwu scans the panicky, suffering throng. She recognizes that all of their frail hopes for life are hanging squarely on her and she is terrified. A small child screams when her mother tumbles backward against the wall. Rita rushes to the woman's side and slowly lowers her to the floor. Knowing their chances are slipping away, Shengwu turns away to escape their demanding eyes. "Uh…well…I don't…I mean…I'm a genome engineer. I work with robots. I need her. I don't know if I…"

Seeing the dread in Shengwu's face, Robert endeavors to persuade her that it is best for her to release Rita to help him. "Now, I realize I'm asking you to do something that you're not comfortable doing, but Shengwu, look at all of these infected people. Now, imagine two or three times this many people sick with Aethon crowding in here. I understand that it will happen, and soon, too. You've admitted that your genome editing method alone cannot save them. Zhou is possibly on the threshold of finding the type of drug we need, but she can't do it with just my poor assistance. We need Rita with her knowledge of Puerto Rico."

Shengwu watches Rita calm the fear filled girl who is tugging at her mother slumped on the floor. Obed kneels next to Rita dabbing the mother's forehead with a damp, sterile towel. "Ok Robert, I will spare her for one day. Tomorrow. But, you must protect Rita. At all costs, you must protect her. With my Peter dying, she is much more important to the future, our future, than you know. Do you understand?"

"You've placed your trust in me and trust me Shengwu, I will safeguard Rita, and I won't stop searching for something that will shield against the Aethon threat." Robert declares attempting to reassure her. "Like Gary Hamel, I believe that a noble purpose inspires sacrifice, stimulates innovation and encourages perseverance. And if your dire warning is accurate, what is a more noble purpose than saving humanity?"

As two American mothers begin brawling, pulling each other's hair and screaming obscenities, Shengwu's face tightens into a scowl. "Just look at those two. Sometimes, I'm not certain I have any desire to save all of these…everyone of this…this so called…humanity, Robert. I can't do it, anyway. I realize that. And I doubt that you and Zhou will succeed either. Right now, I'm only interested in preserving mankind's best. We're better without the rest."

"What! Do you intend to allow these people to die?"

The scuffle between the two mothers is spreading. Kentuckians are clashing with Tennessee victims. Punching and yelling and creating a mêlée.

"Look at these people Robert! Can't you see? I don't have to do a thing. They're unevolved. They refuse to change. They're determined to destroy themselves. Why should I fight to stop them?"

"Because they don't deserve to die, Shengwu."

"And just why do they deserve to live? They're the ones who brought Aethon to Puerto Rico. Sweet innocent Peter is dying because of them. They killed Peter, Robert! Why should I fight to save them?"

"Because some of them are innocent children too."

"I'll leave it to you Robert. You and Zhou and Rita. You can fight to save these…these undeserving, ungrateful…Sists…or whatever you call them. I have other more important battles to fight." Shengwu pivots, retreating into her inner sanctuary.

PATH TO PONCE

Pursuing poison fruit, Robert, Rita, and Zhou depart San Juan at dawn for the La Parguera Nature Reserve on Puerto Rico's southwest coast. Leaving San Juan is uneventful and unquestioned. Negocio's security wave and wish them well. But, Robert notices when a glider approaches to enter San Juan's city boundary that Negocio's security is rigorous with its searching and questioning. Easy to leave. Tough to enter.

Riding with Rita as their guide soothes Robert, who is simultaneously jittery and sleepy. Through the night, nightmares starring the threatening Voleurs rattled his mind and stole his sleep. But now with Rita sitting beside him in the auto-auto glider, he is beginning to relax. She is there to protect him and, in his own way, he is guarding his guardian.

Now, his sleep shortage is demanding attention. His head is pulsing while his eyes ache to close. "I think I'll nap for a while, if you two don't mind," Robert announces as he seeks a comfortable snoozing position in his auto-auto's seat.

"Oh no!" Rita shakes his shoulder. "I want you to see my parents' home town of Caguas. It's a beautiful hilltop city just ahead on the edge of Puerto Rico's Cordillera Central. We'll be there soon."

"What makes it so beautiful?" Robert mumbles from behind his closed eye lids.

"Oh, so many things, since it's the Christmas season, Caguas Plaza is beautifully decorated. I always enjoyed wandering the plaza at this time of year. But, I especially adore the Monumento a la Herencia Taína. It's a monument to Puerto Rico's indigenous women and is a tribute to our Tainan heritage and, especially, to Cagüeña women. Seeing it makes me proud." Rita clenches her right hand into a fist to display her power.

"Are they protected from Aethon in Caguas?" Zhou fearfully inquires, "Have they taken the necessary precautions?"

"Well, I'm not certain Zhou, but I would...I mean...I expect that they have." Rita stutters nervously. "After all, President Negocio required everybody in Puerto Rico to be tested. So well...I think so."

"But, you don't know for certain, so we're not stopping. We can't take any chances or waste time." Robert growls, "Too many people are depending on us finding something to stop this killer. We all need to focus on the reason we are here, not some statue."

Embarrassed, Rita shrivels into her seat. Robert has never berated her before. Insulted and hurt, she shifts away from him and silently stares out the window as their auto-auto glides above passageway 52 south from San Juan and into Puerto Rico's central mountains.

After several miles of sullen silence, they enter the Caguas region. Zhou attempts to cool the conflict. "I'm not certain that was necessary Robert. Negocio and his authorities appear to be gaining some control of the crisis. I must tell you that I'm amazed at how the Puerto Ricans have so quickly come together and worked together to try to subdue Aethon."

Out of the corner of his eye, Robert grasps the hurt he caused in Rita's face. Realizing that Zhou is correct and that he was overly harsh, Robert relents. "Ok Rita, perhaps we can visit some of your Caguas. Is the plaza far from passageway 52?"

"Oh no, it's not far at all. Just take the exit to passageway 1. Goes straight into the city." Rita excitedly inputs directions into their auto-auto's navigation system.

"Beep! Beep! Beep!" Loudly sounds the auto-auto navigation system alarm. "Your request is prohibited. Entry into Caguas is restricted to residents only. Quarantine inspections and Green Aethon badges required. Recommend remaining within passageway 52 corridor."

As they glide toward the entrance into Caguas, law enforcement drones begin clouding the sky. Their auto-auto slows. An identification drone positions itself directly in front of them and begins scanning.

"State your names, your destination and your reason for travel. Indique su nombre, su destino y su motivo de viaje." The identification drone commands via their auto-auto's navigation system.

"Our names are Rita Ayudante, Robert Goodfellow, and Zhou Caoyao," Rita quickly responds. "We're traveling to La Parguera Nature Reserve to conduct research."

"You may continue. Remain within the passageway 52 Caguas corridor. No deviations or departures from passageway 52 are allowed. You are expected to arrive at the entrance to La Parguera Nature Reserve in one hour and forty minutes. Authorities are aware of your travel plans and scheduled arrival time. You may proceed." The identification drone rises out of sight and the auto-auto glides forward.

Traffic in the Caguas corridor is congested with discouraged visitors who also have been refused entry. One confused family hovers in place, blocking passageway 52. Police drones dip and dive, broadcasting conflicting directions and adding to the muddle. Nobody is moving.

"Not exactly the friendly Puerto Rican reception that you were expecting, is it Rita?" Robert teases.

Disappointment shades Rita's face and voice. "No. Not exactly. But, at least we know that Negocio has people in place who are doing their job to prevent Aethon from spreading. Now, why don't you just be quiet and take your nap? Perhaps, you'll wake up a little less crabby."

"Best suggestion that you've made in days. I'll not argue with you. I can use some minor mental maintenance." Closing his eyes, Robert stretches out for a snooze.

His rest is brief. He is just drifting into a dream when Rita begins shaking his shoulder. He opens his eyes to find her pointing toward an air-cycle gliding beside them. The rider is staring into their auto-auto.

"There is another air-cycle behind us." Zhou points backward and whispers, in case they are scanning them. "Should we hail them? They appeared in Santa Isabel and seem to be shadowing us. Do either of you know them?"

"Can't identify them with their helmets covering their faces. But, they don't resemble anybody that I know." Rita whispers, "Friends of yours, Robert?"

"Ha! I doubt it. Since arriving here, I've been collecting far more enemies than friends. I only seem to be popular with those who wish to use me or abuse me." Robert fakes a sad face. "I'm such a kind and lovable fellow too. Wouldn't you agree Rita? Zhou?"

"Oh yeah, you're definitely a corazon de melon *(sweetie pie)*, Robert." Rita smirks.

"What?" Zhou asks confused.

"I just called him a sweetheart. It's a Puerto Rican joke. But, actually he's a manganzon *(man-child)*." Rita snickers. "A man-child."

Zhou titters. "How long have you two been together?"

"Together? Oh no, I can barely stand being near him." Rita playfully slaps Robert's shoulder.

"True Zhou, she's incredibly mean to me, and to think I rescued her from a life of languid leisure and ease." Robert counters.

Zhou motions toward a second air-cycle now gliding on the opposite side of their auto-auto. "Did one of you request an escort? Are they just being friendly or are we in trouble?"

Robert slowly blinks his eye to begin recording the air-cyclists. "Enough chatter. I'm beginning to become concerned about our two unexpected fellow travelers. I don't believe they are just innocent tourists. Did either of you tell anybody about our trip?"

After several moments of silence, an embarrassed Rita confesses. "Well, I did schedule us a guide. We'll definitely need a guide to find a manchineel in the La Parguera Nature Reserve. It's a big mangrove swamp."

"Ok, I can accept that." Robert agrees with a nod. "Can we trust your guide?"

"I certainly hope so. He's my cousin, Guia de Pantano."

"Ok Rita, anybody else?"

Rita drops her head, avoiding Robert's stare. "Wel-l-l-l, yes. My friends in Ponce. But…"

"…how many people in Ponce?"

Still looking away, Rita mumbles, "Oh three or four…maybe six…no more than seven. Yeah, no more than seven."

"And what about you?" Robert quizzes Zhou.

"Only Shengwu and my lab techs at the Instituto."

"I see." Robert sarcastically remarks. "Both of you should take a lesson from Confucius. Confucius said that silence is a true friend who never betrays. Thanks to you two, we're definitely not on a secret mission anymore."

"Why is our trip a secret mission, Robert?" Rita protests. "We're looking for a medicine to save people's lives, after all."

Screeching proximity warning alarms shatter the air, squealing alerts. The air-cycles are squeezing them. Robert attempts to gain a closer look at the riders now hugging the sides of their auto-auto. He is unable to identify them, but they do not resemble the Voleurs. The person on his auto-auto's side is thinner and taller than either of them. Could this rider be one of the men from the beach? He never saw either one of them clearly, so it is possible.

Robert's staring attracts the rider's attention who maneuvers the air-bike closer. The rider reaches toward the auto-auto. Robert hears a soft plop. The rider retracts his arm and slides a few feet away. For a moment, Robert fears the rider may have attached a small bomb. But, the rider never ventures far enough from their auto-auto to survive a bomb blast.

Without warning, the auto-auto's doors and windows unlock and then lock. Their seats move forward and then back. Now, Robert realizes that their auto-auto's controller-area-network is being hacked. Using their hack, the air cyclists can control everything from their auto-auto's indicators to its electric motor and brakes. The riders are hijacking them. They are prisoners within their auto-auto.

Obviously, these two want something. Robert wonders what or who. Or perhaps they are just attempting to intimidate him. Are they giving him the message that they, whoever they are, can get to him whenever and wherever they want? But, then they may be attempting to frighten Rita instead of him.

Worried about the air-cyclists' intentions, he decides it is time for Rita to learn of the threats against her, so she can protect herself. Leaning close to her ear, he uses the screaming alarms to cover his warning. "I have to tell you, Rita. Your life is in danger. That couple you poisoned at the coffee shop are after you. They want revenge."

"And how do you know that?" Rita asks with a scowl of disbelief.

"They grabbed me yesterday. Hauled me out to the beach and threatened me…and you…mainly me, but also you and Shengwu, too."

"Beach? Which beach?" Rita asks with a questioning look.

"Near Area de Descanso 1. Why?"

"Didn't you hear? The police found a man and a woman on the beach near there late last night. Brutally beaten. Unconscious. I understand they're in intensive care now."

"Really?" Robert is surprised. "Well, I guess the Voleurs were telling me the truth after all. Lew warned me that a cabal he called big pharma paid some problem exterminators to come after you, me and Shengwu. I thought they were just attempting to frighten me by threatening you, so I'd cooperate. But, I guess that I was very wrong."

Peeking past Robert at the closest air-cyclist still hugging their rear quarter of their auto-auto, Rita is puzzled. "Why? What do they want?"

"Drugs."

"Drugs? I don't have any drugs. I don't deal drugs." Rita is alarmed.

"Actually, her drugs. Anti-Aethon drugs." Robert motions forward toward Zhou, who is ducking and attempting to shrink enough to hide in the middle of her seat. "If she ever discovers them."

"Drugs that don't exist?" Rita is dubious. "You're telling me there are people sent here to kill me...us...for drugs that don't even exist?"

"Yes Rita, the Voleurs warned me that they are here. And, I believe them. Especially, now that they've been found beaten on the beach. I believe there are organizations determined enough to do whatever they decide they must do to maintain control of the Aethon drugs."

"But, Robert, that makes no sense. Don't they understand that we'll share any anti-Aethon medicine we create?"

Robert shakes his head. "That's what worries them, Rita. It's not about medicine. It's about money. Money, they really don't plan to share. But, they expect us to share whatever medicine we genome edit with them, then they can make the pharmaceuticals that makes them money. The last thing they want is for us to create a cheap medicine. If we develop an inexpensive anti-Aethon drug, we threaten their sales...threaten their revenue. Profit over people. It's not..."

Abruptly, their auto-auto jerks to the right and increases speed, racing away from the passageway toward the roaring waters of Rio Descalabrado. Weaving and twisting, scraping trees and crushing bushes, their auto-auto smashes through the brush. They are prisoners trapped inside a hurtling coffin. Suddenly, at the river's edge, their auto-auto whips left arcing away from the water and back into the trees. Wobbling and shaking, it battles its way back onto passageway 52 barely dodging two other auto-autos. Again the auto-auto lurches right, slamming Robert against the window. Zhou tightens her safety restraint and flattens herself against the seat. Pitching left, the auto-auto recovers its control. It is short-lived.

"What is happening?" Rita screams.

"The air-cyclists hacked our auto-auto controller. Steered us off the passageway and into those trees and almost into that river." The auto-auto jolts right smashing Robert against Rita.

"Do something!" Digging her fingers into her seat, Zhou cries. "Robert! Make them stop!"

Bracing himself and tightening his own safety restraint, Robert thoughtfully analyzes their situation. "I believe the air-cyclist attached a GPS jammer to send interference signals to disrupt our sensors or transmit false sensor readings to our vehicle's sensors so they can commandeer us."

The auto-auto jumps forward and then heaves left hurling equipment against Rita and Robert. Sharply sliding right and steeply braking, the auto-auto regains its self-control slamming the equipment to the floor.

Bleeding from her smashed nose, Rita yelps. "Stop talking and do something!"

"I'm not talking. I'm analyzing." Robert mutters as he searches through the equipment wreckage around his feet.

"You're doing what?!" Rita angrily shouts, as the auto-auto veers left then swerves right then swings left then twists sharply right again, careening closer and closer to the edge of the passageway and nearer to flying into the Rio Descalabrado.

Grabbing Zhou's specimen collection bag, Robert coolly explains. "I have to analyze what they are doing, so I understand what they are doing. Then I can try to stop what they are doing. Understand?"

Veering left. Swerving right. With her head flopping left then right, Zhou moans. "I think I'm going to vomit."

"This may help. Not certain. Just have to try it and see." Robert mumbles as he energizes the collection bag's satellite transmitter. "To stop them from sending us flying into the river, I must establish some form of human driver reengagement, but there aren't any external controls. So, I will attempt to use this bag's satellite signal to block their signal. If I'm correct, we may just be able to escape these two alive."

Stretching forward, tilting side to side, battling for balance, Robert shoves the collection bag against the auto-auto's control system case. Their violent zig zagging slackens. Gradually, they decelerate. Their auto-auto glides left, piloting itself away from the river and easing back into its proper position in the traffic flow.

Proudly brandishing the transmitting bag in his hands, Robert leans left toward Rita. The auto-auto smoothly slides left. Surprised, Robert returns to his original position and the auto-auto follows. Grinning, Robert rotates the bag right. The auto-auto travels to the right. Chuckling, he quickly moves the bag left then right. Following him, the auto-auto wobbles left and then right.

"Look! I'm steering!" Robert announces excitedly, as he again maneuvers the auto-auto a little to the left and then a little to the right employing the bag to guide. "I'm driving! I'm driving. I've never driven before. This is fun!"

"Well stop it!" Zhou demands struggling to straighten in her seat. "You're a rotten driver and you're making me dizzy."

"Sorry, just having a little fun." Robert centers the bag on his lap.

Realizing that they have lost control of the auto-auto, the air-cyclists surge forward and begin squeezing them again. Boom! The rider on Rita's side, kicks the auto-auto. The screaming of the alert alarms intensifies. Bang! Again, the rider slams their boot against the side. Zhou and Rita cover their ears and duck forward, but they cannot escape the noise.

Raising her head and staring directly at the air-cyclist near her, Rita screams. "Me tienes un ojo hinchado *(You are driving me crazy)*! Te cazaré y arrancaré tus testículos *(I will hunt you down and rip off your testicles)*!"

As if responding to Rita's challenging curse, the air-cyclists separate and slide into positions behind the auto-auto. Slowing, the cyclists slip farther and farther behind. The screaming proximity alarms stop. Finally, silence. They all sigh with relief.

Rubbing the sides of her head with her hands while flexing her jaw to pop her ears, Zhou questions Rita. "What did you say to force them to stop attacking us?"

Rita grins. "I simply told them that if they are smart they will go away. Immediately! But…"

Robert snickers. The universal language translator hidden in his ear informed him that Rita was not nearly as civil and proper as she wants Zhou to believe. In truth, the anger and language of her statement surprised him. Obviously, she can get down and dirty when the situation requires it.

"…But actually Zhou, I think the fact that we're nearing Ponce, and those are my friends…you know those friends Robert doesn't approve of…waiting ahead of us is the real reason those air-cyclists stopped attacking us." Pointing ahead, Rita aims a verbal jab at Robert. "Sometimes a few friends can be your best protection. Save you from all kinds of trouble. Don't you think so Zhou? Robert?"

Robert grins as he de-energizes the specimen bag and sets it on the floor. "Well Rita, you can believe that and sing 'I get by with a little help from my friends', like the Beatles sang many, many years ago, all you want. But, personally I am far more thankful for the auto-auto control system's sense-plan-act loops. Without them, we would be dead now, wrapped around a tree or under water in Rio Descalabrado."

"Always the computer's champion, aren't you?" Rita grumbles. "Do you really think computers care about our life or death?"

"It's certainly a different life or death situation than I expected when we left San Juan before dawn this morning." Rubbing her shoulder, Zhou straightens in her seat with a groan followed by a muffled burp. "My stomach is in my throat Robert. I need to walk on some solid ground and get steady. Let's stop."

Reluctantly, Robert searches the sky for enforcement drones. "Will they let us in or will they block us like they did in Caguas?"

"Oh yes! We can definitely get in today Robert. Today is Las Mananitas celebration. In fact if we hurry Zhou, you can settle your stomach at the public breakfast concert at Plaza las Delicias." Rita excitedly bounces in her seat. "Oh, I hope we sing La Marimorena. It's one of my favorite Christmas songs and it's just your type of song too, Robert."

"Never heard of it. I don't believe we sing La Marimor...or whatever you call it...in Canada."

"Or China, either." Zhou adds.

"Oh, both of you are going to love it. Listen, while I teach you the words. I'll even sing it in English, well the version I know, anyway. Ok? Now La Marimorena means the Hurly Burly and this is how it goes." With joy in her voice, Rita begins singing.

"Tonight it's Christmas Eve.
And tomorrow Christmas Day
Take out the wine skin Mary
I want to get drunk

Hurry, hurry, hurry, the hurly burly
Hurry, hurry, hurry, It's Christmas Eve

In the stable of Bethlehem
The mice have come in
And poor Saint Joseph
They've gnawed at his pants

Hurry, hurry, hurry, the hurly burly
Hurry, hurry, hurry, It's Christmas Eve

Here we've arrived
A group of four hundred
If you want us to sing to you
Put out four hundred chairs.

Hurry, hurry, hurry, the hurly burly
Hurry, hurry, hurry, It's Christmas Eve

I've been singing for three hours
Loads of carols

If you don't want me to go
Bring out the Christmas biscuits

Hurry, hurry, hurry, the hurly burly
Hurry, hurry, hurry, It's Christmas Eve"

Looking perplexed, Robert expresses his doubts about Rita's Christmas song. "You have a pleasant singing voice Rita, but your song makes no sense to me. It doesn't rhyme. Although, I must admit I did enjoy the parts about wine and getting drunk."

"It sounds better in Spanish and I did sing you the fun version that I learned on the playground after church, but believe me it's still a Christmas carol." Rita scolds Robert. "You really need to relax a little Robert. Have some breakfast. Listen to some music. Laugh with my Ponceno friends. Aethon may kill us all, if your big pharma thugs don't first, so for just a few minutes let's live. Keep calm Ponce es Ponce."

"What's so special about Ponce?" Zhou asks.

"Ponce is the pearl of south Puerto Rico. Poncenos say Ponce es Ponce lo demas es parkin." Rita proudly declares. "Ponce is Ponce, the rest is parking."

SECURITY PATROL

Fear. Stabbing deep into the heart of Puerto Rico is paralyzing fear. Rita's dream of celebrating Las Mananitas with her Ponce friends vanishes into the silence of Ponce's streets. No mariachis are singing in Ponce this year. No breakfast is being served at Casa Alcadia de Ponce. Decorations dangle with no celebration. Only the singing of hymns and recitation of prayers for healing slice through this morning's stillness in Ponce.

Unlike Caguas, nobody attempts to bar them from departing the throughway and entering the city's center. Because, nobody is there. Only Rita's friends accompany them to the Las Mananitas celebration area. Here, where thousands of people should be eating and singing, it is abandoned. Robert directs the auto-auto to set-down in front of the old courthouse.

Rita's amigos wave at her and shout hellos, but they do not venture close to her or the auto-auto. They stay safely away. Smiling and waving, Rita steps toward them. They wave cautiously, back farther away, then turn and leave.

Zhou wobbles out of the vehicle and vomits. Leaning her back against the side of the auto-auto, she slides down onto the pavement. She bends her knees and drops her head between them.

Stepping out onto the pavement of Calle Villa, Robert stretches and slowly turns in a circle. He is searching the scenery. He fails to see that he is seen.

"He's taller than I remember...quite handsome." One of the two, observing air-cyclists comments as she peers through her electro digital optics.

"How can you forget how tall he is? That's how we were caught. We couldn't fit him into our vehicle, because he's so tall," grouses her male partner.

The dark haired female air-cyclist hiding among trees on Plaza Ponce scolds him. "Look how sick you made Zhou. I think you were a little too rough on them Albern. Almost running them into trees and a river, after all. That was a little unnecessary. Don't you think?"

"Oh, she'll recover, Faul. Better she is a little sick now than dead later." With a smirk, Albern congratulates himself. "I believe I shook them up just enough to wake them up. They need to be more on guard."

As Robert examines the scratches their trip through the bushes affixed to the glider, Rita assists Zhou. Administering a slight tug here followed by a light tap there, Robert determines that the glider's tough graphene sustained only cosmetic damage. He heaves a sigh of relief, straightens and leans against the auto-auto's aerodynamic side. None of them wander from the safety of their glider.

"You told me that Deacon Evoil is supposedly sending three SS Order of Sicarii assassins. Do you think they're here?" Faul apprehensively scans her surroundings.

Just as she fears, she spies two men lurking in the shadows of Calle Amor. A quick scan of their identical, uniform-like clothes informs her they are not Puerto Rican and their skulking reveals they are definitely not innocent visitors. She nudges Albern and directs his attention to the two men. "Are they watching them or are they watching us watching them?"

Through her optics, Faul detects that the interest of the two men is split. One man is focusing on Robert's group. The other man is pivoting his attention between Albern and Faul, and the three others.

"Do you think those two are members of Evoil's three, Albern?" Faul records visuals of the men. "Do you think Evoil may have ordered them to eliminate us along with Goodfellow and Shengwu?"

"You could be correct. Evoil is volatile…and unpredictable. He was furious that we failed and were arrested. He threatened me that there would be consequences, if we didn't stay away. I think he is a brother of Satan." Feeling Faul's fear, Albern contemplates their getaway. "I believe we should start moving so we're not easy targets if they're coming after us."

"What about them?" Faul motions toward Robert and his partners.

"Proverbs tells us that the prudent sees danger and hides himself, but the simple go on and suffer for it. I suggest we be prudent Faul," Albern whispers.

Now silent, Albern watchfully begins creeping out of Plaza Ponce toward his waiting air-cycle. He motions for Faul to follow. She turns and hurries past him. He finds her impatiently mounted and raring to go when he arrives.

"Ok, let's buzz them on our way out. We can't tell them about those two, but we need them to remain stressed and edgy. Alarmed is well armed." Albern directs Faul as he pulls on his air-cycle's Guidance control helmet.

"Then what?"

"According to Rita's intercepted communications, they're going to the La Parguera Nature Preserve. Only passageway two goes from here to there. So we'll ride out of their sight ahead of them. Run interference, you might say." Albern mounts his air-cycle and energizes it.

Faul energizes her air-cycle and adjusts her helmet. "What do we do if those are Evoil's men? What if they attack? What's your plan then?"

"Improvise, ad-lib and trust in God. That's always my plan. My only plan." Albern transmits directions from his helmet to Faul's helmet, as he maneuvers his air-cycle for his assault. "Now follow me. Be loud and menacing. Charge at them."

Kneeling on her air-cycle, Faul poses herself to terrify. "I shall warn them of the evil with the sounds of glory. My speakers will blast them with Handel's Hallelujah Chorus."

Albern jams his air-cycle forward. "Let's roar!"

SEEKING DEATH FRUIT

Never before has Robert beheld such stunningly exquisite blue water. His eyes dive deep drowning his senses in the bay's beauty. Sailing upon the serene bay his thoughts are gliding atop the dancing waters of the Gulf when Arthur C. Clarke's words surface in his drifting mind and dribble out as a mumble. "How inappropriate to call this planet Earth when it is quite clearly Ocean."

"Enchanting view, isn't it." Rita declares as she steps to his side shattering his musing.

"Oh yes, and much more. These waters are as intensely blue as a Lapis Lazuli gemstone." Robert cannot drag his eyes ashore. "Contemplating these waters, I now understand why the Romans believed Lapis Lazuli blue to be a powerful aphrodisiac and a strong medicine thought to keep the limbs healthy and free the soul from error, envy and fear. And, those green islands speckle the bay like the gem's brassy pyrite mottling."

"Lapis Lazuli? Never heard of it." Rita inquires, curious.

"I first saw it when I was serving in Afghanistan. I bought several stones. Like this bay, they're mesmerizingly beautiful."

"Beautiful or not, you're not going to find that Manchineel tree medicine you want in these waters." Interrupts a deeply tanned, weather-beaten, barrel-chested man, as he joins Robert and Rita. "We're sailing my boat inland, deep into the Mangrove swamps where I've seen some native Manchineels."

Pale and wobbly, Zhou shuffles into their conversation. "I certainly hope your boat ride is less perilous than our glider ride here. Two air-cycle riders attacked us along passageway 52 and then again in Ponce. In the middle of Ponce! Came roaring at us like some crazed demons. Extremely frightening."

"Yes, but I believe their ride of terror ended in Guanicas. Sorry, I know you and Rita don't agree with me. But, I still think that I saw those same air-cycles burning in that transporter wreckage outside the Bayer bio tech facility." Robert adds with a touch of anger. "I know what I saw!"

"Me tienes un lado seco *(You're making me crazy)*! Let it go. It was just an accident." Rita chides him.

"Accidents no longer exist! Computerized auto-autos and air-bikes won't collide like that without human interference." Robert argues. "When humans crash into each other, either they meant to or they just made illogical decisions. Give me a logical robot over a bungling human any day."

"Ok Robert, you saw something or you think you saw something in that fiery mess. But we didn't." Rita hurries to change the subject. "This is my cousin Guia. He's our guide. We're searching for the trees using his diving charter boat."

Surveying the marina, Robert notices that the docks are filled with empty, waiting, charter boats. "There's many boats here. Which of them is your boat? I'd like to get aboard and get started."

"Actually, those three are mine." Guia points toward three different sized boats moored along his private pier. "Normally, they would be out by now, but my charters are down. Everybody's charters are down thanks to fear of this Aethon thing."

"That's good and bad for us. Fewer tourists mean less interference and less questions from the curious. But, that also means we are far too noticeable." Concerned about them being too visible to adversaries, Robert is increasingly impatient to shove off. Carrying their sampling equipment, he leaves the others and begins walking toward the boats.

Lugging their own bags and equipment, Rita and Zhou fall in step far behind him with Guia trotting to get in front. Jogging into the lead, Guia directs them to a shallow-draft, open, battery-powered, twenty-five foot dinghy rigged for scuba diving. He jumps into his boat and then assists them and their equipment aboard. Working quickly, he energizes his boat's motors, casts off and is underway into the bay before his passengers find their seats.

Having enjoyed countless hours swimming and boating here, Rita is surprised to see the docks so uninhabited. No fishermen. No snorkelers. Just as Guia predicted, they pass empty charter boat after empty charter boat. Their wake gently rocks them in their moorings. The bay is so empty that Rita hears the boats squeak when they rub against the piers.

As they cruise ahead, the bright sun dances across Rita's face and into her eyes. Blinking and shading her eyes, she struggles to see. Sun blind, she thinks she sees the silhouettes of four men hurrying toward the piers. After her digitized eye lenses adjust to reduce the ultraviolet and visible light, she blinks and looks again. They are gone. She is not certain that she saw what she saw. Probably just some locals, she imagines.

Away from the docks now, Guia accelerates. Clutching the boat's railing, Rita enjoys the cooling breeze, smell of the sea and her view of the verdant, reef islands they will pass heading out of the bay. She focuses her attention forward, missing the ascent of a small surveillance drone above the pier where the silhouettes of the men had appeared and disappeared. Hiding in the sun, the drone trails Guia's boat.

At the edge of the bay, Guia steers starboard surprising Rita. "Aren't we going to Bahia Fosforescente?"

"No Manzanillo left there. All of them were removed years ago. Too dangerous for tourists. We're heading to the Punta Pitahaya area. We should find some Manzanillo there. We may also search in the Boqueroon wildlife refuge." Guia explains as he steers them around some waterway buoys. "It will take some time for us to get there, so just sit back and relax. Enjoy the ride."

Rita follows his advice. She stretches across a wood bench, yawns and is soon snoring. Her concerns are few. Her rest is easy.

Zhou and Robert do not rest. Both engage their PCDs and begin working. Robert connects to his messages while Zhou contacts her researchers at the Instituto. There is no escape from obligation.

Two messages from SPEA greet Robert. The first from Pion is good news. She reports finding no subsequent intrusions or hacking attempts of the data stream between Shengwu and SPEA. He smiles with personal satisfaction, because he knows it is his vigilant, security program that is successfully defending Shengwu's communications. But, at the same time, Robert is troubled. His success is also his failure. He understands that big pharma has not changed its intent, only its tactics. Because of his cybersecurity program, big pharma is rejecting hacking for physical violence.

Robert's second message is also from SPEA. It is a mysterious message from his friendly tormentor, Mugavus Komfort. She is insisting on a covert rendezvous in a public place - a lechonera in the town of Cayey. The exact date and time of their rendezvous will be sent in a separate message, she communicates. She instructs him to buy lunch and eat it at the farthest table in the rear of the lechonera. Mugavus ends her message by dictating to Robert. "Be a tourist, but be on-guard. Don't look for me. I will find you."

For a brief moment, Robert considers requesting more information from Mugavus, but he remembers from experience that she told him all she is going to tell him in her initial message. Mugavus still follows many of the protocols she learned when she was a military intelligence officer in Estonia. She is trained to tell nobody nothing more than necessary. Frustrating as she is, Robert trusts her completely. More than once, he has trusted her with his life. If he needs to know, she will tell him. If he doesn't then she won't.

Wondering if Shengwu is progressing in her genome editing fight against Aethon, Robert accesses the data flow from Stamina Vitae to SPEA. Many of the algorithms and other information transmissions are familiar. Shengwu has used them before. But, as he works his way backward through the data packets from recent transmissions to earlier transmissions, he discovers a radically different group of algorithms. The transmitting of these distinctive algorithm packets began shortly after midnight and ended at two ten this morning. Robert also notices their coding is different. Thanks to his NATO and Coalition experience of working with the US military, he recognizes that the coding is similar to that used by the US Department of Defense, but not exactly. Something in the coding technique is familiar, yet different. He is studying one of the packets when his concentration is shattered.

"Have you used scuba gear before?" Guia interrupts Robert by shoving a lengthy, neoprene scuba wet suit toward him.

Robert requires a moment to digest Guia's unexpected question. "Well, uh yes, but it's been a while. About fifteen years ago in the Red Sea off Djibouti. Why do you ask?"

"Because you're going to need to wear it soon." Guia drops the wet suit onto Robert's lap. "This suit is hooded, so very little of your head will be exposed to Manchineel burns."

"The rest of your head will be covered with this full face mask." Guia retrieves a large scuba mask from a locker box and gives it to Robert. Next, he pulls out a pair of gloves and scuba boots and drops them at Robert's feet.

"I'm a little confused Guia. I don't understand why I need all this scuba gear. I'm not diving. I thought we were just going to collect some samples of the tree and maybe some of its fruit." Robert questions as he sorts through the scuba clothing Guia has dropped into his lap.

"Not we. You! My boat and we aren't going near those trees." Guia shakes his head. "Too dangerous! Deadly! You do know that it's called arbol de la muerte…tree of death, don't you?"

"Well, yes, I read. I heed. I've read about it, so yes I know the Manchineel is very hazardous, but…"

"Hah! Reading will teach you respect, but what you really need is fear." Guia wags his finger toward Robert. "There is no part of this tree that won't kill you. Do you know that Rita's Taino ancestors tortured Spanish soldiers to death by lashing them to Manchineel trees so they had to breathe the tree's poisonous fumes? If they lived through that, they would leave them there so rain would drip from the leaves onto them burning and blistering them. The Tainos also dipped the tips of their arrows in the tree's sap. Supposedly, that's the way they killed Ponce de Leon. Did you know that?"

"No, I didn't know that. But, I do know that the sap in the leaves, twigs and bark will burn you like acid and that you never eat the tree's apples. So then, I suppose you're correct, this scuba gear is necessary. I just…"Robert notices that he is talking to himself. Guia is gone. He is back at the helm, steering them through the reefs toward the forested shore.

Carefully, Guia skippers his boat into a channel cutting through groves of dwarf mangrove trees. They are entering the Boqueron state forest near Punta Pitahaya. As they cruise deeper into the Boqueron, the channel narrows. Knobby mangrove tree roots stand guard above the soggy soil. The trees reach out to touch each other. Intertwining their branches, they create a shady, deep-green tunnel.

Unnoticed, behind them, the trailing drone softly touches down on the water. Turning onto its side, it sinks into the channel. The drone is now subsurface with its propeller blades pushing it through the water instead of the air – an unseen shadow.

Rita awakes, groans, stretches and joins Guia, as he slowly edges his boat ahead. Zhou, who is intensely entranced in her research communications with the Instituto, is startled when her connection is cut by the dense canopy of branches and leaves. For a few moments, she is confused, lost in the leaves along with her electronic lifeline. Zhou stands, climbs onto a bench, twists, turns and struggles to re-establish her connection. Only after almost falling overboard does she finally accept that she is incommunicado.

Grumbling, she moves next to Robert who is studying the thickening forest on the starboard side of the boat. "I certainly hope we find something here that we can use. Shengwu is desperate. I fear that she is losing her sanity. She keeps talking about creating a new human species to survive Aethon...actually a new Peter. She's always talking about some future Peter. Like he will be reborn."

Robert nods his head in resignation. "Yes, I'm worried too. I know she is distressed. And, she said something about genetically engineering a new human species to me, as well. Something her father was doing for the US military. I believe her father..."

"There she is!" Guia hollers and points toward a tree several yards off the starboard bow growing at the end of a channel so narrow that it is actually little more than a deep ditch.

The boat goes dead in the water. Rita steps first to the port side and drops a small anchor overboard then on the starboard side, she tosses another small anchor into the greenish channel water. Now securely anchored, Guia depowers the motor.

Twenty-five yards behind them the small drone drifts to the surface. Soundlessly, the drone positions itself and its electronic eye to observe and transmit.

"Time for you to dress and go swimming, Robert." Rita cheerfully goads him.

"You and Zhou aren't going too? Just me?"

"No. Guia only has enough scuba equipment for you." Rita continues with a devilish grin. "Zhou and I must stay aboard to handle the specimen bags and tell you what to do."

"I could drown, you know." Robert jokes as he gathers the scuba gear.

"Oh, I doubt it." Rita jabs back. "This water is much shallower than you are tall. But if you do drown, just remember, we'll be sad. But on the other hand, you'll finally be quiet. You are expendable, you know?"

HARVESTING DEATH FRUIT

Singularly unimpressive. Robert's immediate reaction to Guia's Manchineel is disappointment. If he did not see the small, yellow-green, apple-like fruit balls scattered around its base, he would not realize that he is staring at the world's most dangerous tree. Standing less than thirty feet tall with a mix of dark brown and gray bark, the Manchineel melts into the background of the surrounding trees. Only its lack of knobby-knee mangrove support roots and its growth on sand distinguish it. But then, looks can be deceiving.

"Are you going to stare at it all day or are you going to pull on your scuba gear and retrieve the samples I need?" Zhou gripes impatiently. "Do you see those clouds? It may start raining soon and we don't have any cover."

"Just reconnoitering. Developing my plan." Considering Guia's warnings, Robert is reluctant. "As you probably know, Moliere said that unreasonable haste is the direct road to error."

"Well Zhou says, I'm hungry and you're wasting valuable time." Zhou firmly pushes Robert forward. "Now, get in your gear, get in the water and get me my samples, so we can get some lunch."

"Ok. Ok. But where do I change?" Robert finds no privacy on the small, open dinghy.

"Robert! Como las tetas del toro *(useless, like tits on a bull)*!" Rita barks, as she begins tugging at his shirt. "Just strip to your undershorts. Nobody cares about your boney body."

After slapping away Rita's hands, Robert hurriedly yanks off his shirt and shorts. He is especially thankful that he left Shengwu's hot, protective skin on the floor of his room, this morning. Tugging and dragging, grunting and groaning, he successfully envelopes himself in the neoprene from his ankles to his hooded head. The suit is an inch or two too short making it crotch crushing snug.

After Rita and Zhou slide on his boots and gloves sealing him in synthetic rubber, Guia straps on his full face mask and oxygen tank rig. Robert tastes the artificial air entering his mask. Next, Rita straps a tool belt around his waist containing a knife, a hatchet, a garden trowel and a pair of shears.

Directing and lifting, Rita and Guia guide Robert into the shallow water. He is mid-thigh deep. Around his ankles, water begins seeping into his wet suit cooling him.

"Here Robert, these are for the samples." Zhou slides a large mesh bag onto his right shoulder. Inside the mesh bag are ten, five-gallon size biohazard sample collection bags. "I need at least a dozen Manchineel apples, two bags of leaves, one bag of stems or young, small twigs, one bag of bark and some samples of the soil beneath it. It is out of season for the tree to have flowers, but if it does, gather some of them too. Now, it is important that each sample be in a separate biohazard bag. Understand?"

Robert nods his head, turns and begins slogging toward the tree. Near the boat, the water reminds Robert of his favorite green tea. As he walks, he studies the sandy bottom for stumble hazards. As he nears the tree, waterlogged Manchineel apples scattered on top and hidden in the sand bottom skid and slide beneath his feet. He stumbles and tumbles to his knees at the edge of the channel bank.

Here, beneath the tree, Robert notices thin, oily streaks on the water. He also senses an irritating stinging gnawing on his legs and groin. As the stinging begins burning, Robert realizes that the Manchineel's oily sap is riding the water into his wet suit. His genitals are aflame.

"While you're down there, collect at least six of those sunken apples." Zhou hollers from the boat.

Hurriedly digging in the sand, Robert retrieves and bags three buried apples and three waterlogged apples. Lunging forward like a seal onto an ice floe, he heaves himself out of the irritating water and onto the bank. He finds little relief. Cupping his hands, he compresses the neoprene down each of his legs squeezing out as much water as he can. That seems to ease, but not end his pain.

Robert knows he can only end the burning attacking his groin by removing his wet suit, and he can only safely remove his wet suit when he is back in the boat with Zhou's samples. So, he grits his teeth, curses and endures.

Still on the ground, he pulls out the garden shovel and collects her soil sample. Kneeling where he just landed, he begins feverishly grabbing and bagging dry apples. Ten, eleven, twelve apples, done with her dozen.

"Robert, I want at least six apples straight from the tree. You know. Six that haven't dropped." Zhou requests, much to Robert's chagrin.

"Well, of course she does." He mutters, as he straightens and stands.

One, two, three, four low hanging apples, he tears from the tree and throws into their selected bag. Robert stretches and reaches. The final two apples he needs swing teasingly just out of his reach. He removes his bag with bags and sets it on the beach. From below, he circles the two high-hanging apples seeking an advantageous spot, then he leaps. Actually, he barely hops. The weight of his tools and his scuba tank keep him ground bound.

Off balance and out of control, he lurches ahead slamming his shoulder into the Manchineel's trunk. Boom, he drops to the ground. Plop, plop, the two apples drop onto the beach. He fears his shoulder may be broken, but at least now he has Zhou's six freshly picked apples.

"Hurry it up! It's starting to rain!" Rita shouts, believing she is encouraging him while actually, she is only aggravating him.

After collecting the two apples he knocked loose, he decides to cut sections of bark from the area where he brutally beat the tree with his aching shoulder. A few whacks from his hatchet and he is shoving two large sections of sap oozing bark into a bag. His gloves and the hatchet are sticky with sap.

Rita's rain, starting as a soft, warm shower, escalates quickly into a squall. Robert chuckles, as he watches the trio on the boat searching frantically for protection that does not exist. But, his amusement is short lived.

As the downpour showers sticky, wet sap onto him, Robert realizes just how true are Guia's stories about the Tainos using rain through the Manchineel as deadly torture. It is certainly tormenting him. Each sap laden drop splatters and sticks to his wet suit.

On his face mask, a vision distorting glaze is growing in size and density. Attempting to wipe away the thickening slime with his gloves only smears it. Each moment, his ability to see is growing worse. To complete Zhou's assignment, he needs a bag of leaves and limbs, but everything is blurry. He is hesitant to blindly cut and hack.

The drenched trio waiting aboard the boat do not appreciate Robert's vision struggles or understand why he is hesitating. They just know that they are wet and he is still standing staring into space. In unison, but with each making different demands, they begin shouting at him. They squawk like a murder of crows.

Peering through the thick rain, Robert approaches the overhanging shadows that resemble limbs and leaves. His right hand clutches the shears while his gloved left hand feels for leaves. He touches the side of the shears against his left hand before sliding it away to the right. Snip. Snap. He cuts free a small limb with leaves. Sap flows along the shears and drops onto his wrist and saturates the palm of his glove.

He pulls his prize close to his mask. Success. But, now he realizes another problem. He cannot see well enough to find the bag for the limb and leaves. After unsuccessfully, blindly searching and struggling, Robert rams the limb into the big bag.

Working with more confidence, he quickly cuts and bags five more limbs and leaves. The sixth limb is the largest. It is a branch. He strains to force the shears' blades to gnaw through it. When he finally twists and turns and tugs it loose, he discovers that there is no space for it in his bag. It is stuffed full.

But, this bough is his prize. Now that he has it, he refuses to leave it. Turning toward the boat, he raises his trophy above his head. He hears no cheers. They stand strangely silent.

His job done, Robert plods into the water toward the boat. Only after escaping the sap dripping Manchineel, does he realize that the rain has stopped. His plan for the rainstorm to clear his facemask and wet suit of some of the sap collapses. He must remain a gummy skin-burning mess. He is untouchable.

Clutching the bough bleeding Manchineel-sap in his left hand and with the shears glued to the palm of his right hand, he slogs to the boat. Struggling to maintain his balance, he keeps his head down scrutinizing the water as best he can through the glaze. Lugging all of Zhou's samples on his back, while encased in the tight, hot, wet suit is draining him. He is sucking hard for air. He cannot find enough oxygen in his mask. Staggering and fading into unconsciousness, he collapses against the boat then sinks to his knees. He is done.

SAP SLAP

Smack! A boat push-pole hook-point slams into Robert's left shoulder. Crack! The hook whacks his head.

"Air ya daid?" A male voice demands in a Tennessee drawl.

"Hit im agin, Joe." A second man urges twanging a similar, southern drawl.

"Good ideya, Billy." The push pole hook pokes Robert in his neck.

"Stop!" Robert yells, as he struggles to his feet.

Five foggy images float before Robert's fuzzy eyes. Manchineel sap clinging to his facemask still distorts everything. Squinting to focus, he identifies Rita, Zhou and Guia huddling together on the far side of the boat. Her action is blurry, but Robert believes he sees Rita making a slashing sign across her throat. A warning.

Nearest to him, two fat, bald blobs in clashing, garish shirts and shorts tip the boat. The man-blob to Robert's left wields the push-pole hitting him. He must be Joe.

The other man-blob, Billy, is waving, what Robert cannot clearly see, but by its shape he suspects is a pneumatic pistol. After all, a pneumatic pistol is the only logical weapon for Puerto Rico. Laser-aimed pneumatic pistols are silent, clean and deadly, and 3D printable, so they can be smuggled into countries prohibiting regular weapons. Definitely dangerous dudes.

"Git in the boat!" Joe orders then leans forward and whacks Robert's shoulder with his boat pole.

Stab! Robert spears Joe in the face with the sap slobbering butt of his Manchineel bough. He grinds the burning juice deep into Joe's eyes and nose, blinding him with acid fire. Screaming, Joe drops his pole into the water and claws at his face scratching the sap deeper into his flesh.

169

Thrusting with his right hand, Robert plunges his sap drenched shear blades deep into Billy's calf. He yanks the shears out and then drives them into Billy's other leg. Cursing and staggering, Billy fires his pistol at Robert's stabbing shears, burying a ball into his own foot. Hopping and careening along the boat's edge, Billy lurches into Robert's sappy bough, slavering the pasty poison onto his thigh and groin. Yelping, he shoves away the bough coating his hands in scorching sap. His pneumatic pistol bounces off Robert's shoulder and sinks with a burble into the channel's sand bottom.

Both men lurch past Robert into the water. Seizing their chance, Rita and Guia rammed their shoulders into their two wounded attackers heaving them soaring off the boat. Blinded, blubbering and bawling, they flail about in the water behind Robert.

"Rita, you and Zhou take their boat and head back to the marina." Guia directs, as he swiftly lowers a boat boarding ladder over the boat side. "Robert, climb into my boat and let's get out of here."

Robert tosses his battle bough into the boat then using his left hand he pulls the shears from his right hand and drops them next to the bough. The bag of bags is tossed in next. Finally freed, Robert clambers up the ladder and rolls into the boat.

Less than a breath later, Guia is piloting them out of the narrow channel. Ahead of him, Rita and Zhou are yelling and pointing at a drone floating in the water. Rita lifts a set of First-Person-View, drone control goggles from their boat's deck. She waves the FPV goggles above her head for Guia to see before throwing them into the water next to the drone.

Guia heads for them. Crunch! He smashes his boat's bow into the spy drone shattering it. Steering his dinghy over the bits and pieces, he sinks part of it and scatters the rest.

"Now, I know how they were able to find us and sneak up on us." Guia proclaims into the wind, as he pilots his dinghy through the narrow channel. "We were watching you and didn't see them slipping in from behind. Ea' Diantre *(Wow)*! Suddenly, they were here, and we were their prisoners."

Lying on his side, with his tacky, gloved hands, Robert is struggling to remove his face mask. It is sap glued to his wet suit hood. He cannot unstrap his oxygen tank harness, either. Flopping like a fat flounder on the dinghy's deck, he is stumped.

"Hey! I need some help here!" He yells at Guia.

When Guia ignores him, Robert kicks him on the side of his leg. "Hey! Sorry to bother you, but free me from this strait jacket! Will you?"

Guia slows the dinghy to a crawl. Then he turns his attention to Robert. "Do you think I'm stupid? I'm not going to touch you. You're covered in poison."

"Sorry, but you can't just leave me like this." Robert protests.

Guia surveys the deck for some gadgets to help Robert. With a clap of his hands, he concocts a plan. He uncovers a length of tow rope from a pile of gear.

Displaying the rope to Robert, he explains his scheme. "I'm going to tie this end of the rope around this cleat here." Guia secures the rope around a cleat on the aft end of the dinghy.

"This other end, I'm going to wrap around your chest." Carefully, without touching him, he slips the rope around Robert's chest, just below his armpits.

Using the rope, he helps Robert stand. "Now, I want you to jump back into the water."

"Sorry? What!" Robert objects.

"You hop back in and I'll pull you through the water back to the marina. By then, you should be clean enough to touch." Guia directs with a confident smile.

"Are you crazy?!" Robert tugs at his rope harness.

Guia chuckles. "Some people say I'm Locó, but I just think I'm imaginative. Now are you heading back into the water or do you want to wear that hot neoprene the rest of the day? It's up to you."

Robert shakes his head in resignation, walks to the stern and drops off into the shoulder-high water. He watches Guia gradually ease the boat forward. The rope tightens around Robert's chest and pulls him off his feet. He is soon bobbing and twirling along, up and down, chest-up, chest-down, behind the boat. At first he fights, but soon he relaxes and enjoys the ride. The water flowing through his suit is cooling and flushing the sting off his legs and cooling his fiery crotch.

Guia slows until the dinghy is dead in the water next to his pier. Refreshed, Robert swims to the side of the dinghy. Guia slides the boarding ladder over the side and he climbs aboard. After he unties Robert, Guia completes mooring.

Some parts of him remain a little sticky, but now Robert is finally able to shed his facemask, tank, tool belt and wetsuit. The bay breeze flows across his skin and begins calming the flaming blotches puffing out on his legs. But, the gentle, saltwater wind cannot extinguish the smoldering in his midsection.

Grabbing a two-liter water bottle from the deck, he pulls his boxer shorts away from his belly and douses himself. If one is good, three are better. Desperately, one bottle after another, he drenches his genitals. Only when Rita wolf whistles at him, does he remember that he is wetting himself in public wearing only his clinging, wet undershorts, his diving boots and his scuba gloves.

"Acho que fiebre *(What a fever, dude)*!" Rita blows on her fingers like they are hot and she must cool them. "You are looking good, especially the diving boots and gloves. They're so…oh, I don't know…you. Yep, it's a fashion statement only that dapper man, Robert Goodfellow, would or could make."

After feigning a smile at the approaching Zhou and Rita, Robert peels off his diving boots. Next, he yanks off his gloves and tosses them onto the deck. Guia hands him his shorts, shirt and shoes and he swiftly dresses with his back turned to the women. His water-soaked boxer shorts are a welcome, wet compress pressing against his enflamed skin. Carefully, he inspects the Aethon badge attached to his shirt. It is still lucky green.

"Don't lose those gloves." Zhou advises. "You'll need them to transfer my samples to our glider."

"And we need to do that now and get out of here." Rita points toward a man untying the boat she and Zhou just returned. "He told us that the two men we left swimming back there were thugs brought here by two other men. I think the men out in the channel were their muscle."

"Well they certainly weren't their brains." Robert sneers with swagger, stretching to his full height and puffing out his chest, as he savors his triumph in combat over the two tough guys.

"Yeah…well anyway…" Smirking, Rita continues. "The two men who left are mean looking fellows according to him. He told us he overheard them telling the two thugs that they were going to meet some associates in Guanica, while they collected the packages here. He expects them to return soon and he's scared of them, so he's going out to find the two goons who attacked us."

Guia, Rita and Zhou wave at the other boat as it passes. The man distractedly returns their wave. He is concentrating on the bay ahead, searching it for the two men.

Zhou motions for Robert to hurry, as he pulls on the diving gloves. "He may be looking for a while. We told him we found the boat abandoned off the point near Boquerón Faro, so he won't look in the channels immediately. But, like he told us, he expects the other two to return at any time. So, we need to leave here, now."

Lugging all of Zhou's Manchineel samples the half-mile from the boat to the auto-auto is a painful, exhausting chore. The sample bag is a heavy burden when it is not floating on water, especially as Robert struggles to keep it away from his body. Each brush of the bag or bough against his skin scalds him. Flinching, wincing and cursing, he wrestles his balky harvest of death apples, leaves and limbs up the pier, through the landing lot, and finally, into the auto-auto's rear storage.

Hauling Zhou's samples from the boat has drained Robert of all of his victorious, gladiator bravado and most of his strength. He struggles to find enough power to pull off the diving gloves. He drops them onto the samples and closes the glider's hatch. He is drained and dizzy, and leans against the side of the glider for support.

"Darse prisa *(Hurry up)*! We must go now, Robert!" Rita shouts from inside the auto-auto.

The entry panel slides open. Zhou and Rita grab his shirt, yanking him inside onto the floor. The glider bolts ahead with a jolt.

"We're taking a different route back. We're not using major passageways. Rita says it will take a little longer, but only locals know to travel this way. It should be safer." Zhou explains excitedly. "And she says that we'll stop at a place in the hills called Maelo Chicken Fever. It's a roadside restaurant that has spectacular smoked chicken. Since, it's not in a city, she says they'll feed us. I hope so. I haven't eaten at all today. I'm starving!"

Robert drags himself from the floor onto the glider seat. "Well, Lewis Carroll said that if you don't know where you're going, any road will get you there. So let's go look for some chicken to chew. I'm hungry too."

CLEAN GREEN

Perfect plans fail eventually. Bad plans flop immediately. Travelling the lone passageway connecting La Parguera's piers to the rest of Puerto Rico never enhances your chances of avoiding detection. Bad guys always monitor the main routes.

"Duck! Get down! Get down!" Rita shoves Zhou out of sight onto the seat. Her safety restraint slapping her across her throat, nearly strangling her. Robert instinctively pops his safety restraint and drops to the floor. Rita plops on top of Robert knocking his breath out of him.

Robert squirms for breathing space beneath Rita. "Why are we hiding and why are you crushing me?"

"The other men! Didn't you see them? Two guys wearing the same ugly, bright shirts." Pushing on Robert's back, Rita rises and peeks out the side window. "Ok, I don't think they noticed us."

"Oh, they'd have to be blind to have not noticed us. We're probably in the only auto-auto glider in Puerto Rico sporting bush scratches. Our rumble with the air-cycles left distinguishing marks, you know." Robert grumbles.

Zhou props herself up and peers out their back glass. "If that's their glider that I see, we may not be safe, yet. I think they're slowing. They may be stopping."

Rita and Robert join Zhou at the back glass to spy on the glider that passed them. It hesitates, but does not stop. A few feet farther it accelerates, returning to normal speed. Breathing easier, but not relaxing, the trio continue watching backward. Only when nothing appears for several minutes do they adopt a jittery normal and exchange crouching for sitting.

Rita exhales and rubs her fingers across her forehead. "Phew! Salió el tiro por la culata *(that plan backfired)*. I thought for a moment that we were trapped. But, I think we'll be ok now."

A distressed expression etching her face, Zhou is not as confident as Rita. "Can this thing go any faster? We need to get far away from here, as fast as possible. I dread what will happen once those men learn that their companions are missing…or worse yet…they find them and see what Robert did to them."

"Sorry, but auto-autos will not exceed the allowed maximum speed. It's going as fast as its program permits." Robert's explanation does not soothe Zhou's concerns.

Beyond her sight, Zhou's forebodings are transforming into reality at La Parguera's piers. Arriving at the bay, the two bosses discover Guia calmly tending his empty, moored dinghy. They are perplexed. They expected to find their two men in possession of the trio and their samples awaiting them. They certainly did not expect to discover Guia healthy and alone. According to their plan, he and his dinghy should still be out in the bay.

Hurrying from pier to pier, they complete a brief search of the port. No luck. They cannot locate their own men or their rented boat. Standing at the water's edge, scanning the bay and then looking back, the truth smacks them. The two suddenly grasp that they just allowed their quarry to glide by them.

In less than a minute, they initiate their pursuit sending a speedy surveillance drone shooting skyward to hunt that glider they just passed. One of the men dons a pair of FPV, drone control goggles to view what their drone views. Searching the only passageway exiting this small town proves an easy task. Whizzing through the air on drone wings, his camera eyes swiftly spot the trio's solitary auto-auto gliding along the single thoroughfare.

"Got them. They're traveling north on thoroughfare 304," announces the goggles wearer. "In a few minutes, I'll have the drone within audio surveillance range, too. All we have to do is look and listen. They can run, but they cannot hide."

Grabbing the drone pilot by his arm, the other man hustles him to their auto-auto and shepherds him inside. Then he scrambles in beside him. After he punches a few buttons synchronizing the FPV drone control goggles signal with the auto-auto's guidance system, their glider is underway. Robert, Rita and Zhou's glider has a thirty-five minute lead on them, but with their spy drone leading them they know they will catch them eventually. They can be patient. There is no escape.

Thirty-five minutes distance ahead, as they climb into the mountains, Zhou is growing impatient. Her mind is racing far ahead of their glider. Questions, questions, questions plague her. Can she transform the Manchineel poison fruit or toxic sap into an Aethon killer? Does a weakness exist in the Aethon RNA that she can exploit?

Mentally, she inventories her Manchineel samples and contemplates a range of possible genome modification algorithms. But, her mental manipulations provide no solace. She aches to be working in her lab microscopically ripping apart the Manchineel's genetic structures to reveal its secrets.

Zhou concedes that examining any of her Manchineel samples inside the glider is too dangerous, but she wonders if she can learn anything by probing Robert's sap burns. "Robert, do any of the places where you came in contact with the Manchineel still burn?"

Robert is unprepared for Zhou's question. He must mentally self-examine himself for a moment. "Uh yes, well my calves...and...uh...my groin. My groin burns the worst."

"Ah, tender skin...good. The groin is where your body would most easily absorb Manchineel sap." Zhou taps her nose in thought and then reaches toward Robert. "Let me see it."

"Sorry?" Robert throws Zhou's exploring hands away. "Whoa! Wait one minute, now. I don't think so."

Giggling, Rita immediately seizes her opportunity to pester Robert. "But, it's for the sake of science Robert. I say, let's see some bare bum buddy. You were flashing it on the pier. Why not here?"

Zhou points at the Aethon badge on Robert's chest. "I wouldn't ask, but your badge is glowing green. It's much greener than mine or Rita's. So, something special is occurring inside you. Must be because you're the only one who had Manchineel sap on their body. I just want to analyze..."

"Look at my calves. Take some of my blood. But, I'm not taking off my shorts." Robert grabs his short's waist.

"I wonder. I'm not as smart about this genetics stuff as you guys but..." Rita reaches toward Robert and lightly touches his Aethon badge. "...couldn't this be a good sign? Like a positive, positive? Since green is good isn't glowing green better? Perhaps your badge is telling us what we want to know."

To protect himself from being stripped, Robert releases his tight grip on his short's waste and activates his embedded PCD. "Pion will know. She developed the analytic parameters for it."

Robert receives no immediate response from Pion to his initial inquiry. He waits five minutes before he attempts again. Again, she is silent. Five minutes later, he tries his third time. No answer.

Robert completes some mental time travel. "If my calculations are correct, she is eighteen hours ahead of us here, so it should be six thirty-seven in the morning there. Actually, I guess you could say tomorrow morning. Perhaps, she's eating. If she is, then interrupting her structured schedule will upset her. Better not to bother her, again. When she's prepared, she'll respond."

Pion appears on Robert's PCD fifteen minutes later. She is not the woman he expects to see. Her room is dark. Her face is haggard. She is gently rocking to and fro with her eyes closed, mumbling. Robert recognizes that she is stimming.

Seeking not to agitate Pion and worsen her condition, Robert approaches her cautiously. First, he ensures that she cannot see Rita, who upsets her, or Zhou, who is a stranger. He places his finger across his lips motioning for them to be silent. Without speaking, he watches and waits for her to indicate that she is prepared and willing to receive him.

His patience pays. Her rocking gradually slows to a stop. As if awakening from a deep sleep, she opens her eyes. Still repeatedly mumbling something that sounds to Robert like "Shengwu" and "babies". She stares ahead.

Believing that she is attempting to tell him something, Robert nods his head and gently, calmly agrees in his most reassuring, soothing voice. "Yes, I understand. Are you ok? Can I ask you a question? I need your help."

Eventually, her mumbles become whispers and then stop. She closes her eyes. Droops her head. Silence. Robert waits. Slowly, she raises her head and nods.

Robert ventures his question in a voice just above a whisper. "Some Manchineel sap absorbed into my skin and now my Aethon badge is glowing green. What could cause it to glow green? Is that good or bad?"

"Glowing green? Please show me." Pion requests.

Robert displays his badge to her. She waves her hand in front of her face to energize her Artificial Intelligence interface. Soft light bathes her face from this type of heads-up display. In Pion's own voice, the AI greets her. "Good morning Pion."

"Access Aethon badge parameters." She directs.

Shadows and colors prance across Pion's face. She moves her eyes to the side and one shadow pattern dissolves into another. She leans a millimeter forward and the shadow patterns enlarge. After minutes of study, she nods and the shadows disappear and the light melts away.

Pion focuses on Robert. "When we created your badge, we combined dynamic DNA nanotechnology with high resolution electronic sensing and integrated wireless electronic devices to detect the presence in the wearer's blood of the genetic mutation Aethon, as a single nucleotide polymorphism. Our graphene-based Aethon detector operates by directly incorporating DNA itself into the graphene sensor. So…"

Robert's eyes widen. A small smile dances onto his face. He jumps into the conversation. "So, for the Aethon badge to accurately detect the presence of Aethon, it must be able to establish a flawless match between Aethon DNA in my body with an Aethon DNA strand in the detector. Is that correct?"

"Correct, to ensure the detection badges are able to recognize Aethon DNA in the wearer's blood, a strand of Aethon DNA is required for matching. Therefore, an Aethon DNA strand is required in all of the badges. The Aethon DNA strand is 3D printed within the graphene of the badge." Pion explains without emotion.

Robert's smile widens. "Is it possible that my Aethon badge is glowing green, because the Manchineel sap that I absorbed, killed it? Do you suppose chemicals in the sap made my blood poison to the Aethon DNA strand in my badge?"

"It is possible. But, I never suppose anything." Pion declares, "More genome analysis is required to prove it. I will await a sample of Manchineel sap for examination."

Without further comment, Pion abruptly ends their communication. Blip, she is gone. Her behavior is no surprise. Although, Robert does wonder why she was stimming in the beginning. She does not resort to stimming unless she is distressed.

Zhou waves her hand and whispers, "Is she gone?"

178

Robert nods and explodes with joy. "Manchineel! The tree of death is our tree of life!"

"Can it be? Do you think it's true?" Zhou hesitantly probes.

"Yes!" Robert taps his badge. "Jeff Bezos was so correct when he said that there'll always be serendipity involved in discovery. I inadvertently absorbed some Manchineel sap diluted in water and you witnessed what it did. It killed the Aethon in my detection badge, but it didn't kill me. Manchineel eradicates Aethon!"

Bouncing on her seat, Rita shouts, "Wepa *(All right)*! Now, we celebrate. I'm in a fervor for Maelo Chicken Fever. I'm buying the beer!"

CHICKEN FEVER

Sweet smelling, savory smoke swirls and spirals, singing a song of delicious delight. Seducing scents summon Robert. He is starving. Sniffing, smelling, searching, Robert discovers a hungry man's heaven in a simple, tin-roofed, square, half-open, block enclosure – a chicken cooking coop. Enslaved by his senses, he stares in salivating disbelief at row after row of plump poultry riding eight long spits, round and round, slow roasting to exquisite perfection above beds of sizzling embers.

"I do not believe that I have been this excited about tasting a food since the time I ate my first peameal bacon sandwich at the Carousel in Toronto's Saint Lawrence market." Robert exclaims, as he steps into line to order. "This is real meat! Not that lab-grown, processed protein that I normally eat, but real meat."

"Their sweet potatoes and yucca are also fantastic." Rita edges in line in front of him, dragging Zhou along behind her. "Follow me. I know what's best, so I'll order for us. Ok? You two just follow me and be prepared to carry your heaping plates. No meal is small here."

Since Rita is taking control of procuring their meals, Robert is now free to enjoy the people, the music and the life enveloping him. First, he notices everyone's Aethon badge is proudly and prominently displayed on their chests. He smiles. All of them beam green, but only his glows. He struggles to prevent himself from shouting, we found the cure.

Robert watches a small girl, waiting with her parents, begin wiggling and dancing to the Reggaeton tones embracing her. Without realizing it, he is soon wiggling and swaying, too. Robert cannot escape the infectious combination of hip-hop and Jamaican dance beat pumping out of large speakers hanging in every corner of the open-air restaurant.

Puerto Ricans live loud. Riding atop the music is a layer of laughter and lies, rumor and recrimination – cháchara *(chatter)*. The rhythmic, cacophony consumes Robert. His mind swoons in the suffocating smells and sounds.

"Gracias, buen provecho *(bon appetite)*!" The woman behind the counter shouts over the music and chatter at Robert, as she swings her arm, motioning for him to move ahead.

Startled awake, Robert hurries toward Rita and Zhou. At the end of the serving counter, he waits his plate. Half of a chicken, slices of sweet potato, a large serving of yucca, plus some vegetables Robert does not recognize, piled high into a food mountain flooding over his plate. Both of his hands are required to transport his weighty feast to their table. Rita has already arrived, deposited her dinner, and departed to acquire their promised beers.

"Finally, we have something to celebrate." Rita announces as she hands Zhou and Robert their beer bottles.

Robert tips his bottle toward Zhou and Rita. "As we say in Toronto - Cheers. Or, if you rather, as we say in Quebec - a votre santé."

Zhou lightly taps Rita's bottle and nods. "Ganbei *(drink up)*," She toasts in Mandarin.

But when she taps Robert's bottle, she looks at him directly with worry in her eyes and her personal warning. "Xún xù jiàn jìn".

"One step at a time", is the statement, Robert hears from Zhou via his inner ear translator. He eyes her quizzically. She avoids his questioning gaze to concentrate on tearing into her plate of food. Is it her hunger hurrying her or something else? Her chomping decimation of her dinner is not a pleasant sight.

Robert focuses his attention on his own plate. Rotating it, he deliberately studies each delicacy. Leaning forward, he sucks in the tantalizing, tempting aroma of the chicken. Unlike the lab-grown poultry portions he routinely consumes when his body demands protein, this hunk of hen excites his every sense. It dizzies him.

With his fork and knife, he surgically carves the chicken's breast and then slides a slice of meat into his mouth. He does not chew, but allows it to lay upon his tongue so its juices can caress his taste buds. Slow-roasted flavor is baked into every fiber.

This chicken is a traditional masterpiece created today just as it has been for centuries. He closes his eyes, chews slowly to capture the flavor and finally swallows. It is divine.

His second bite is enjoyed with the same relish, as is his third and his fourth. When Robert opens his eyes to taste his next bite, he meets the disapproving glares of Rita and Zhou. While he is savoring each succulent morsel, they have grazed their way across most of their plate. Ignoring them, he selects a slice of sweet potato as his next taste treat. He smells the sweet potato slice, as if he is a sommelier chasing the bouquet of a fine wine.

"Are you about finished?" Rita asks impatiently.

Robert waves the forked sweet potato slice like a magic wand across his body. "I remember Hippocrates taught that you should let food be thy medicine and medicine be thy food. So, I'm allowing this food to heal my Manchineel pains."

Zhou pushes away her plate. "Are you planning on living here, Robert? I'm itching to analyze my Manchineel samples. Just because some diluted sap killed the Aethon DNA strand in your badge, is no guarantee that it will work on anyone else. But, I cannot learn anything about that here. Every minute we sit here is another minute less that somebody suffering Aethon in San Juan may have to live."

Rita is growing equally impatient. "I know this is a special taste treat for you, and normally, I am quite willing to spend the afternoon here eating and drinking and enjoying the music. But, there are lives at stake. People are depending upon us. Shengwu and Peter are depending upon us."

Humiliated, Robert apologizes. "Sorry, sorry, I lost myself in this unbelievably, delicious meal. I've never tasted anything like it before. Está pasao *(It's awesome)*! Most of my meat is printed in a protein processing lab and is tasteless."

"Yes, it's awesome. But we must go. Bring it with you." Rita collects her meal remains along with Zhou's for disposal and leaves for the exit.

As Robert carefully prepares his food for transporting to enjoy in the glider, Zhou energizes her PCD and accesses her research lab at the Instituto. Concentrating more on her PCD than her walking, Zhou stumbles along behind Robert. She watches his legs and reads simultaneously. He is stepping precisely, so he does

182

not lose one speck of his precious banquet from his plate. His feet are her guides.

From their table, winding through the other diners and into the street, Zhou does not remove her attention from her PCD and Robert's heels. She is intensely engaged in preparing to examine possible relationships between Aethon genomes and Manchineel genomes. Abruptly, Robert halts. Zhou only stops when her forehead bumps into his back.

"If my conjectures are correct…because it's all conjecture until we analyze it in the lab…Manchineel could be an almost free treatment for Aethon." Zhou tells Robert, with her head resting against his spine and her eyes glued to her calculations.

"Zhou…" Robert flexes his back nudging her head attempting to gain her attention and stifle her talking.

"Do you know that there are Manchineel trees in Florida, Robert?" Robert slides to the side, leaving Zhou standing alone. "More than in Puerto Rico."

"That would make it accessible on the mainland close to Tennessee and Kentucky. It could be…" Searching for Robert, she raises her eyes from her PCD to discover a pneumatic pistol pointed at her head.

"Shut up." Robert murmurs.

"…almost free…" She continues, mumbling into silence.

"Almost free, eh. Well unfortunately for you, that's not really good for us." A tall man dancing his laser aiming dot across Zhou's forehead declares in a threatening growl.

Rita, Robert and Zhou are standing face to face with the two men from La Parguera. The ominous warnings of the Voleurs flood Robert's mind. These two men are almost certainly here to kill them.

Zhou steps away from Robert toward the two men. Since Robert did not warn her, she does not grasp that anything she says is putting them in peril. Naively, she is expecting the two men to celebrate her good news.

Smiling broadly, Zhou points toward Robert's Aethon badge. "Look at how his Aethon detection badge is glowing. Just a little Manchineel tree juice did that. Now, I need to return to San Juan to do more research, but it's possible that just a few drops of Manchineel sap can knock out Aethon. If I'm correct then with

Manchineel trees here, in Florida and the Virgin Islands, people can be protected for pennies. Isn't that great?"

The glowering expressions of the two men confuses Zhou. Nervously, she asks again, "Don't you think that's excellent news? I mean I think we can save a lot of people. Don't you think…?"

"Yes, we know all about it. We heard your conversations with that freak, Pion." The man nearest Rita snarls at Zhou. "That's exactly why we're here. You talk too much. We're here to shut you up, so only our employers know your excellent news."

"I don't understand. You're not going to help all of those people with Aethon? You're just going to let them die? You can't let them die…" Zhou pleads. "…not when we have a cure."

"Oh, our employers will help save people from Aethon. But, they will be the right people. People who can pay. Medicine for the masses no longer exists." The man rubs his thumb and index finger together indicating money. "You have to pay to play in today's game of life. If you can't pay then you can't play. Game over."

The man with the pistol smirks. "It's a billion dollar deal, lady. A deadly disease, a desperate public and nearly free Manchineel. Almost one hundred percent profit. But, we can't allow you to spread the word and save the Sists. The Sists must continue to suffer, because it's only when they're afraid that the people with the money buy our medicine. Fear is medicine's best salesman. Our employers will make a killing by not stopping the dying."

While Zhou is holding the men's attention, Robert notices Rita stealthily activating her forearm-embedded PCD. After triggering her PCD, she sneaks her left foot back and then her right foot. Clank. She smacks an empty bottle knocking it onto its side. Rattling, the bottle rolls down the street.

"Stop right there!" The man without the pneumatic pistol grabs Rita's arm and yanks her back.

"We've talked enough. Why don't we take a little walk in the trees over there?" The tall man waves his pistol toward a path that leads into the wooded area behind Maelo's.

With his pistol pushing against Zhou's back, forcing her to walk close to Robert's side, the tall man herds them off the street, down a slope and into the thicket. Squeezing her arm, the second man drags Rita along behind. In the brush, the path quickly narrows.

Robert keeps his eyes moving, searching for Palo Bronco trees or Dumbcane hoping to employ their stinging nettles as a weapon. But, he sees none. They do not grow here. This is not the rain forest.

"Robert, why are you still carrying your chicken plate?" Rita shouts at him from behind. "Why don't you share your delicious meal with your friend?"

"Excellent suggestion." Robert counters. "I think I shall."

"Yes, you shouldn't let it go to waste." Rita persists.

"Would you like some chicken?" Robert offers, maneuvering his plate between the man and Zhou and upward closer to the man's face.

Instinctively, the man glances down. Robert slams his plate up into the man's face. The bare chicken bones slice deep into the man's cheek and eye. Robert drops the plate, grabs the man's gun hand and rams his knee against the back of his elbow, shattering it. Screaming, his arm twisting backward with the end of a bone peeking through his skin, the man drops his pistol and falls to his knees. Robert rams his extended fingers deep into the man's throat. Snap. Crack. Pop. Silence.

Behind him, Rita is driving her man to the ground. A violent kick against the side of his knee ruptures his right leg. He buckles. Her knee crushes his nose. Spewing blood, he slumps against a bush.

"I think you may have killed him, Rita." Robert concludes, after he kicks the bottom of the man's shoe without a response. "Where did you learn those moves?"

"Dance class." Rita smiles and nods toward the man Robert crippled. "You didn't do too bad yourself. Where did you learn that elbow crushing action? I've never seen anybody's arm bend backward that way before. Appears to be suffering a lot of pain."

Robert pulls the man's pistol out of the dust. "A dead Russian taught me that move in Ethiopia. After he knocked out four toughs, he told me that Americans rely too much on their weapons instead of their wits. I believe he was correct."

Her hands shaking and her voice quivering, Zhou hesitantly asks, "What are we going to do now?"

Rita points back the way they came. "You need to leave. Take your samples to San Juan and create some magic Manchineel medicine. Robert and I will keep guard on these two fellows until Negocio's people arrive. Isn't that right Robert?"

Robert nods his head while waving his hand for Zhou to leave. "Yes, we've wasted far too much time. Please go. Go now. Save Peter."

"I should be in the lab at the hospital when you return, Robert. I would appreciate your assistance. I will definitely need some samples of your blood, so try not to die." Zhou turns and jogs away, out of the brush.

"I will join you there as soon as I can, and trust me, I will try my best to follow your advice concerning my death." Robert calls after her.

With a groan, the man Rita crippled regains consciousness. He opens his right eye and gingerly touches his broken nose. His left eye is swollen shut. He spits out some blood and a tooth.

"You're going to die!" He snarls at Rita through his swollen lips, as he lunges at her.

Rita easily steps out of his reach. "Collera o Coyera *(good for nothing dumbass)*! Stupid American! I don't believe you've learned your lesson. Do not provoke Puerto Rican women. We'll gut you in revenge for things you haven't even done yet."

Rita points to a large leaf centered directly above the two men. Glued to the leaf's underside is a six inch by three inch, cream, honeycomb nest surrounded and covered with paper wasps. "Robert, if you jump can you reach that leaf?"

"Yeah, no problem." Robert practices hops to measure his reach.

Rita slides past Robert moving several feet away. "Ok now, in a moment, I want you to jump, slap the top of that leaf as hard as you can and then run back here with me. Ok?"

"Ok, but why?"

"Don't ask, Robert. Just do as I tell you."

With a skip and a jump, Robert leaps and slams his hand against the top of the leaf. Perfect! The leaf with paper wasp nest ridden by a horde of enraged wasps crashes to earth between the two men. Robert hits the ground running. Safely out of the wasps' reach, he joins Rita.

A veil of furious wasps cling and sting the men's heads and faces. They scream and swat and swat and scream, but they are broken and cannot flee. They have no escape. It is torture. The more they flap and flail, the more the wasps attack, burying their stingers in them again and again.

Robert shudders at Rita's fiendishly, mocking chortle. She is relishing every stinger's stab. Every shriek of pain feeds her hunger for vengeance. Death is dancing in her eyes.

"You are always quoting somebody, Robert. Well now, you can listen to one of my favorite quotes. This is my warning for all of these Americans that come to Puerto Rico to cause us harm." Rita points at the writhing, groaning men. "Stieg Larsson wrote that to exact revenge for yourself or your friends is not only a right, it's an absolute duty. Well now, I've done my duty."

PROMISE PETER

"Rub some on him! Now!" Shengwu commands Zhou. "Give me that!"

"No! Too much of it could kill him." Zhou wrestles Shengwu's hands from a small bag of Manchineel sap.

Tears flow across Shengwu's face dropping like rain upon comatose Peter. Shengwu clasps her hands together pleading, begging Zhou. "Don't you see? He's already dying. You must help him. Please. Please save him."

"I'm very wary of this stuff, Shengwu. I must test it first. It won't take me long, I promise, but I need some of Peter's blood to determine a safe dosage. Just a little blood and a little time. That's all I want." Zhou forces a venipuncture blood collection kit into Shengwu's hands. "If you want to help save Peter, get to it. Do it now. Don't wait for a nurse-bot."

Shengwu rotates the kit in her hand. She is reluctant. She considers taking Peter's blood an unnecessary waste of time for a little boy with so little time left.

Zhou pushes open the room exit. "As soon as you have Peter's blood, bring it to the lab. I'll be there preparing the test media."

In the lab, Zhou discovers Robert napping. He is draped across an empty table wearing his dirty, sweaty clothes. He stinks of the day.

Zhou sets her bag of Manchineel sap on the table and shakes Robert awake. "Where have you been? I expected you hours ago."

Jerking awake, Robert hops off the table. "I came as soon as I could. Straight from Maelo's. There were some unexpected complications with the two men."

"Complications? What kind of complications?" Zhou removes two test kits from a cooler and places them on the table next to the Manchineel bag.

Robert frowns. "Actually, Negocio's security people required some explanations. Since the faces and lips of our two attackers were too swollen for them to talk, telling their tale fell to us. We didn't want security to know we were responsible for their wounds, so we had to create a convincing cover story. After all, paper wasps aren't capable of crushing a man's larynx, then shattering his arm and another man's knee and nose before they sting them into Anaphylaxis shock."

"Paper wasps? I don't remember seeing any wasps." While Robert is distracted and talking, Zhou begins extracting a test sample of his blood. "But yes, I imagine the two men's injuries would be difficult to explain. So what story did you concoct?"

"Actually a very simple story. We told security that we were leaving Maelo's when we heard them arguing...possibly about the plate of food splattered on the man's face. So, we went into the woods to see what was happening. They fought. Each injured the other. Then, during the fight, the tall man accidently shot the paper wasp nest leaf off the tree onto themselves. All very plausible. Don't you think?" Robert asks with a mischievous grin.

"Did they believe you?" Zhou is barely listening to Robert as she concentrates on exchanging test containers.

Robert glances down at his blood flowing into Zhou's test container. He wonders if there is actually an Aethon cure hiding in his corpuscles. A cure worth killing and dying for, like the two men they left behind. "Well, nobody in the security detail wanted to venture too close to the swarming wasps to investigate the scene, so they were willing to agree with our explanation. Also, the head of the security detail is one of Rita's cousins, so he accepted her story with minimal questions. Later, Rita and he talked for several minutes beyond my hearing, so I expect she may have told him the true details. When they finished their private conversation, he made it a point to return and tell me that he has seen stranger things happen. I guess to reassure me. After waiting more than an hour, two robot hospital drones arrived and airlifted the men out of the trees."

Robert shakes his head. "Both of those men appeared to be barely alive, when the drones hauled them away."

Zhou hesitates. Scowls at Robert and then slaps him. "How can you be so flippant about this? They were planning to kill us. I vomited three times in the glider before I arrived here. I've taken four tranquilizers, just to stop my hands from shaking, so I can work. Unlike you, I don't think being threatened with death is humorous."

Zhou slaps Robert's face again. Her hands tremble. She struggles to continue collecting his blood.

With his free left hand, Robert strokes his sore, reddened cheek. "Sorry, but you don't understand. If I dwell on these attacks, I'm no help to anyone. Right now, I'm more concerned with saving the dying than I am with actually dying. I don't consider myself fearless, Zhou, but their attacks…these attempts by these amateur assassins to stop us…well, they're telling me just how important our effort is. We're not just fighting Aethon. We're fighting the greed that would murder millions of innocents for money. At this moment, I refuse to fear my own death when so many others are dying. You can say, I'm following the old Chinese proverb that I'm certain you know. 'When people are no longer afraid of death, there is no use threatening them with it.' I'm no hero. I'm just outraged. I made a promise to Shengwu and I'm planning to fulfill it."

Relief slips into Zhou's face. Her hands calm. Robert's anger gives her strength. "Thank you, Robert. Thank you. I'm still afraid, but with your help, I shall proceed. We shall succeed."

"Sorry, but, enough is enough. I'm tired. I'm dirty. I'm sore. I smell so bad that I don't like being this close to myself. Perhaps, I'm out of my mind, too. I just…" Robert is startled when the lab door opens.

Shengwu enters the lab delivering Peter's blood samples. Robert watches Zhou remove her final blood sample from his arm. While she is labelling Robert's blood container, she directs Shengwu. "Set Peter's samples next to my Manchineel sap and Robert's blood, so I can compare effects on them."

"How is Peter?" Robert reaches toward Shengwu, attempting to console her.

Shengwu drops her head. Her tears pitter patter upon the table. Her voice trembles. "He is very, very weak, Robert. Where have you been? What took you so long?"

"Didn't Zhou tell you? We were attacked…twice."

"Three times!" Zhou snaps.

"Sorry, three times. Once on the passageway by two air-cyclists and twice by Americans. The Americans…"

"Americans! I've had enough of them. All day today…whining and complaining…demanding and fighting." Fuming, Shengwu straightens, grabs Robert's hand and pulls him toward the door. "Come along. I must return to Peter."

Entering the room, Robert gasps. Peter's skeleton lay on top the bed. Aethon emaciated. His yellowed skin stretched so thin, Robert sees Peter's laboring heart beating through it.

Scanning the bank of monitors, Robert immediately notices that Peter's functional magnetic resonance imaging is indicating no brain activity. His blood pressure is critically low at fifty over thirty-three and his heart rate is registering a feeble thirty-seven beats per minute. Peter is a mechanically supported human husk.

"I'm going to rub some of this on his chest." Shengwu pulls a stolen bag of Zhou's Manchineel sap from her lab coat and opens it. "It killed your Aethon. It will kill Peter's. I know it will."

Robert grabs Shengwu's hands. "No! No! You don't know what you're doing."

Shengwu struggles to wrestle free. The sap bag slips from her hands dropping to the floor. Smack! Manchineel sap spews from the bag splattering across the tiles. Startled, Robert jumps backward. She is free.

"No!" Shengwu plunges to her knees. With her right hand, she scoops Manchineel sap into the palm of her left hand. Instantly, burning blisters bubble and boil Shengwu's skin.

"Stop! Don't touch it!" Too late, Robert lunges forward, slamming his hands against Shengwu's shoulders, hurling her away from the Manchineel pools.

Sliding in the sap, Robert crashes against the bed. Blood spurts from a gash on his forehead. He slumps onto the floor.

In a bleary daze, he watches Shengwu crawl on her elbows and knees through the Manchineel pool to Peter's bed. Kneeling, she stretches her Manchineel wet fingers as far as she can reach. Onto the boy's chest, she wipes a small circle of sap.

"I love you Peter. I love you." Shengwu sobs. She clasps her fiery red, blistered hands and collapses upon the floor. Excruciating pain knocks her into unconscious shock.

"What have you done?!" Zhou demands, storming into the room. Instinctively, she slams her hand against the emergency alarm.

"Help Shengwu!" Robert yells. "Her hands are covered in Manchineel. She is in shock. It will kill her, if you don't get it off."

"What about you? You're bleeding. Your face is covered with blood." Zhou asks while she hurries to Shengwu.

"I'll survive. She may not." Robert pulls himself into a standing position.

Swiping some blood away from his eyes, Robert focuses on Peter. Scorching the middle of his chest is a pool of puss and sap. His mouth is gaping open in a silent scream of agony. He bucks. He jerks. He gasps. He falls silent. The flat line hums of his attending machines mourn his death.

"Take her to emergency." Zhou orders the emergency nurse-bots. "She has Manchineel burns on her hands and Manchineel poison in her blood. We have to hurry."

As Zhou starts to exit, she turns to Robert. "What about Peter?"

"He is dead." Robert chokes. Tears fill his eyes. "I fear her Manchineel finished him. But, don't tell her that. Don't ever tell her that. Promise!"

"I promise." Zhou disappears through the door.

MEDICINE CRAZE

Zap! Flinching, the young girl jerks. Zap! Eyes tightly closed, the girl's mother shudders. Zap! A teenage boy yelps. Zap! At the speed of sound, magnetic jet injectors shoot nanobot micromotors containing Manchineel vaccine through the arm skin of an anxious Puerto Rican man. Before the man completes his blink, the nurse-bot is injecting his wife standing next to him.

Across Puerto Rico, nurse-bots are rolling up and down row after row of young and old, male and female Puerto Ricans vaccinating them against Aethon. Each free inoculation requires less than three seconds. A startling sound, a sting and the nurse-bot moves to the next person. Five minutes after inoculation, the Aethon detection badge begins glowing green signifying preventative safety.

"Puerto Rico is alive and well and preparing to share its medical miracle with the world. Just ask, and we will provide." President Negocio announces in front of a crowd awaiting their visit with the nurse-bot. "In less than forty-eight hours, Puerto Rico expects to complete vaccinating all of its populace. That will leave more than six million anti-Aethon doses, which Puerto Rico is making available to anyone who needs it."

With his green badge glowing almost as much as his face, Negocio cheerfully broadcasts Puerto Rico's success story. He is spreading his message early and worldwide, using all the methods available to preempt any additional interference or attacks. Also, he is enjoying taunting big pharma and the US on the international stage. To the world, his small, nascent nation is generously offering to save its big northern neighbor.

But while he is happily and loudly telling them that Puerto Rico has what they need to stop their Aethon plague, he is not sharing the source of the vaccine with them. Why? Because, he does not know it. Only Rita, Zhou, Pion and Robert know the secret of the Manchineel miracle, and they have sworn to tell no one. Even, Rita and Robert do not know the vaccine's final formula. That is a secret only Zhou and Pion share.

Unfortunately, Zhou and Pion have only been successful developing the vaccine. So far, their efforts to create a medicine to heal people already sick with Aethon are proving less effective. But, they are not stopping their research. At Stamina Vitae, Zhou and Pion are working without rest, striving to discover a universal cure.

Nearing exhaustion, they are finding that Aethon is an elusive and wily organism. As Shengwu had observed, once inside an individual, Aethon spreads and multiplies quickly by hiding itself and mutating. How it proliferates and into what part of each body it invades is different for each victim. All they do know for certain is that the end result of an untreated Aethon infection is always the same. Death.

Each Aethon sufferer's reaction to Manchineel medication is also unique and unpredictable. To some, Zhou's injection of a measured Manchineel serum is retarding their Aethon and strengthening their resistance. They are recovering. In other victims, the same strength serum is not repressing their Aethon as effectively while causing painful blisters and fevers. For them, the Manchineel treatment is slowing the Aethon progression, but the side-effects are almost deadly.

Fearing that their Manchineel medications will unexpectedly kill, rather than heal, Zhou and Pion have halted all treatments. But, stopping their treatments has not stopped more and more sick Americans from flooding into the facility. They just keep coming, by the boat load. Crammed inside the lobby are the sickest Aethon sufferers.

"We need Shengwu. Where is Shengwu? Why is Shengwu not here? Shengwu would know what to do. Where is she?" Frustration and fatigue are punishing Pion. She begins rocking and moaning. Before Zhou can react, she withdraws into stimming.

Still, Zhou attempts to reach her. "Shengwu is in the hospital. She is ill. Robert is with her."

Pion continues rocking. Her eyes are closed. She does not respond to Zhou.

"Shengwu will be back soon," Zhou tells Pion, being more hopeful than truthful. "Robert told me that she is much better already."

As Zhou silently watches Pion, exhaustion crawls into her own body and captures her mind, drowning her thoughts in dreams. She staggers to Shengwu's revitalization couch. Seconds after crawling upon it, she is unconscious in sleep.

Beyond the protective walls of the Stamina Vitae workspace, in the lobby's reception area, Rita and Obed are struggling to contain the anticipations and expectations of an increasingly restive crowd of Aethon infected Americans. When Zhou was still experimentally treating patients, she conducted a triage. Those still waiting watched some of their more sick friends or family vanish inside the clinic for treatment. But, they have not returned.

Those waiting worry, "Where did they go? Why have they not returned? Are they alive? Are they dead? When will I receive some medical help myself? Am I going to die waiting in this room?"

Their fears and agitation only escalates, as over and over again they view President Negocio declaring the successful vaccinating of his fellow Puerto Ricans. His optimistic statements cause their hopes to soar, but as their fevers rise and their bodies weaken, they begin questioning his promise to share his Aethon vaccine. They wonder if this miracle medicine actually exists, and will it truly be shared. Or is it Puerto Ricans yes and Americans no.

"My baby is so hot! Why aren't you helping her?" An Aethon infected mother angrily shouts at Rita. Cradling her feverish child in her arms, the mother staggers ahead. Weak and woozy, she stumbles and topples against another woman.

"Get off me!" A fist flies into the mother's face hurling her backward. She crashes against an elderly man. Both collapse in a groaning heap. A weak squeak escapes her dying child.

"You didn't need to hit her!" A strong slap staggers the second woman. Retaliating, she swings wildly, slugging a surprised, innocent man. He shoves her sprawling onto three children.

A minor disagreement erupts into a riot. Flailing bodies fly into each other and fall to the floor. A father and his daughter attempt to escape the mayhem. With his shoulder, he forces the lobby door open, banging and bruising a man waiting outside. Fighting explodes and spreads like a wildfire into every corner of Shengwu's complex.

Shocked, Rita and Obed stare in horror as the fighting engulfs them. Rita grabs Obed's shoulder shouting, "A juyir! Let's get out of here!"

Hauling Obed backwards, Rita accesses the inner hallway-door. Swish, the door slides open. She yanks him out of the lobby. Swoosh, the door closes.

"Oh, my Lord!" Obed exclaims. "That woman is a member of my church back in Tennessee. I've never seen her act crazy like that. I fear, Satan has her in his grip."

Ignoring Obed, Rita accesses Negocio's security officers appealing for help. "Send officers and paramedicos to Stamina Vitae immediately. We desperately need assistance here. Se formó un corre y corre! It's a huge fight. Salpafuera! More than a hundred people are involved. Women are fighting. Men are fighting. Babies and little kids are being hit and hurt."

After she completes her emergency call, Obed and Rita press their ears against the closed lobby door. Loud arguing and yelling vibrates through the metal. Bang! They jump backwards. Something crashes against the other side. Bang! Bang! Bang! Desperate pounding. People are slamming their fists and themselves against the wall and door.

Rita retreats deeper into the hallway. "This reminds me of those old zombie shows I used to watch. You know, where hordes of living dead bodies break through windows and doors and devour regular humans, like you and me. Ever watch those shows, Obed?"

Staring at the loudly throbbing door, Obed lowers himself onto his knees. Squeezing his eyes shut, he clasps his hands together and begins bellowing Psalm 28. "Unto thee will I cry, O Lord my rock; be not silent to me: lest, if thou be silent to me, I become like them that go down into the pit. Hear the voice of my supplications, when I cry unto thee, when I lift up my hands…"

Increasing, ceaseless, thunderous pounding on the door, yanks Obed's attention away from his prayer, although he continues spouting the Psalm from memory. With each explosion against the door, he jerks and jumps, but his praying never ceases.

His eyes exploding with fright, he scoots farther away from the door. "…and he is the saving strength of his anointed. Save thy people, and bless thine inheritance: feed them also, and lift them up forever. Amen."

Finished, Obed silently bows his head. He listens. His prayer did not succeed in soothing the demanding swarm beyond the door. Their beseeching banging intensifies.

"Uh, Obed, you do realize that I was only joking about the zombies, don't you?" Rita asks, unsettled by Obed's sudden supplication shouting.

Obed climbs to his feet and returns to staring at the rumbling, drumming door. "Yes, I figured you were, but I thought throwing a little of the Lord at them might help. I certainly feel better now. How about you?"

"I would feel much better if you had prayed for a stronger door."

WARNING WORDS

Machete clutched in his fist, the broad-shouldered, dark-haired man advances toward Robert. He raises his razor-sharp blade. He grins. Swoosh! The machete slices through the air. Schwack! Deep into the shoulder it cuts. He yanks his knife free. Swinging again, he buries it deep into muscle again. Jerking his heavy blade back with one hand, he strips a chunk of meat from the bone.

Closing his eyes, Robert sucks in lung flooding smoky air. He plunges into the smells surrounding him. With a smile and sigh, he licks his lips. The aroma of several whole pigs roasted over an open flame is intoxicating. Mingling and mixing with the roasted pork perfume is the bouquet of Puerto Rican rice and pigeon peas, yucca, morcilla blood sausage, tostones, turkey, chicken and a host of other local dishes. Robert swoons in the nose nectar.

"I didn't think it would be possible, but I think this is as good as Maelo's Chicken Fever." Robert mumbles to nobody in particular, as he slides his tray along the open-air serving line. "I do relish Puerto Rican food. Thank you Mugavus!"

Alone in a crowd of sociable strangers, he is loving it. Just forty-five minutes outside of San Juan, he is hiding in plain sight in an open-air lechonera. Two days before Christmas and this tiny town of Cayey in Puerto Rico's Guavate sector is crowded with celebrants. The smell of joy in the air is as intoxicating as the smell of smoked pork.

Carrying his platter heaped high with food in his left hand and a cup of cold beer in his right, Robert wanders out of the restaurant. Leisurely, he meanders toward the row of sheltered tables behind the lechonera. It is a scenic sight. Shady shelters overlooking a mountain stream bubbling and burbling through a lush, grassy corridor of banana trees and palms. Robert pauses to inhale the natural beauty. With each breath, tension slides away. Flooding his lungs with a mix of roasted park and forest air, he closes his tired eyes and sighs. Oh, he needs this.

Puerto Rican salsa music envelops the families partying in the shelters and tables nearest the lechonera. Cautiously, they monitor his approach until they spy his glowing green, *Aethon Free* badge matching theirs. When they realize he is safe, they smile, flash their own bright badges, and motion for him to join them.

Seeking soothing solitude, he smiles, politely declines and ambles to the last shelter, as Mugavus had instructed. Sliding into a seat at the table farthest from the lechonera and nearest to nature, he prepares to savor every bite of traditional Puerto Rican lechón he can eat. But, as much as starving for a piece of authentic pork, he is starving for peace of mind.

Robert had not realized the depth of Shengwu's emotions and passions until he watched her sacrificing herself to save Peter. Recalling her torment, he gently touches the artificial skin tissue covering the gash on his head from Peter's bed. Unwanted tears begin escaping down Robert's cheeks, as images of Shengwu's anguish and pain flood his mind.

For many long hours, he had been keeping vigil. Through day and night, he sat in the hospital monitoring her. Filled with painkillers, she floated in a special solution to ease the agony of her hands, feet and face disfigured by excruciatingly painful Manchineel burns and blisters.

Just an hour ago, he was still by her side when the robo-aides lifted her from her aqua-bed and transported her to see Margarete. He chokes recalling Shengwu sobbing to Margarete, "I am sorry. I am so sorry. I failed. I tried everything. Everything. Your Peter is gone Margarete. But, I will not allow him to die. He will never die."

Sucking in a deep breath to collect himself, Robert rejoins the festive families surrounding him. With a napkin, he dabs his cheeks and blows his nose. Shaking his head and shoulders, like a dog shedding water, he sheds his sadness. He leans forward and inhales deeply to regain the sweet smell of his holiday meal. Plop! His badge drops into his platter of food.

"If you had designed those badges better, that wouldn't happen." Mugavus Komfort's Estonian-accented, scolding voice arises from the grass outside the shelter, startling Robert.

199

Rising from his seat and leaning over the railing, he scans the lawn and bushes surrounding his shelter. Seeing nobody, he searches the shelter. First, he peers under his table, then he inspects the beams and roof above him. Feeling foolish and wondering if she is pranking him, he sits. With a napkin, he lifts his badge from his platter and carefully swabs away the pork grease.

"You may be a super hacker tracker, but you stink as an engineer." The bodiless voice sarcastically teases.

"Sorry, but I stopped talking to my imaginary friends when I was six years old." Robert forks a saucy hunk of pork into his mouth. His tongue cradles the meat. He closes his eyes. The smoky flavor dances across his taste buds. Finally, he chews and chews and chews, squeezing the flavor from each tangy morsel.

"You still have your Neanderthal weakness for devouring dead animals, I see." Invisible Mugavus interrupts Robert's contented chewing. Her voice sounds, as if she is within a meter of him, now. "I thought I cured you of that nasty, barbaric habit."

"Oh, you and your environment-saving entomophagy. You may chug all the bugs you want, Mugavus, but for me human cooked real mammal meat is a true treat that can't be beat and is becoming impossible to find." Robert cuts loose another portion of pork. "Besides, as the great philosophizing comedian John Cleese once said, 'If God did not intend for us to eat animals, then why did he make them out of meat?' And, if you didn't want me to eat meat here, then why did you tell me to come here?"

"Safety in numbers and location. I know that if I have to, I'll be able to sneak you out this back way with less chance of people noticing." As if magically materializing from air, Mugavus' hand appears, snatches some yucca from Robert's plate, and disappears. "Besides, I heard they have great yucca."

"Hey thief!" Robert flips a fork load of pigeon peas in the direction where the hand appeared and disappeared. The flying, flung peas crash against a wall of air that is not there, bounce backward and scatter across the table, except for two. Two peas, appearing to defy gravity, float in the air in front of Robert.

He chuckles at the curious sight, then reaches out and swipes the peas away. "Why do you think you may need to sneak me out of here? These people are happy. It's the holidays. We have Aethon under control here, and…"

Smiling, Robert tugs on his shirt. "...see the Maple leaf on my shirt? See it? That tells everybody that I'm Canadian. Everybody likes Canadians, ya knahw...especially this Canadian. Eh?"

"Evidently, not everybody, Robert. I'm here to tell you that three men are in Puerto Rico to eliminate you." Mugavus dryly delivers her intelligence. "Actually, they've been ordered here for both you and Shengwu. Maybe more, but we don't know for certain."

"Well thank you Mugavus, you certainly know how to ruin my excellent meal." Robert slides his plate away. "Do you know why? Why now? Why me? Don't they know what a sweet, generous fellow I am? Are they some big pharma goons? Rita and I just sent four of them to the prison infirmary. I suppose that would upset them. Yet, in spite of their interference, we have the Aethon vaccine. The entire world knows about the vaccine, now. Negocio told everybody, Mugavus. Free vaccine! They can't stop it. They're too late."

"Actually, Negocio's announcement of a free vaccine created massive problems. Fear sells medicine. Free vaccine will cost big pharma and Abaddon's government billions of dollars. They don't like that. So they are banning it. Claim it is untested poison." Mugavus groans. "In the metrostates, they're rioting. In the wastedlands, lots of people are still dying."

"Keep the people dying to keep the people buying?" Robert laments. "Big pharma always has its profit sharing plan."

"But, these guys after you, they're not big pharma and they're not interested in the Aethon vaccine. Although, I don't believe these three would have complained if big pharma's boys had succeeded and you had failed." Mugavus explains in a disembodied voice too loud for the sudden, silent lull between salsa songs.

She waits for the music to return, then continues. "They've been in Puerto Rico waiting and watching for events to align for them, just as they have. By announcing the vaccine, Negocio opened the door for them. With the world's attention focusing on Negocio freely sharing the Aethon vaccine, they doubt that anybody will notice their moves against you and Shengwu. They're anticipating exercising that old magician's trick of distraction hiding action. Also they assume Negocio will relax his security. They expect you to lower your guard, as well."

"Ah yes, but they fail to understand what a wily warrior I am." Robert glances over his left shoulder, then his right. A boy eating at the nearest table is eyeing him, suspiciously. "Why don't you remove your digital, background-duplication, camouflage, concealing cloak and join me? Talking to empty space is too strange. People are beginning to suspect I'm crazy."

"I'd consider crazy an accurate diagnosis by them." Mugavus jokingly goads him. "It's safer for both of us, if I remain unseen. So, why don't you just stop interrupting me? Go back to gnawing on your dead beast like a caveman and listen."

Robert considers throwing something more than peas at her phantom voice, but decides to accept her advice. He retrieves his plate, loads his fork with meat, slides it into his mouth, chews and listens.

"The worst news is that Evoil escaped Ethiopia, Robert, and he's grown even more insane. He's gone mad and is seeking revenge on you and me. That's why, I'm remaining covered. I can see without being seen."

Robert chokes on his meat. "Evoil is still alive and in Puerto Rico?!"

"No, not in Puerto Rico. Our intelligence tells us that Evoil's operating out of a bunker somewhere in the ruins of D.C. But, we received some information from a Faul Dusslig about his plans. Shortly before she was murdered, she messaged us that he had dispatched three of his Sicarii assassins, code named Willy Wanker, Billy Bollocks and Pour LeNuls, to Puerto Rico."

"Only three? Lucky me." Robert swigs his beer to flush the lodged lump of pork down his throat. He coughs followed by a burp.

"Well, there may be one more to make it four. Evoil's pastor, a Reverend Diaboli, is returning to San Juan to provide spiritual guidance to the three Sicarii. Our sources told us that he is the leader of those religious protestors outside Stamina Vitae. He's been using them as a cover, so he can spy on Shengwu for Evoil." Mugavus voice is moving. Robert turns following her words.

"Those protestors are gone. Many of them died from Aethon. I had nothing to do with them and Shengwu is treating those still alive, so I don't understand why this Diaboli is after me." Robert swallows another bit of beer.

Mugavus' camouflage cloak rustles as she changes position. "Actually, my fellow SPEA analysts believe they want you, so they can use you to get to Shengwu. They're after her because they're certain she possesses the program and data for some US Department of Defense genetic engineering project called ELF. Heard of it?"

Robert's eyes widen with recognition. Reacting quickly, he recovers his nonchalance. "Yes, she may have mentioned it, but only as a project of her father's."

Mugavus' background digital regeneration flickers for a moment, as she moves, creating a ripple in the recreated, projected-through background veiling her. Another background misalignment occurs when her cloak brushes against Robert. The boy at the other table is intently studying Robert's table noting the unnatural changes to the scenery.

Finally, when Mugavus sits on the bench next to Robert her cloak's reconstruction of the scenery stabilizes. Making it too late for when the boy convinces his father to glance Robert's way. Seeing nothing unusual, the boy's father gruffly warns him to pay more attention to his food and less attention to other people. He obeys his father's reprimand for a few seconds, but his curiosity rapidly returns his eyes and attention to Robert.

Whispering, Mugavus continues her revelations. "When Shengwu's father escaped Abaddon's SS Deacons, the ELF genome engineering project disappeared. At least, the SS Deacons could not find it when they searched his lab. But with their hatred and ignorance of science, they probably wouldn't have recognized the ELF data, if they had found it. They tortured one of his assistants to death and destroyed his lab searching, but…"

"So, he stole it to save it. Good for him. He's a hero in my eyes." Robert murmurs, acting as if he is concentrating on his plate, ignoring the cloak concealed Mugavus now sitting next to him. "But, since both you and I know that Righteous Rightists despise science and genetics especially, why do they want it bad enough to kill for it?"

"SPEA's intelligence sources have heard two reasons." Robert hears Mugavus suck in a deep breath. "I consider both of these very disturbing. First, they wanted Shengwu's father to create a huge army of mind-controllable Christian soldiers that they could use to enforce their will. Then second, and this really frightens me, they were reportedly wanting him to develop a method for enslaving the general US population. A type of enshrined obedience, if you will. We're still investigating both claims."

Again he questions her innocently, as if he knows nothing about Shengwu's involvement with ELF. "But, why do you think Shengwu has it, if her father took it?"

"We suspect Shengwu possesses the ELF digits, because she synthesized a human embryo using it. Just by happenstance, Pion discovered a series of clandestine interactions between Shengwu and SPEA's AI involving ELF algorithms. She conducted her DNA synthesis with SPEA's AI quantum computer using a covert interface."

Mugavus pauses for a thought before resuming. "But, what Pion considered most extraordinary was that Shengwu was able to simultaneously conduct research involving both Aethon and ELF genome engineering algorithms. Pion suspects that she was using Aethon genetic engineering algorithms to distract her, so she wouldn't notice the ELF genetic engineering algorithms. It was like she was two people."

"What do you think she is endeavoring to do?" Robert decides to continue withholding his personal knowledge of Shengwu's activities until he learns exactly what Mugavus and SPEA know and want from him. If Shengwu is not revealing her plans to them, then Robert certainly will not divulge what he has seen. Shengwu has earned his loyalty and, at this moment, his silence. She protected him. He will protect her.

"We're not certain what her plan is. But, she doesn't need to hide. She needs to know that SPEA wants to preserve ELF and shelter her. That's why I'm here and that's why we've hidden our air transportation on the Bahia de San Juan just off La Perla. Remember Dijaineo's sky whale? Well, now it's floating digitally camouflaged invisible, ready and waiting." Again, Mugavus is caught talking loudly when the music stops.

Mugavus' plan surprises Robert. "La Perla? Why did you hide the sky whale there? Negocio told me it's a poverty-stricken, hide-out for smugglers and drug dealers."

Unable to contain himself any longer, the observing boy stealthily creeps away from his family's table toward Robert. On his tip toes, he sneaks closer and closer until he ducks into Robert's shadow. Hiding behind Robert's back, he barely breaths as he listens and scrutinizes the space to Robert's left.

Robert hears Mugavus chuckle. "Did you learn nothing in Ethiopia? When you want something hidden who better to hide it than smugglers. Besides, I've always trusted the poor. There is a certain honesty in poverty."

Robert places his finger to his lips. "Shh. I sense we're being watched."

Speaking in a soft voice, Mugavus whispers, "Pion told me that Shengwu codenamed her ELF synthesis work, Operation Resurrect Peter and that her first interaction was when…"

"Ha!" yells the boy, jumping and punching his small fist into Mugavus' digitally hidden hip. When his hand collides with her cloaked back, he is as surprised as Robert and Mugavus. They swivel to watch him. Silently, he glances away at his father, whose eyes and attention are on his sister.

With the boy's attention diverted, Mugavus slides away from Robert's side. "I've got to go. I'll contact you or you can contact me. Watch yourself, Robert."

"Papi!" The boy calls to attract his father's attention.

"Papi!" He hollers again, but the music buries his small voice, and his father ignores him. Returning his interest to Robert, he hesitates, then he thrusts both hands forward. He grabs air.

With his hand on top of his head, Robert gently guides the dispirited boy to his father's side. "Little man, you can't catch what you can't see. Yes, she was there, but now she's air. She had to flee, just like me."

TUNNEL VISION

"Shengwu Kexuejia is dead. She died suddenly from myocardial infarction." Doctor Salud dictates for Shengwu's death certificate and her social media report. "Results of the autopsy to be conducted by the San Juan coroner's office will be included when they are available."

Wearing a coroner's cold composure, Robert accompanies the robotic corpse-cart containing Shengwu's bio-bagged body out the rear of the hospital. Two mortuary assistance-robots transfer the corpse-cart into the waiting coroner's transfer auto-auto. Robert climbs into the rear of the coroner's carriage and sits next to Shengwu's body. As they leave the hospital complex, he opens the bio-bag. She is at peace.

In two auto-autos hovering just outside the hospital complex, four men wait and watch their aerodrone's visuals. They were approaching the hospital when they received Doctor Salud's death announcement. They paused to consider their options. Not entirely convinced by Salud's vague statement, they launched the aerodrone now surveilling the complex. When the coroner's transfer auto-auto departs, the aerodrone shadows it. The two, waiting auto-autos interface their navigation systems with the aerodrone and begin pursuit.

Inside the leading auto-auto, Reverend Diaboli issues his orders to his three accompanying Sicarii. "Deacon Evoil's latest commandment to me was that if we cannot capture and get Shengwu or her father out of Puerto Rico, then kill them. Do whatever is necessary to recover ELF, if it is here. Then destroy all traces of it. Above all, we must ensure nobody learns of ELF. Do you all understand?"

The three Sicarii respond that they understand. Each of them then retrieves and prepares their pneumatic pistols. Their hunt begins.

Stealing a corpse is so much easier than sneaking a pained, blister-covered Shengwu out of the hospital, so that is exactly what Robert is doing. One, carefully measured injection of the general anesthetic methohexital by Doctor Salud temporarily sedated Shengwu into the comatose condition required for his plan to work. Add sufficient pain-killing medication to suppress any possible groans and to the uninformed observer, she is dead. Nobody challenges the removal of her body.

"Rita, I'm approaching Stamina Vitae. I should arrive in approximately ten minutes." Robert alerts Rita.

"No! You can't come here now. We're surrounded by Aethon infected Americans…basically under siege. Negocio's security has established a perimeter. They put the facility on lock down. You won't be able to enter."

"Hold here." Robert orders the auto-auto transport onto a side pad. Rubbing his fingers against his forehead, he attempts to generate a contingency plan. He did not consider the possibility of them not being able to covertly enter the facility and sneak into the lab.

Scratching his head, he gazes at Shengwu's placid face. "Well my friend, I'm out of ideas."

For many long minutes, Robert and Shengwu hold in place, while Robert considers his options and attempts to develop a contingency plan. To ensure he stays away, Rita interfaces his PCD with Stamina Vitae's security drones providing him with continuous visual situational awareness. What he sees, he does not like. More desperate, Aethon infected Americans are arriving, overwhelming Negocio's security. Sick with fever and scared of dying, they are shoving and shouting and fighting. A poisonous shower of Aethon transmitting blood, sweat, spit and tears rains death upon all. They are the dead living.

Finally, Shengwu's mouth opens and closes. Blinking repeatedly, she begins to recover from the anesthesia. Again, she attempts to speak, but her brain is still floating in an anesthetic fog. Robert leans close to her face. She puffs slurring sounds into his ear.

"Canal Oeste?" Robert repeats what he thinks he heard Shengwu say. "Did you say Canal Oeste?"

Shengwu weakly nods her head. Through her mouth, she sucks in a large breath of air. She is fighting her way back to full consciousness.

"Five zero three." Shengwu breathes into Robert's face. "Go there."

"Go to five zero three Canal Oeste?" Robert simultaneously questions Shengwu while directing the transport to that address.

During their ride to the Canal Oeste address, Shengwu's strength increases and she regains her mental clarity. She formulates a plan. When the transport holds outside the door of a garage attached to the small house at five zero three Canal Oeste, she directs Robert. "Use the access code – H3CH3CN2HOOH - to enter the garage."

"What?" Robert is not prepared for her unexpected directive. "What is that? What are you saying?"

"I'm saying that the chemical formula for the amino acid Leucine is my access code for entry. Leucine is an essential DNA building block for human life. I'm surprised you don't know that." Shengwu commands him impatiently. "I can't input the access code with these healing wraps on my hands, so you have to. Just enter it into your PCD and transmit it."

"Easy for you to say." Robert stares at his PCD. "Give me the formula again. Slowly, this time."

With irritation in her voice, Shengwu dictates her access code to Robert. Upon transmission, the garage door slides open. The transporter slides into the darkened interior. After the garage door closes and locks, the floor descends into an underground chamber. When the floor clicks to a stop, the chamber illuminates.

Outside the garage, the shadowing aerodrone circles the Canal Oeste house. As their auto-autos arrive, the four men are now certain that Shengwu's death announcement was a ruse. No coroner transports a body to a private house.

"I believe we've been duped by mister Goodfellow." Reverend Diaboli splits up the three Sicarii. "Billy and Pour, you two wait here in case they come back out. Stay alert, you guys. Remember, capture or kill. Willy, you and I'll go to Stamina Vitae, so I can provide some religious reassurance to those in need. And while I'm comforting, you and I'll be searching."

Beneath the garage, after adjusting to the dim lighting inside the underground chamber, Robert notices a smaller entrance panel and access pad, similar to those installed in Stamina Vitae. "Where are we?"

"We're at the entrance of a tunnel into my private project lab." Grimacing, Shengwu sits up on the corpse-cart. "As I remember, you desperately wanted to see what was inside. Well, now you have your opportunity. All you have to do is follow my directions and cart me down there."

"And what are your directions?" Robert asks, as he converts the corpse-cart into a self-propelled carriage.

"Actually, it is all reasonably easy. Within five seconds of me informing the security computer that I am entering the security code, you must enter it. Understand?" Shengwu scoots into the middle of the cart, allowing Robert access to the security pad.

"$H_3CH_3CN_2HOOH$. Correct?" Robert reads his last transmission from his PCD.

"Oh no, Robert, Leucine is only for the garage. Using the same code for both entrances would not be smart security. You should know that." Shengwu answers with disbelief. "The access code for this portal is the amino acid Serine – $C_3H_7NO_3$."

"Well of course it is. How unbelievably simple minded of me." Robert sarcastically remarks.

Through the portal and into the tunnel, Robert guides Shengwu's carriage. As they proceed, pressure power-panels covering the floor generate dim overhead lighting directly above them. Only they are lighted, and only where they are. One step forward and the lighting behind them extinguishes. Robert can ascertain little about the construction of the tunn

"How did you dig this tunnel?" Robert touches the wall. He discovers it is roughly smooth.

"It wasn't dug, Robert. It was vaporized with lasers. So, there was no dirt or rock waste disposal to hide. Fast and relatively clean." Pointing toward the ceiling, Shengwu sweeps her arm in a circle. "What mineral residue remained was 3D printed into the overhead and the flooring."

"I see. Well then, I suppose you would agree with innovative tunnel maker Elon Musk when he said that floors are underappreciated, but not as much as tunnels." Robert snickers.

Shengwu flashes a grin at Robert, but then becomes earnest. "This is more than a tunnel, Robert. This is my self-preservation, escape route. I wasn't prepared when Evoil's SS Deacons unexpectedly banished me from the US. I lost everything…everything except my genetic engineering knowledge and skills. Thankfully, Negocio allowed me to establish my clinic here. So, I've been able to use the one thing the SS Deacons couldn't take away from me…. my genetic engineering, my ability to heal people, to improve human life. That's all I've ever wanted to do."

"Yes, and because of your work, Negocio swore to protect you and your clinic." Robert reassures her. "That's why I'm here and Rita is here."

"I know, Negocio is trying. You are trying. But, fear of the future that I can provide for mankind is too strong in America. Ignorance and hate are in control there." Shengwu shakes her head in resignation. "Ignorance always hates change and always seeks to destroy it."

Robert nods his head in accord. "Yes, I agree with you and I also agree with Emma Goldberg who said that the most violent element in society is Ignorance. But, at least for a while, I hope Negocio, Rita and I can protect you. I think you will be safe here."

"No, I'll never be safe." Shengwu sighs sadly. "Even before Mugavus warned you and you snuck me out of the hospital, I knew eventually the US Righteous Rightist regime would attempt to destroy me and my work. So, I prepared. I created my escape. I will not lose my work again. I have progressed too far…far too far. I cannot wait any longer. I must immediately begin arranging to transport my creations to safety. It's my only way to save Peter…to enable humanity to evolve…to survive."

The last overhead light glimmers, displaying another sliding panel and security pad. With a groan, Robert steps to the security pad. "Ok Shengwu, tell me the secret word to open this one."

"Simply the formula for amino acid tyrosine - $C9H11NO3$." Shengwu leans toward the security pad and announces. "I am entering the security code."

"Well, why so simple, Shengwu?" Robert derisively comments as he enters the tyrosine chemical formula.

"At the time, I considered it appropriate. I was tired and tyrosine helps humans fight fatigue from stress." Shengwu explains, appearing weary.

Swish! The panel slides open. Blinding bright light and the burning stench of antiseptic slam Robert. Covering his eyes and nose with his hand, he staggers out of the tunnel. Smack! The heel of a foot drives deep into his stomach. Oof! Robert drops to his knees grabbing his gut.

"Welcome to my secret lab, Robert. I apologize for forgetting to warn you. You just encountered the defensive kick of my very protective and paranoid father. He guards my lab." Impatiently, Shengwu commands Robert. "Now stand up, we must begin our work."

CURE CHASE

Uumph! Another heart explodes. Another mother slumps onto the floor. With a whimper, she dies. Two coroner-bots accompany the corpse-cart into Stamina Vitae's lobby. Together, the coroner-bots lift her body onto the cart and remove her from the room. The dying surrounding her watch her disappear. The few that knew her mumble prayers in her name. The rest pray louder to save themselves.

"Mommy! Mommy!" Her face fever-flushed, a bawling, young girl toddles behind the departing cart carrying away her mother.

Stretching forward, another Aethon stricken mother captures the girl and hugs her tightly against her breast. The girl screams and twists and struggles to follow her mother. Clenching the child tighter, the woman begins rocking and softly singing. The girl slips into exhausted sleep, too sick to continue fighting.

"Can't we do anything to help them? We must do something!" Obed pleads to Rita as they witness the increasing suffering via projected visuals from Stamina Vitae's security cameras.

Obed and Rita remain safely ensconced outside the reach of the fear-filled, panic-stricken, mob of Aethon sufferers crushing Shengwu's facility. Negocio's security forces suppressed the near-riot fighting and a few security remain to maintain control. But, they can do little else than minimize the mayhem, caused by the growing number of Aethon-ill Americans flooding the clinic.

"How many times must I tell you Obed that we can't do any more than we are already doing?" Rita is vexed at Obed's repeated pleading. "Zhou and Pion are working desperately to genetically engineer a Manchineel medication for all Aethon strains, but they don't possess the knowledge and skills they need to succeed. Without Shengwu's expertise to guide them, they are floundering."

Rita shifts her viewing to a drone's visual of the facility's exterior grounds. "Negocio is doing about all that we can do too, keeping them fed, watered and comfortable enough that they don't try to kill each other again."

Taking control of the drone Rita increases its altitude to provide a wider view of Stamina Vitae. Although, hundreds of ailing Americans are encamped in the open, in and around the facility, they are not being ignored. Scattered among them, Negocio's security monitors and calms the crowd. Red Cross service-bots circulate among the unhealthy horde, distributing water and food. Nurse-bots are also active, issuing medications for non-Aethon illnesses. Portable toilets and showers, stationed strategically for convenient accessibility, are surrounded by lines of increasingly desperate users.

"I pray that they create some remedy soon, Rita. I see too many people I know waiting out there…dying out there." Obed begins silently praying while he watches.

"Isn't that against the teachings of your Reverend Fili Diaboli?" Rita quizzes Obed, who looks with confusion at his praying hands. "No, not your praying, Obed. I mean Shengwu's genetic engineering."

Obed returns his attention to the scenes of the Aethon afflicted. "I believe if Reverend Diaboli could see the suffering that I see and the healing that I have seen through the workings of Zhou and Shengwu and Pion, that he would change his commandment. For as it is written in Romans, 'Do not be conformed to this world, but be transformed by the renewal of your mind, that by testing you may discern what is the will of God, what is good and acceptable and perfect.' I believe I shall bring him in here to observe Zhou and Shengwu's labors of the Lord's love. Once he sees their good works, he will understand that they are not evil, I believe."

With a skeptic smirk, Rita shakes her head in disbelief. "I believe you expect a miracle that I doubt shall transpire. So if he comes, don't allow him inside here until I am long gone. Ok? No, on the other hand Obed, just don't allow him in here. Ok?"

Obed returns his focus to observing the anticipating sick, ignoring Rita until he mumbles, "My Lord shall guide my hands."

"Well, Shengwu shall guide mine." Robert startles them as he and Shengwu arrive behind them.

Whirling around, Rita squeals happily. "Shengwu! You're here. Oh, how we need you…they need you." Rita points at the visuals projections.

"You're the answer to my prayers!" Obed pronounces.

Drawn by the noise, Zhou ventures away from her work with Pion. She smiles with relief when she sees her colleague. "Shengwu, at last, Wǒ hěn gāoxìng kàn dào nǐ jiànkāng *(I am so thrilled to see you healthy)*. We're so happy for your return."

Robert maneuvers Shengwu and her cart into her work room where Pion awaits, as an augmented-reality hologram. Immediately, he notices Pion's face relax. Of course she does not smile, that is one step too far. Yet, he considers less tension with no stimming a certain sign that she, in her own Asperger's way, is pleased to see Shengwu.

With as severe a demeanor as Pion, Shengwu begins her crusade. "So Pion, what have you and Zhou tried so far and what results have you received? What have you found effective? I'll require a complete genetic breakdown of your Manchineel samples and the individuals you've treated."

Pion responds straightaway. Genetic algorithms, amino acid compositions and the genetics of Manchineel swarm into the room.

After her initial review of Pion's data dump, Shengwu grimly shakes her head. "I am less than confident that we'll find some way for Manchineel to break the death grip Aethon has on these people. Once Aethon is inside, I've found it to be a merciless killer. Today's humans are weak, almost defenseless. I've fought it and lost so far. I lost Peter. I do not want to lose anyone else…regardless of who they are."

Shengwu is the calm eye in the center of whirling storm of formulae. She studies an algorithm. Then, with a wave of her bandaged hand, wipes it away. Pion offers her another She contemplates it, then eliminates it. Robert, Rita and Obed silently watch in awe.

"Aha! This looks interesting." Abruptly, Shengwu freezes her genome ballet. "How is this individual, Zhou?"

"He is improving." Zhou compares the information floating before Shengwu with the heads-up display on her AR glasses. "Pion, display our latest blood sample from Aethon case number eight hundred and eighty eight."

After reviewing the blood sample, Shengwu grins at Zhou. "Patient eight hundred and eighty eight? Eight, eight, eight? I believe that's the luckiest number possible in Chinese numerology. Is it not? Lucky for him and lucky for us...or for them. I think I see a possible genetic chink in the Aethon attacking this man."

Shengwu points toward a series of floating formulae. "These Manchineel genomes seem to be teaming with his own body's defenses to exploit this single crucial gene. That gene may contain the instructions for building his personal Aethon antibiotic. Basically, he is generating his own in-body antibiotic. Of course, the trick is to find a means for duplicating that ability to produce personalized antibiotics in other sufferers."

"She is a messenger from God." Obed too loudly whispers, "I am reminded of a writing from the book of Matthew, 'Then great multitudes came to Him, having with them the lame, blind, mute, maimed, and many others; and they laid them down at Jesus' feet, and he healed them'. Only it is she, not he, now."

Obed's glorifying interrupts Shengwu's manipulation concentration. "This is only the beginning, Obed. Only, the initial...well, it's a clue...that's all...a vague connection. This is no guaranteed remedy. We have much more analysis to do, so why don't you see how the people outside are doing?"

Hanging his head in embarrassment, Obed wanders out of the room. With him gone, Shengwu returns her full attention to solving the mystery of Manchineel and Aethon. Robert, Rita and Zhou solemnly witness her wizardry. They are afraid to breathe heavy, lest they disturb her again.

Finally, after many minutes of contemplation, Shengwu taps her bandaged fingers together, nods her head and frowns. "I believe I see our problem. If I edit this Manchineel..."

"He's here! He's here! Reverend Diaboli is here!" Obed exults, crashing into the room shattering Shengwu's thoughts. "He is praying with the Aethon victims in the lobby, right now. Laying hands upon them. Wiping their pain and their sweat of death away. Sharing his healing breath of health with the babies."

Immediately realizing what he plans to do, Rita strains to restrain Obed. He is just beyond her reach. The others stand frozen in stunned silence.

"It's a miracle! Just as I prayed. He has come. You must meet him, Shengwu. You must!" In a breath, before he can be stopped, Obed is gone, racing to usher Diaboli inside the heart of Stamina Vitae.

Panic! Horror slashes across Shengwu's face. She barks, "Robert! Our plan! I'll alert Mugavus. You, take Rita to the lab. Run! Get out! Save my Peter, Robert. Save Peter!"

PETER PRINCIPLE

"Okay Rita, open wide and say…"

"Say one more word Robert and you'll regret it for an extremely long time." Rita sternly shakes her fist at Robert, before she twists onto her back flexing her hips and knees, and separating her thighs to assume her lithotomy position.

"So, I guess asking you if you have a womb for rent would be completely unacceptable." Robert nervously teases her. Hidden behind his back, so Rita cannot see, are his trembling hands. He is attempting to joke away his apprehensions.

Scowling, Rita scolds him. "What is wrong with you? You're definitely not providing me with the sincere assistance and support that I require at this moment. If I had known that you were going to act like this, I would never have asked you to stay."

"Sorry. Nerves." His right hand quivering, he lightly swipes across his forehead. He begins pacing. "Aren't you concerned? In a few minutes, you'll be hosting the embryos for Shengwu's genetically-engineered, designer babies. Embryos that she personally created. A new species of human soon will be living inside of you. You'll become the incubator for future mankind. Life as we know it, or don't want to know it. What if she is creating a…

"Stop babbling! What you need is a good strong dose of this benzodiazepine that he gave me. Settle your nerves." Rita slurs slightly as she points toward Shengwu's father and two nurse-bots approaching her.

Wearing a pair of AR glasses and a comforting smile on his face, Shengwu's father gently grasps Rita's hand. "Please call me Yisheng, Rita. You are very lucky. We have twelve embryos in the two-to-four celled stage. The perfect level of blastocyte development for transfer. Six male and six female. Ok?"

Yisheng's statement, along with Robert's concerns, begin to arrive in Rita's drug dulled brain. "A dozen babies? Inside me? Twelve!

"Well, only until you arrive at SPEA's city of Venus. Several SPEA women are waiting for you there. They've volunteered their wombs for transplant and full-term pregnancy. Then, these babies will be born and raised on Venus, where they will be safe and protected…enabled to achieve their destiny as the next human species. The humans who save humans." Yisheng reassuringly pats Rita's hand. "So, are you ready to begin?"

Rita hesitates, thinks for moment, then nods her head. "If I have womb for one, I have womb for a dozen. Always womb for one more!" She giggles, a bit dope dazed and goofy.

Yisheng motions for the two nurse-bots to begin. Continuing to hold Rita's hand, he explains the procedure the nurse-bots are following. He is monitoring the transplants with his AR glasses. "Now, relax Rita. First, this sterile bivalve speculum is inserted to visualize your cervix. Whoo! I should have warned you, it may be chilly. Ok, I see that your cervical canal and uterine cavity are aligned now. Good. Very good. Now, what you feel, Rita, is insertion of the Teflon catheter containing the embryo and tissue culture medium. Ah, there! The first embryo is implanted! That's one, Rita. Only eleven more to go."

"Hunh, I didn't feel a thing, except for that cold speculum." Rita closes her eyes and relaxes.

Yisheng captures Robert's attention. He points toward a nurse-bot waiting across the room. "You will receive your injection of computerized brain implants, there."

"Sorry?" Robert hesitates. "Nobody told me about this."

"Oh, it won't hurt you, Robert. The implants are laser imprinted on nano-biochips. Smaller than your smallest red blood cell. That nurse-bot will inject them into your blood stream where they will float around until it's safe to remove them. We'll be able to locate them, because I implanted in each of the biochips an addressable transmitter operated as magnetic spin, which will transmit their locations in your blood stream. Rita is transporting Shengwu's embryos. You're transporting Shengwu's Peter…actually Peter's personality, captured by my daughter…plus massive data bases of consumable memory…and ELF version 2."

"Again, sorry?" Robert glances at the waiting nurse-bot and then disbelievingly questions Yisheng. "Nano-chips? Why?"

"Shengwu calls it her Peter Principle. Makes Rita the mother and you a type of father. Besides, she also used genomes from both of you for these dozen darlings." He flashes four fingers to Rita signaling the implanting of the fourth embryo.

She smiles and closes her eyes. Obviously, lying there unable to move while the nurse-bots methodically load her with embryos is boring her.

Rita does not see Yisheng flash her his four fingers and thumb, before he returns his attention to Robert. "You and Rita are preparing to become the surrogate parents of the next human species…super-intelligent, transhumans. Shengwu has designed the embryos residing inside Rita so when they're born, their bodies will have the physical ability to withstand the heat and survive the diseases of the future. Their genetically engineered cells are self-healing and anti-aging. If Shengwu's genome engineering is correct and if they are not murdered, these twelve humans may never die. Also, thanks to her gene drive engineering, neither will their offspring."

Without looking away from Robert, Yisheng displays a count of six. "She embedded the embryos' advanced intelligence and ability to fully interface with Artificial Intelligence in the nano-biochips you will carry. The ELF nano-biochips contain both the upgraded version of ELF and the instructions for the embryos' intelligence insertion."

Robert is skeptical. "So, what do these nano-chips do to me…floating around in my blood? Why not just send them in a normal container?"

"Because, like the embryos, the biochips are human cells requiring presence within a human body to survive…a hospitable host…your body. Ninety-six hours from now, the embryos should be transplanted from Rita into their full-term wombs. By then they will have grown sufficiently for acceptance of the intelligence biochips." Yisheng flashes eight fingers at Rita. Her eyes remain shut, so she does not receive his count down. He turns to Robert. "You should go now. Get your injection."

"And what if I say no?" Robert defiantly shakes his head.

"You can't say no! If you say no, you're dooming the human race." Robert's unexpected refusal alarms Yisheng. "I have seen Evoil's plans Robert…an army and a nation of minions with submissive minds they can control. But even if I prevent them from creating millions of obedient slaves, if we allow the anti-evolutionists and science deniers like Evoil to remain in control, mankind will breed itself into extinction, Robert!"

Robert hears Shengwu speaking with Yisheng's voice. "Our current bodies are unevolved, weak and vulnerable. Aethon is just the first…the first superbug, super killer to be spawned by Earth's collapsing environment. Many more superbugs are coming, causing mass extinctions. Do you really want to be responsible for the death of humanity?"

"Ok. Ok, I'll get the injection. I promised Shengwu. Just stop preaching that everything is an end of the world catastrophe." Robert begins walking toward the waiting nurse-bot. "I can only panic so many times, and as Richard Bach wrote, 'what the caterpillar calls the end of the world, the master calls a butterfly.' Perhaps a deadly disease is just what humanity needs to clear out the clutter. Maybe much of mankind deserves to die."

Yisheng straightens nine fingers. "You may be correct. I think it's inevitable, Robert. Most of mankind is driving itself to annihilation, just like Neanderthals. Darwin's old belief in survival of the strongest and fittest is no longer true. Now, it's survival of the adaptable. People who do not adapt will not escape from their self-created, self-destruction."

Ignoring Yisheng's sermonizing, Robert slides into a chair next to the nurse-bot and presents his right arm. The nurse-bot inserts an IV needle and activates an intravenous transfusion. Doubting what he has heard, Robert skeptically scrutinizes the pale pink substance entering his body.

"This goo is the future of mankind?" Shaking his head in disbelief, he questions Yisheng. "I'm the host holding the hopes for humanity?"

Yisheng nods. "Yes, you are and you are doomed to watch humanity's survival or demise happen, Robert. When Shengwu engineered your genomes to fight Aethon, she also applied her epigenetics skills to lengthen your life. You should live for another one-hundred and fifty some years."

"Sorry? What?"

Yisheng smirks. "Shengwu cursed you with a long life fraught with unending responsibility. You're now the founding father of her homo futuris."

RELIGIOUS INSPIRATION

Reverend Diaboli slams his palm against Shengwu's nose. Blood sprays into the air, onto her clothes and across the floor splattering Zhou's body. Her knees buckle. She crumples. Painfully squeezing her arms behind her back, Willy Wanker forces her to stand. She wobbles, half conscious.

"Leave her alone!" Pion screams. She grabs for Diaboli, but she is only Augmented Reality - a flickering, holographic light. Her hands are colored air grabbing air.

Locked outside the room, Obed paces in the passageway. He is watching for Negocio's security, as Reverend Diaboli ordered him when he shoved him out of the room. He does not understand why. Pressing his ear against the door, he cannot hear what is happening inside the room. He fears for Zhou and Shengwu. What has he done? He is sick to his soul.

Raising his hand high, Diaboli again threatens Shengwu. "As it is written in the bible, 'He that covereth his sins shall not prosper: but whoso confesseth and forsaketh them shall have mercy.' I can show you mercy or I can strike you down. Do you wish to join your friend on the floor?"

Blood oozing from her nose and a cut on her face, Shengwu's head hangs limply forward. Grabbing her hair from behind, Wanker yanks her head back. "Answer the Pastor!"

"What do you want? I don't know what you want." Shengwu mumbles through bruised, swelling lips.

Wanker shakes her "ELF! We know that your father stole it, and we know that you know where he is hiding. You must return them to Deacon Evoil. He sits at the Lord's right hand...the hand of God. Only he is blessed and wise enough to use ELF to save the world from evil non-Christians. But even with God's help, Deacon Evoil cannot complete his earthly mission without your father and ELF."

Bleeding and rattled, Shengwu pleads, "Please stop. I'm just a genome engineer trying to save these sick people…your people. Please don't hit me again."

Crack! Reverend Diaboli slaps her ear. Shengwu's head rings with a clanging, banging. She cannot see. Her eyes refuse to focus.

"They are sinners!" Diaboli screams into Shengwu's face. "God has visited this plague upon them for their sins. Unsaved sinners will die. Those who have supported my ministry, I have touched with my prayers…with my saving grace. Those who have given unto me, I have laid my hands upon. They are saved…are freed of sin. They will live. It is the way of the Lord."

Zhou groans. Her left leg twitches. She is still a lump of flesh on the floor, too weak to move. Slowly, consciousness is seeping into her brain. Her Nsep induced paralysis is easing.

Diaboli kicks Zhou in her ribs. "Do you care about your friend? Do you want to see her hurt, because you refuse to cooperate? Just give us ELF!"

Diaboli kicks Zhou again, a little harder. Zhou grunts. Her eyes flutter with the pain.

Shengwu begs him. "Don't. Please don't hurt her. She knows nothing about ELF."

Diaboli drops his foot onto Zhou's throat and shoves down. "In the book of John it is written, 'the one who does what is sinful is of the devil, because the devil has been sinning from the beginning. The reason the Son of God appeared was to destroy the devil's work.' The Son of God lives in me and I am here to destroy the devil's work. Now, if you don't want your friend to suffer, return ELF."

"The time has come, Shengwu." Pion unexpectedly announces. "There is no reason to resist, anymore."

"Is Peter well?" Shengwu calls back.

"I was told that Peter is preparing to leave." Pion responds quietly.

Wanker yanks and twists Shengwu's arms. "What are you two chattering about? Who is Peter?"

Bang! Bang! Bang! Obed slams his fist against the door. "Reverend! San Juan police! Police!"

"Tell us now! Right now! Or I will crush her throat." Zhou chokes, struggling to breathe, as Diaboli mashes his foot against her throat.

"Don't! Don't hurt her. Leave her alone. I'll cooperate." Shengwu surrenders.

Bang! Obed kicks the door. "The police are trying to break through the lobby door."

From behind them, Pion enquires, "Shall I enable them access, Shengwu?"

"Yes!" Shengwu shouts. Diaboli smacks her silent.

"Let's go!" Wanker drags Shengwu backward toward the door. "Where's ELF? Tell me! Tell me now or Pastor Diaboli crushes your friend's throat. Now!"

Stumbling and grimacing against the pain, Shengwu moans. "In my lab. ELF is in my lab."

"Take us there." Wanker releases Shengwu's arms, opens the door and heaves her into the passageway.

Shengwu crashes against Obed, knocking him onto the floor. Whack! Diaboli's boot toe crushes Obed's chin, knocking him unconscious.

As he follows Shengwu and Wanker to her lab, Reverend Diaboli steps over Obed's bleeding body. He glances down upon him, then graces him with a few words of faith. "Heed well these words from Proverbs my son, like a dog that returns to its vomit, a fool does the same foolish things again and again."

NIGHT MOVES

Sun sets on old San Juan. Reds and golds flower across the Bahia de San Juan. The San Felipe de Morro Fortress glows. Christmas lights sparkle aboard the yachts and cruise ships plying the bay. Across the Bahia, competing Christmas songs and music mix and mingle. The holiday music and singing dances upon the bay waters.

Robert and Rita cautiously edge the coroner's transporter out of Shengwu's tunnel complex garage and into the twilight. Flash! The glider's automatic lights bloom brightly. They are a blazing star.

Pop! Pang! Crash! Pneumatic pistol pellets pepper the auto-auto. Rita dives to the floor. Robert scrambles to shield her. The transporter rolls forward and then stops.

"Go! Go!" Robert orders, but the auto-auto settles onto its spheres and refuses to proceed.

Peeking through the transporter's pellet shattered glass, Robert sees two men blocking their passage. Its auto-guide jolts to a halt with them barring its way. Their pneumatic pistols pointing at the auto-auto, the two men warily advance. Robert ducks a breath before another pellet crashes into the glass where his head had been.

"We're trapped!" Robert warns Rita, as he feverishly scours the transporter's interior for something, anything that can save them. He finds nothing. "This auto-auto is so safe, it's going to get us killed."

Tap. Tap. Tap. Robert hears knocking on the transporter's corpse carriage access panel. Tap. Tap. Tap. Crawling over Rita and across the carriage hold deck, he stretches and activates the access panel. It slides open, revealing nothing.

"Get out! Get out now!" Mugavus' formless voice commands.

A fusillade of pellets shred the cabin windows. Robert grabs Rita's shoulder, yanking her toward Mugavus' voice. She scrambles past him and rolls out of the access panel and onto the ground. Robert slides out behind her.

"Get under here." Mugavus raises her digital, concealing cloak and motions to them.

Rita and Robert clamber beneath Mugavus' protective, invisibility cloak. They huddle together, struggling to hide three under this covering for one. Robert bends and twists, but still fails to squeeze all of himself out of sight. Hearing the two men nearing, the three freeze. Robert futilely attempts to shrink his uncovered legs and feet.

"Ok Billy, where do you think they are?" Pour LeNuls illuminates the transporter's interior. "I don't see any blood or anything."

Standing on the opposite side, Billy Bollocks pumps several more pellets into the interior to ease his frustration. "Willy isn't going to be happy to learn we destroyed this coroner's auto-auto for no reason."

"I'm more worried about Reverend Diaboli and his hell fire." Pour randomly swings his light around the ground and garage entrance. "I suggest we keep silent and wait. Tell Diaboli nothing until we know something."

Watching Pour and Billy taking seats on the ground in front of the transporter, Mugavus whispers. "We need to leave. I have a glider waiting less than one hundred meters away."

"Mugavus, you and Rita go. You can stay camouflaged. I'll hide here until you're in the glider." Robert unwraps himself.

"What about you?" Rita clutches Robert's arm. "I'm not leaving without you."

Pulling loose, Robert slips from beneath the cloak. "Get going. I'll follow."

"How?" Rita reaches for him again.

"Don't know, yet. I'm making it up as I go along." Robert slides away, seeking cover below the auto-auto's body.

Scrunched beneath the edge of the transporter and barely breathing, Robert waits, watches and listens. Sitting at the opposite end, blocking the exit, Billy and Pour are doing the same. Robert searches his mind for a method to escape their notice. He craves a distraction to lure them away.

Mugavus delivers. Safely within her glider, beyond the range of Billy and Pour's pneumatic pistols, Mugavus shatters the night with light and noise. Like moths to a flame, she is calling them. They take her bait.

"Who is that? I wonder what they want." Pour rises to his feet and begins jogging toward Rita and Mugavus.

Billy jumps up and follows Pour. As they near her glider, Mugavus moves a few feet ahead. She is luring them farther away.

Now is Robert's opportunity. Avoiding glass shards and other dangerous debris, Robert climbs inside the glider. With the push of a button, he activates its silent electric motor. A whisper and the transporter rises to life. No bodies stand in front of it. Like a ghost, it eases forward.

Seeing that Robert is safely on the move, Mugavus decides to stop playing her cat and mouse game with Billy and Pour. She directs her glider to accelerate full-speed ahead. "Instituto de Neurobiologia hover lot at maximum speed."

As Mugavus and Rita dissolve into the darkness, Billy and Pour realize that they have been suckered. They turn around just in time to watch Robert hum by, out of their reach. Angrily, Billy pumps two pellets at the fleeing Robert.

"Stop wasting your time and pellets, Billy. Your pellets won't puncture its graphene body." Pour jogs to his auto-auto. "Let's go! The longer we delay, the farther they'll get away."

Wheezing from his run, Billy kicks the door. "We'll never catch them in this, Pour. Auto-autos are programmed to follow all the traffic regulations. He's already out of sight. We can't go fast enough to find him."

"So, we send the drone." Pour yanks open the portal. "Pull it out and launch it. With all the damage we did, his transporter will be easy to spot."

Pour's prediction is correct. Less than five minutes later, their drone is hovering above Robert. Leading him by two blocks are Rita and Mugavus. They are racing to their get-away sky whale, as fast as San Juan's traffic laws allow.

Following legally behind in their auto-auto, Billy is increasingly nervous. "Should I tell Reverend Diaboli what we're doing, now?"

"Are you crazy or just stupid?" Pour snarls. "We don't tell him nothing, until our job is done. Just shut-up and keep your drone on top of that transporter. Don't you dare lose it!"

Riding uncomfortably in his shelled, breezy auto-auto, Robert nervously searches ahead for Mugavus and Rita. Only Mugavus knows the location of SPEA's flying whale aero-transporter. If he does not find them, he will not find it. And although he cannot see them, he is certain that his two attackers are not far behind him. Robert restlessly rocks in his seat hoping his motion will propel him forward faster. It does not.

Kilometer after kilometer, the pursued and their pursuers impatiently trudge around the bay from Catano to the center of old San Juan and La Perla. Normally a twenty minute trip, Robert swears it is requiring twenty hours, tonight. Nervous sweat soaks his skin.

Intensely concentrating on searching for Mugavus and Rita, Robert does not hear the holiday music blaring from speakers. He does not see the revelers crowding Calle Norzagaray. His auto-auto does. Without him realizing it, he is no longer moving. Holiday celebrators spilling out of Plaza de Colon are blocking him to a halt.

"Are you ok, mister?" A young girl asks Robert, as she and her parents walk past him. "Why happened to your transporter? It's all broken."

"Unh? What?" The girl's question shakes Robert from his trance.

Recognizing that Calle Norzagaray is an inescapable, human river, Robert abandons his crippled transporter. Standing on the ends of his toes, while stretching to his full height, he examines the crowd for Rita or Mugavus. Nothing. Not a trace. He is alone and on his own. He decides his best chance to find them is near La Perla where Mugavus' hid the flying whale.

"Where is La Perla?" Robert asks a man carrying a small girl on his shoulders while leading his young son by his hand.

"Follow us. You can't miss it. We'll pass it on the way to the La Sinfónica de Puerto Rico Christmas concert." The small boy excitedly giggles and skips at the mention of the Christmas concert.

Robert smiles at the small boy, who grins in return. The boy points toward Robert's chest and then at his own. He wants Robert to notice how he has proudly decorated his own glowing-green,

Aethon badge with a paper ornament. Robert nods his approval with a wide smile. Beaming happily at his new friend, the boy holds out his arms.

Robert decides walking close to these three may protect him. He lifts the giggling boy onto his shoulders. As a disguise, it is not perfect, but Robert decides that it is better than nothing. Besides, what insensitive boor would ignore a boy who wants a ride?

Not that far behind Robert, Billy and Pour are wriggling and squirming through the growing crowd. They are gaining ground. Instead of flowing, they are fighting the flow causing concert goers to intentionally block their progress. It is a battle. Shoving with a shoulder, punching and pushing, they muscle their way closer and closer to Robert. Closing the gap.

Ahead, Mugavus and Rita wait and pace. They stand at the edge of La Perla on Calle Bajada Matadero, ready to disappear into the slums upon their first sight of danger. Mugavus is especially uneasy. Protecting Rita and transporting her and her embryos to Venus is her primary mission. Nothing must be allowed to prevent her safe delivery. Robert's escape is secondary. He is important, but she is prepared to sacrifice him, if necessary to protect Rita.

"We'll allow Robert ten more minutes, then we need to go, Rita." Mugavus sets the alarm on her PCD. "I'm not going to lose you and your packages."

"No! We will wait. I know that sometimes, he is slower than an old wobbly people caravan, but I will not leave without him." Rita steps away from Mugavus, out of her reach. "We go together or not at all. When I was receiving the embryos, I may have had my eyes closed, but I heard every word Yisheng said. I may carry the babies, but Robert carries their brains."

BAHIA BOUND

"Terminate with extreme prejudice. Do you understand your orders, gentlemen? Deacon Evoil wants Robert Goodfellow and anybody with him eliminated ASAP. They must be silenced. Make it so." Wanker's directions to Billy and Pour are terse and blunt. "We have completed our recovery mission here. We will meet you at the rendezvous point when you complete yours. Do you copy?"

"Affirmative, sir. We understand and we shall complete our mission." Billy replies confidently to Wanker. While shaking his head, he silences his PCD.

"We have to find him to kill him." Pour reminds Billy. "We may never find him in this crowd."

"Well, if we don't find him, then we better disappear along with him. If we fail, it will be us Evoil terminates with extreme prejudice." Billy stretches, trying to see over the human wall in front of him.

Less than one hundred meters in front of Pour and Billy, Robert is enduring the endless singing into his ears of the boy he is carrying on his shoulders. Every song the boy learned in school, he is now repeating for Robert's enjoyment. Only, Robert is not actually listening. Instead, he is scouring every inch of Calle Norzagaray for Rita and Mugavus.

To gain Robert's attention, the boy rocks on his shoulders and lightly taps the top of his head. "Hey mister, do you want to hear a special rhyme we learned in school? Do you?"

Tired of hearing him repeatedly singing holiday songs, Robert is definitely ready for a change of tunes. "Certainly. Tell me the rhyme you learned in school."

The boy claps his hands together to establish his beat before loudly beginning to chant. "Do you see? I am Aethon free. Do you see my badge on me? It is glowing. It is green. It says I am Aethon free. Get your shots. Wear your badge. Every Puerto Rican must be. Aethon free!"

"Hey, you know what? I really like your rhyme." Robert taps his badge. "Do you see? I am Aethon free."

"Yes, you have a shiny green badge. So does that man and that lady and that man and that baby." The boy twists and turns on Robert's shoulders, pointing at all the badges he sees. "He has one and she has one. Hey! They don't have one! Why don't they have badges, mister?"

"What?" A chilling thought stabs Robert in his chest. "No badges equals bad men."

Grabbing Robert's face, the boy steers him until he turns him around. "See! Those two men don't have badges."

Less than ten meters away stride Pour and Billy. Instantly, Robert recognizes them. It is difficult to forget people who attempt to kill you. Luckily, they do not spot him as quickly.

"Well, my little friend, I have to run along now." Robert hurriedly lifts the boy off his shoulders and sets him onto the ground. Still walking, he bows down to the boy's level, temporarily out of sight. "Grab your father's hand. There you go. Stay close to him. Ok?"

Tears begin forming in the little boy's eyes along with a catch in his throat. "Why are you going? Don't you want to hear the music with me?"

Walking bent double, keeping his head down, Robert decides to employ the boy in an attempt to buy himself some time. "Those two men you saw without badges are bad men. They want to hurt people who have badges…like you…and me. So, you must tell everybody about them. Yell really loud now, so everybody will know that they are bad and don't have badges. Ok?"

The little boy wipes the tears from his eyes and nods. He tugs on his father's hand pulling him to a halt. His father turns to see his son excitedly motioning toward Pour and Billy.

"Those men don't have badges! They want to steal your badges!" The boy points and screams his alarm, as loud as his little lungs allow.

Robert's ploy works. The boy's yelling is more effective than a siren. Within seconds, an outraged, threatening throng surrounds Billy and Pour, delaying and confusing them. They are caught badgeless, without a reason or an explanation, in a country fighting a killer disease. Angry shouting soon escalates into violence.

While the mob menaces and batters them, Robert runs. Weaving and winding through the multitude, while still searching for Rita and Mugavus, he is not escaping fast. Up the hill he jogs, jumping every few feet to scan above the crowd. His final jump is his downfall.

"There he is. I see him." Pour shouts to Billy.

They are close behind him. Flourishing their pneumatic pistols, they quickly part the sea of people surrounding them. Waving their weapons, they charge forward. No one dares challenge them or stand in their way, clearing a path for them to him. Pursuing police are not as lucky, finding their way clogged by too many helpful citizens wishing to tell them what they saw and what they heard.

"Here, Robert! Over here!" Rita and Mugavus sing out his name. Never have their voices sounded so sweet.

Rita and Mugavus jump and wave, calling Robert. Breaking free of the throng clogging Calle Norzagaray, he races toward them. Waving his hands wildly and yelling, he shouts for them to start running. They begin slowly jogging down Calle Bajada Montadero, as it worms its way into the gut of La Perla.

"Go! Go! Go!" Robert is running beside them in a heartbeat. "They're right behind me."

Huffing and puffing, their lungs burning, Rita and Mugavus hurtle down the steep street after Robert. His long legs propel him ahead of the two women. Alone, he races through the old fort wall at Puerta de Santa Rosa and into La Perla. He skids to a halt in front of a menacing mountain of a man pounding an enormous baseball bat into the palm of his gigantic hand.

"Qué pasa pai *(What's up dude)*?" Loudly popping the bat into his grizzly bear sized paw, the giant growls, "Creo que estás perdido en el lugar equivocado *(I think you're lost in the wrong place)*. You don't belong here."

"Está bien *(It's ok)*, Luis. He's with me." Mugavus shouts using her last breath, as she and Rita stumble-run into the intersection.

Rita grabs Mugavus by her arm and pulls her forward. "Come on. We have to keep moving. I can hear them coming."

"Where is the flying whale, Mugavus? Which way do we go?" Spreading his arms, Robert points left and right. "Those guys will be here any second. How far away is it?"

"Not far. Al cantio de un gallo *(The distance a rooster can be heard when he crows)*. Follow me." Luis leads them into the hallway of a crumbling building. It is dark and stinks of rot and rats.

"Arrempujate pa ca *(Come this way – get closer)*. Hang on to each other." Luis commands, as his hand swallows Mugavus' hand, wrist and forearm.

Grasping each other's hands they grow into a human chain that Luis pulls deeper and deeper into the guts of La Perla. He is their guide and protector escorting them in and out of buildings, across streets and down alleyways. Stumbling along as the last link in their human chain, Robert soon realizes that in La Perla, Luis is a leader of the lost.

Slithering out from their dark dens, scarred, hulking thugs growl and threaten, then hide their weapons and step aside when Luis snarls and advances toward them. Tall, skinny Robert, on the other hand, poses them no threat. He feels them close in around him. Their stench surrounds him. Like a pack of wolves they circle and nip at his back, waiting to pick him off if he stumbles or falls behind his herd. He hurries ahead until he is walking beside Mugavus, who he pulls close to Rita.

After tramping through too many derelict, collapsing buildings for him to remember, they escape into a narrow alley. In the open, the wolf pack scatters and Robert discovers that not every resident of La Perla is a deadly threat. Skinny, grimy children playing in a dimly lit, abandoned scrap yard shout Luis' name and wave frantically, as he passes. An arguing man and woman fall silent and force smiles when Luis steps from the alleyway into their building's hallway. For the moment, he brings peace.

As they near the rising ocean, they begin slogging through buildings flooded with deepening, stagnant, stinking seawater. When they wade out of the last collapsing building, the seawater is knee deep on Robert and thigh deep for Rita and Mugavus. Luis stops them in the shadows of a grove of drowned trees. According to a half-submerged sign, they are standing on pavement that was once Calle San Miguel.

Luis points across the seawater stream which was once the street. Moving his arm, he directs their attention to two figures hiding in the shadows of a building ahead and to their right. Their trackers have beaten them to the beach and are waiting to pounce. Taking a secretive, circuitous route through the innards of La Perla had done nothing more than provide them with a frightening walk on the wild side.

As soundlessly as his deep voice will rumble, Luis explains his plan. "To get to the boat waiting to take you to your sky whale, you'll have to go through that red building. Your boat is tied at the other end. But, don't go yet. I'm going to walk over there and talk to those men. Don't go until I am standing in front of them, blocking their view. Then go. Stay low in the water. Buena suerte *(Good luck)*."

Robert watches Luis slog through the rising waters to the two men. Amazingly, he appears to magically expand and widen himself into a tall wall in front of them. When Luis' bulk blocks the two men's view sufficiently, Robert, Rita and Mugavus silently sink into the water, bending and twisting so only their heads show. Without raising a ripple, they sneak across the street and slide into the building.

Drenched with filthy scum, they slog toward the pale moon peeking through the open doorway at the far end of the corridor. It is their only light. In the dark, dank hallway, Rita's foot crushes a rotting cat's carcass. Maggots and guts explode onto her foot and leg. She jumps, shakes her foot and screams - loud and long. Dogs bark and howl. Sleeping birds awake, squawk and explode into the sky. More dogs bark and howl.

"Well, I don't think you could have announced our location to those killers any louder than that, Rita." Mugavus snarls.

Still struggling to rid herself of maggots, Rita snaps back. "If you were covered with this gruel, you'd be upset too."

"Be silent and be strong Rita. For, it is in the midst of disasters that bold men grow bolder, according to Henry the fourth." Robert whispers, attempting to bolster her.

"Oh, shut-up!" Both Rita and Mugavus hiss, simultaneously.

First outside and then behind them, they hear the two men. With Mugavus leading and Robert at the rear, they race to the end of the hall. Just as Luis promised, a small man is waiting in a small, open boat. One after another, they leap aboard. The man slams his boat into reverse and churns away from the building.

Cursing and shaking their fists, the two men storm into the doorway. Too late. The boat is beyond their reach. Both men aim their pneumatic pistols. Mugavus and Rita dive onto the boat's bottom. Trapped kneeling in the front, Robert ducks.

Foomf! Foomf! Foomf! Robert hears the pellets sail by. He squeezes lower. Foomf! A pellet nicks his earlobe. Fwack! A pellet burrows deep into his forehead. Robert falls back. All is black.

BRAIN STRAIN

"Who am I? No. What am I? Am I still a man? Am I a human or am I just a computer's mammalian container and power supply? Are these even my thoughts? Do I still have my own thoughts? Or are these some programmer's algorithms?" Silently contemplating his confusing new life as a transhuman, Robert drops his head into his hands awaiting his inner voice.

"American educator Stephen Covey wrote that every human has four endowments – self-awareness, conscience, independent will and creative imagination. These give us the ultimate human freedom... The power to choose, to respond, to change." The computer voice inside Robert's brain responds, then queries. "Is this sufficient information? Do you require additional definitions or data?"

"No that is sufficient." Robert thinks, gritting his teeth in frustration. "Now, I am really talking to myself...or am I talking within myself. Either way, I don't like it. Except, I'm not talking. I'm thinking. At least, I think that it's me thinking. I think therefore I am. I think. Or am I? Am I going crazy? I think I am! I think I am going crazy!"

"Are you wondering if you are becoming mentally unsound or are you wondering if you are becoming distracted by desire or excitement?" Robert's constant computerized cranial companion inquires. "Both are dictionary definitions of crazy. Please be more specific."

Groaning, Robert rubs the small scab on his forehead. Behind the scab is where Pion and SPEA's robo-surgeons inserted the brain prosthesis into his frontal lobe after they extracted the pneumatic pellet. The silicon chip implant was expected to perform the same processes as the damaged part of his brain it replaced. But, it is doing that and much more - too much more.

When he awoke from his prosthesis implant surgery, Mugavus told him that he had undergone an experimental procedure done in an emergency to save his life. According to her, he was brain dead by the time they arrived on Venus. She was also kind enough to congratulate him for taking the pellet to his head instead of in some body part that would have bled. According to her, all of Yisheng's biochips were recovered from his blood thanks to the pellet lodging in his skull. Instead of, as she teased, somewhere important.

Mugavus also told him that while he lay unconscious in a coma induced to allow his brain to heal and accept the prosthesis, Yisheng's biochips were removed from his body. Simultaneously, the twelve embryos, Rita transported from San Juan were also removed. The biochips were implanted into the growing embryos and the transhuman embryos successfully transplanted into the welcoming wombs of the SPEA volunteers.

She also told him that when Mugavus informed Shengwu that the human mothers and her transhuman fetuses are healthy and flourishing, Shengwu cried celebratory tears. She realized that although Reverend Diaboli and Wanker had beaten her father to death, they did not kill his dream. Knowing that the contributions of both her father and her Peter will continue, she has returned to her search for an Aethon cure.

Shengwu and Zhou are temporarily fighting Aethon from her lab at the Instituto, while Negocio rebuilds Stamina Vitae. Always a man with a plan, Negocio negotiated a deal with the Voleurs and Terra Sigillata allowing them to distribute Puerto Rico's Aethon vaccine for a small, reconstruction fee. Terra Sigillata's pure Puerto Rican Aethon vaccine is selling well on the pharmaceutical gray market while big pharma continues to flood the commercial market with their high-priced placebos.

Once Mugavus completed her - while you were sleeping - current events briefing to Robert, Pion had induced what she called a mind upload that she converted into a mind upgrade. She interfaced Robert's brain implant prosthesis directly into the Cloud via SPEA's AI. He is now in constant interaction with all of the world's data and receives continuous intelligence updates. Information overload.

As with every upgrade, there are new functions and changes that require time for learning and adjustment. He is struggling to adjust. His brain is always processing. He constantly hears the debate of his inner voices. He cannot sleep in silence.

"I pity the digital dozen having to grow up suffering through this agony. But, then they'll never know anything different. They'll be born chip children. They won't need to relearn to think or control their thoughts." Robert ponders as he stalks a loud location where he can rest. "Better a chip in the head, than dead. I guess."

Sitting in the center of the crowded, noisy Venus plaza, Robert concentrates on gaining control of his mind. He is attempting to employ the cacophony surrounding him to overwhelm his mental noise. He is seeking that level of sounds where he can happily say, "I can't hear myself think." Adding thunderous music, he achieves a deafening decibel level, closes his eyes and captures sleep.

Five hours later, Robert's personal peace in pandemonium abruptly ends. His neurotransmitters erupt. It is too quiet. Venus' plaza is vacant and still. His bloodshot eyes fly open.

"Good evening, Robert. Welcome back." Sitting in front of him, Rita quietly greets him. She leans forward and kisses his cheek. "I have important news, Robert."

Robert nods and meekly smiles. He thinks thanks, but fails to speak. Rita looks at him, first quizzically then peevishly.

"Use your words!" Rita commands him. "I can't hear your thoughts."

Embarrassed, at not realizing he is not projecting his thoughts beyond his cranial cavity, Robert clears his throat and coughs out his first words in days. "Sorry, I forget that you're not wired like me."

Rita tenderly caresses his cheek with her hand and smiles softly. "I have important news."

"If you're planning to tell me that Reverend Diaboli and Willy Wanker died last night in Tennessee, don't bother. Alarms sounded in my head with that several hours ago." Robert sneers. "My sources communicated that they both died excruciatingly painful deaths from Aethon. I guess the diplomatic immunity that protected them from prosecution in Puerto Rico for killing Yisheng didn't give them immunity to Aethon. You'll pardon me, I hope, if I fail to shed any tears of sorrow for them."

"Yes, I feel the same, but…" Rita begins tapping her fingertips together.

Robert continues wandering within his own wonderings. "Their agonizing deaths actually please me, but I worry about the ELF programs they stole. Who has ELF?"

"SPEA has ELF. Yisheng packed all of the real ELF inside of you. Diaboli got nothing." Rita stops for a breath then smirks. "Well actually, in exchange for Shengwu's and Zhou's lives, Yisheng did give them some genome editing programs code named ELF. And I truly hope Evoil is successful implementing his stolen ELF programs..."

"What!" Robert feels betrayed.

"...Yes, I definitely wish Evoil success." A mischievous smirk caresses Rita's face. "Because Robert, Yisheng told me that if Evoil's minions edit genomes following those particular ELF algorithms they will actually produce millions of Extra Large Flies."

Robert chuckles. "I imagine Yisheng died laughing."

"Yes, I suppose, Robert. But, I need to tell you something important." Rita leans closer to Robert's face to secure his attention. "Do you remember our first night together?"

"Well, of course, I do. I haven't lost my memory. I've lost my identity." He pulls back. "So what?"

Rita cups Robert's chin between her hands. "Robert, when they started to suck those twelve embryos out of me, they found thirteen."

"Thirteen?" Robert frowns.

"Actually, they found twelve embryos and one fetus. Our fetus. Our baby." Rita bounces and giggles. "Robert! I'm pregnant!"

"Say again." Confusion clouds his face and mind. "Suddenly, his consciousness is unconscious."

"You and me, Robert, we're pregnant!" Rita pats her stomach. "And whether it's a boy or a girl, guess what we're naming it."

Still lost, Robert shrugs.

"Aethon, of course. Aethon!"

THE END

About the Author

"The best way to predict your future is to create it," Abraham Lincoln said and as bestselling author, entrepreneur and agent of change Seth Godin wrote, "If you are deliberately trying to create a future that feels safe, you will willfully ignore the future that is likely." Now, you may ask why I am beginning this semi-biographical discussion with these two quotes. I am beginning with these two quotes because they represent the type of thinking that shapes my reasoning and my writing.

I am not a scientist. I am a future fanatic. As far back as I am still capable of remembering, I have always been interested in what is next, what is over the horizon, what will be the next innovation or invention and how it will change the world. So, I adopt, adapt and employ inventions and innovations in my efforts as a writer to investigate, consider and discuss what the future may hold for the world. I don't know what I don't know I admit, but I am always ready and excited to learn something I didn't know and then to share that information with others. For as Charles F. Kettering said, "My interest is in the future because I am going to spend the rest of my life there." So, I hope you will join me as I look around and ask, "What if?"

Connect with R. E. Kearney

Website:
http://rekearney.com/

Facebook:
https://www.facebook.com/RE-Kearney-
956373567787029/?ref=bookmarks

Twitter:
https://twitter.com/rekearney

Did you enjoy this book?
Please write a review.

Made in United States
North Haven, CT
07 June 2023

37471536R00137